New Perspectives

New Perspectives

A COLLECTION OF PROSE AND POETRY

from

Writers West of Alameda, Inc.

Alameda, California

ACKNOWLEDGEMENT

Our thanks to those who helped turn an idea into reality: the writers who contributed to this collection, the editorial committee, and our families and friends, who encouraged and supported our endeavors.

© 1988 Writers West of Alameda

All rights revert to the authors

No portion of this book may be reproduced
without the written permission of the publisher.

Published by
Writers West of Alameda, Inc.
P.O. Box 2692
Alameda, California 94501
ISBN: 0-9616107-1-9

Cover: Historic Alameda High School

Book design and typesetting: Alameda Words Words Words
Photographer: Ray Young
Cover design and typesetting: Ken Debono, Ankh Press
Printer: GRT Book Printing, Oakland, California

Dedication

Writers West wishes to express special thanks to Bert and Shirley Johnsen for graciously hosting our annual dinner parties. Our applause also goes to Ray Wiermack for his spirited piano playing at these gatherings that have enriched our lives and expanded our perspectives.

Contents

The Soul Man/Roberta Debono	1
Ages Past/Grant Lowther	10
Good Bye, Minnie/Lola Curtis	11
Jubilation?/Frank Bette	18
Water Borne/Cecil Fox	19
The Company President/Delbert B. Campbell	21
A Man Tonight/Helen Cannon	24
Full Circle/Grant Lowther	30
Druid's Eve/Marilyn K. Dickerson	31
Camels Are for Eating/Petey Brown	38
Dorothy Richardson/Delbert B. Campbell	41
Passing Through/Joe King	44
Second Chance/M. L. Archer	45
Genesis/Lucile Bogue	50
A School for Madina/Sybil McCabe	53
The Bagman/D. Leah Miller	60
Promised: Chapter 19/Betty Matulovich	69
City Boy, Oakland 1959/Roque Gutierrez	76
Back to the Bagley/Jean Tucker	77
Bunce Island/Don Donovan	80
Grandma's Airplane Ride/Allen J. Pettit	84
Stone/Linda Marlow	92
Bavarian Chocolate Fudge/Mary Jo Wold	93
The Glass Bowl/Wanda Giuliano	94
I Remember Sousa/Cecil Fox	103
Fernando Flamingo Can Do the Flamenco/Gail E. Van Amburg	106
The Car Igniteth Not/Mary Jo Wold	109
Go Back! Go Back!/Genevieve Bonato	111
Radio Dispatch (Station KFY207)/Delbert B. Campbell	114

Eyes/Linda Marlow	115
Someone Cares!/Ann C. Krauss	118
Sons of the Valley/Roque Gutierrez	119
Let Us Say So/Jean Tucker	127
The Briarwood Witch/Marilyn K. Dickerson	128
Beige Box/Grant Lowther	134
A Birthday Dare/Jean Albrecht Lucken	135
Party Time/Lola Curtis	140
Witch in the Vicarage/Lucile Bogue	142
In an Ashen Land/M. L. Archer	153
Holy Moses/Genevieve Bonato	160
Spring/Joe King	162
Tokyo Interlude/Allen J. Pettit	163
The Carrot/Frank Bette	174
Ribbons Retied/F. "Perky" Peling	175
Can the Sun Melt the Sidewalk?/Roque Gutierrez	179
The Day the Piano Arrived/Shirley Johnsen	180
The Master Painter/Ray Weirmack	182
Away from It All/Helen Cannon	183
It Takes One to Know One/Marjorie Nesbit	190
The Unwelcome Guest/Don Donovan	195
The Wedding: Chapter 20/Betty Matulovich	199
Vernal Equinox/Ann C. Krauss	206
Mother's Day/Gail E. Van Amburg	207
The Nest/Wanda Giuliano	208
Aren't I Pretty?/Andrea Crankshaw	214
About the Authors	218

Foreword

New Perspectives, the second collection offered by Writers West of Alameda, sings with the songs of many cultures, speaks with voices of many hearts, and sparkles with the varied styles and talents of its members.

As individual as are the writers who created them, the selections contribute their special slices of human drama. Whether they tell of a war widow's painful journey into a long buried past, the last tenuous hope of a discharged prisoner, or the angry song of a "soul man," the stories evoke some hidden memory within us. The terror of a young woman caught in a supernatural web, the quiet dignity of Mexican field workers, or the gentle gift of a teacher to her husband's memory elicit our own identification and interest.

This volume marks another milestone in the growth of Writers West, a group of over forty men and women of diverse ages and backgrounds who meet twice a month to read and critique in an atmosphere that embodies the best aspects of a writers' workshop. As their teacher, friend, and fellow writer, I have watched this group grow in skill as well as in membership.

This eclectic collection reflects the many aspects of life and the many facets of its authors -- many viewpoints, many insights, many voices. Best of all, it fulfills the writer's first obligation, to keep the reader interested and entertained.

Eleanor Chroman

The Soul Man

Roberta Debono

He stood on the low stage in a bar on Grove Street: a long-bodied, supple-throated young Black man, singing now like a prophet and moving when he sang like a man treading water, his eyes swinging, shiny-black, his face a kaleidoscope of purple, yellow, pumpkin-colored lights, his body quivering. And it wasn't water holding him up, but a swarming smell of beer, sawdust, and urine, chopped by a saxophone, stiff and husky in its deepest sighs. That and a steady staccato beat on a drum skin, illuminated at the corner of the stage by one pale thrust of blue light, buoyed him up and pulled him down at once, like quick bright water, nursing and drowning the lonely swimmer. And there was smoke to swim through as well, and murmurs and shouts: "Get down, Man! Get hot!" until the last notes were wrenched out of his throat and his hands left the microphone. His feet were over the side of the stage; Crazy John the blond mulatto drummer shut it down with a flourish, applause washed around his ears, ran into the corners of his eyes in a salty stream, and he stood in the back hall, a laugh of triumph growing in his throat.

In the darkness of the corridor a fleshy hand touched his arm, leaving a moist imprint on the sleeve of his jacket. As he turned and peered into the shadows, one arm, taut with the muscle of youth, drew back almost mechanically for defense.

"Easy, Boy!" and a ponderous man whose body seemed to stand in coils, like a pile of curtain rope back of a stage, took him by the shoulders. "Boy, you ready for L.A. now. You ready to go and sing for my Man."

New Perspectives

"Eddie," he managed to murmur, though his wind had left him from the shock of joy, "Man, you wouldn't put me on? You mean it?"

Slowly the older Black man reached for a light cord. A yellow bulb lighted up the walls, scrawled with obscenities, phone numbers, and one masterwork, a life-size couple in an embrace, sketched with a charcoal stick.

"Donny, I wouldn't put you on," he said, benevolently patting the boy's shoulder. "Ever since I first let you sing here I been waiting for you to get ready. Now you done it." He jerked his head toward the partly opened door to the nightclub. "They dig you. You bring 'em to the Jazz Box, Donny. I ain't forgettin' that." He slowly eased his bulk onto a straight-backed chair, almost filling up the tiny hall. "Billy Rollins, my old buddy in L.A., wants to see you and you got to oblige. He got a place. The Sportsman's Club. It's big time! You get on down to L.A. on Sat'day. Oakland to L.A. take you maybe seven hours driving hard."

Donny was breathing rapidly. His eyes felt filmy; his lips parted in excitement. "I'll be ready!" he cried, "I'm gettin' ready now!"

As he headed for the back door and the alleyway, the fat man called out, "Cool it till Sat'day! Get yourself straight, and tell your pretty little wife, tell her Uncle Eddie loves her!"

But the younger man was out the door before Fat Eddie had finished, out the door where Della was waiting, grabbing his wife by the waist, dancing around and around with her in his arms, feeling her small hands fasten in his thick hair and her laughing quick breaths against his cheek.

"Honey, Honey, we're on the move now!" and he patted her tight buttocks, high as a fawn's rump, kissed her skin, darker than his own coffee-milk complexion, a shimmering mahogany in the bright backdoor lights of the nightclub.

Then he set her down and put on a mock swagger, while Della smoothed her skirt with one hand, trying to erase the wrinkles that sitting in a hot room for two hours had put into the yellow silk. She laughed huskily and her voice was vivid with pride: "You were so great, Donny! You put 'em all down. Can't none of 'em sing like you!" For a moment he stood watching her, his head tilted slightly to one side, hands in his pockets, and thought, *Should I tell her now, tell her about L.A.?*

But his silence and the way his eyes seemed to deepen into black flares had already told her, and she cried, "This is it, isn't it, Donny?" She took his hand in both of hers. They were trembling, he thought, like two small brown city sparrows. "What did Uncle Eddie say?" she cried.

The Soul Man

He expanded his chest in one deep breath and spoke.

"I'm going to L.A., Della, next Saturday. They've got me an audition lined up! It's BTSB, Honey—Big Time Show Biz!" He watched her face and saw a look—certainly it was a look of pain—flicker across her eyes. But it was instantly embraced and hidden by a smile, as the woman's lips turned up to him, full and dusky pink like a dark forest rose.

He could sense her thoughts were all pictures: pictures of him leaving, of wild nights in L.A., of other women, but pulsing through the images, sometimes obliterating them, was his own likeness, as he stood on the spotlight circle, and the sound of his voice, singing. He knew that all of this was in her mind; he felt her lips on his and then heard her whisper as she stepped back, away from him and yet touching him.

"I've been knowing this for a year, since we married. I've been knowing what you wanted, what you were working for. Now the chance has come," she hesitated, "and you got to go. Now don't you get mixed up with none of those show gals down there, Donny!"

And as she laughed a low, poignant laugh like a dove's call, made up of desire and longing, he grabbed her hand and did a clowning dance of triumph that made her giggle. He began a mad tear down the alley and out onto the street. It was an old game between them, and Donny called as he ran, "Come on, Sweet Woman! You can do better'n that!"

But he had left her far behind, at a red traffic light, and when he reached her side and wanted to begin the game again, he was suddenly aware of sweat on her dark throat and a tremor at the corners of her lips. "What's the matter with you?" he whispered.

"Nothing, Donny. I'm just a little tired. We best get home, Honey." Arms interlocked, her head coming just up to his chin, they moved down the sidewalk, walking through the long city streets, turning finally up a steep flight of stairs that led into the hallway of a worn Victorian house, fringed with crumbling elaborate woodwork.

The passion that always followed them from the frenzied show and into the old apartment had abated, and the man wondered at it, wondered if she were sick. . .really sick. . .like his own mother had been that last time. "Shit!" he muttered angrily, crushing his fear before it had a chance to take hold in him. "Nothing wrong with her! Just let her rest awhile. . .later, I'll lay down next to her, quiet, and just hold her. . .just hold her for awhile . . ."

New Perspectives

She had slipped into the bedroom of the small flat, and for a few minutes he could hear the soft padding of her bare feet, water running in the bathroom, the opening and closing of drawers as she prepared for sleep.

Then it was quiet, and he sat in the kitchen, his lips tasting coffee, his fingers toying with an ashtray, but his mind caught in a web of drum beats somewhere in the streets, drawn by the rhythm into remembering evenings when the city was a forest of brick mountains and steel liana vines, and tall conga drums or knee-sized bongos tore the wind apart and sewed up the night until it was never again the same.

Four years ago, when he was sixteen, he had first heard the drums, really heard them, so that their rhythm crept into his mind and it was hard for him to study in school. He was drawn, every evening, to the periphery of a mandala, a magic circle on the corner by an old lumber warehouse.

"Hey, Baby!" a drummer might yell to one of the youths in the circle, "get me some beer! The bread's in my back pocket!" All this with no slack in the flailing motion of their hands against the drumheads.

He remembered the first time he had seen a man's hands bleed onto a drum, after a day and a night of pounding, taut Black fingers beating the blood into it, the skin of the conga and of the hands fresh with dark liquid, the men silent in the circle, almost afraid, but unable to leave.

He remembered the first time he had sung on the corner, a fierce throbbing chant which he had improvised as a tribute to the musicians and which had made him one of them from that night on. All of this was in his mind and he knew that someday a part of him must also bleed for this music.

In the bedroom, Della whimpered faintly in her sleep, and he went to the door, watching her for a moment. Then he returned to the kitchen and began the remembering again: his first real job, after the talent shows, the private parties, the street theaters.

It was at a bar called Eight Levels, and they rehearsed in the afternoons, squinting and sweating through the dusty spotlights.

One afternoon, he had stopped halfway through a song, and after a few bars the man on piano and then the drummer had stopped, too, because an old drunken man had heard the music from the street and staggered through the door. It was eerie to see a man drunk in sunlight, a man dirty and unshaven, his gray stubble of beard rough against a pockmarked face. Donny stood on stage looking down as the man lurched into the center of the smoky room. The others watched and heard him speak in a cringing tone that turned into sneering belligerence.

The Soul Man

"The great Donny James! You dumb bastard! You think you gonna be a singer? You think you gonna make it? You ain't worth a fuck!" He rubbed his mouth with his coat sleeve. "Y'all need the strap like I used to give you. No-good bum, dropout!"

"Get on outa here, ol' man," Donny said softly.

The man was tall, but bent over to one side, listing like an ancient ship. He pulled a greasy leather cap lower on his forehead. He did not move until the boy jumped down from the stage and came toward him slowly. "Awright, I be goin', I be goin'," he mumbled.

"You better split, Daddy!" called the drummer.

As the man stumbled out the door, he shouted, "You never be no singer! Should be a pimp, not no singer!"

The atmosphere was momentarily tense and embarrassed. The piano player shifted on his bench and played a few chords as Donny leaped back onto the stage like a cat.

"That really your ol' man?" someone finally found the courage to ask, and Donny turned slowly, his eyes blank and dark.

"Some old wino, Harry! My Daddy? Not a chance. He's just a crazy old man, that's all. Let's get hot! We got work to do."

Thinking of it now, he absent-mindedly reached under his shirt and fingered an old scar on his rib cage, a raised circular welt that could have been made by a belt buckle.

A soft rustle at the door startled him and he turned abruptly. "Della, Baby, what you doing up?" She stood half-leaning on the door frame, her bare feet on the cold linoleum, her small dark hands folded across her stomach, the fingers interlaced. "Della, you're just a little old country girl," he growled in mock rebuke as her eyelids drooped down and then opened wide again in a motion of desire.

"Donny, Honey!" She took one step toward him, and as she held out her hands to him, he turned in his chair to pull her into his lap, she whispered, "Honey, I have to tell you tonight! I wanted to wait till tomorrow, but I couldn't sleep. I'm so happy. . . . " Her smile flowered into a tropical rose, laughing in the rain forest of the city, and he put his hands around her waist.

"I've got your baby in me, a little boy or a little girl with your eyes, Donny . . . " She stopped as he took his hands away from her and stood up. "Your eyes and my lips," she whispered, watching the faint flush that colored

New Perspectives

the skin below his eyes, the widening of his nostrils as if he sought to breathe more deeply. His chest felt full and sick.

"Della, why did you do this to me, Girl? Damn it, don't you have no sense?"

She felt for the door frame and leaned back against it, one hand at her lips and that hand trembling. He heard her breath begin to mount up in choking speed inside her throat, so that it rattled harshly in the silent room.

His glance ricocheted from her face to the peeling walls, the window space he'd covered with a board, anticipating winter rains. "Christ, Della!" he cried, bringing both fists onto the table top so hard that a cup spun away over the edge and shattered at his feet. "You want to rot in this ghetto? You gonna start dropping one kid a year, bring 'em up on that corner, talking to whores and junkies before they're half grown?" His hand knotted a fistful of her robe's cottony front, where it hung in loose folds over her stomach. A flash of her gleaming dark flesh was exposed as he held the material and she stood rigid, drawn up into herself until he released her.

She raised her eyes and seeing them like copper orbs in the yellow light, infused with a fierce radiance, he was glad that he had not struck, had not crushed her. "Don't ever tell me you didn't want this! No, Donny!" she cried as he moved to place his hands on her shoulders. "When you loved me that time we didn't use anything, you knew it too! You cannot ever say you did not know it!"

His head felt tight and his lips were dry. "You'll get rid of it, Della! I can't take it! It is too much, and I will not get up-tight over this!" He raised both palms, the fingers pointing up stiffly, his shoulders lifted, as if he wanted to absolve himself in a gesture. Then he turned swiftly away from her and stood at the window, looking out. She stood behind him, waiting.

"Della, it's no good." He spoke slowly, and in his own ears the words sounded tight and cool, like the voice of a different man. "I got to be in L.A. awhile before I really start to make some money and can send for you. I won't know where I'm staying from one day to the next. Maybe . . . maybe the Sportsman's Club won't work out like Uncle Eddie said it would." He turned and faced her, thinking, I know I'm right! We got to do this! "Don't you understand? I got to get some good clothes, pay rent up here and down south too, maybe have to hire my own group down there. Fat Eddie says that's the way to do it."

She looked down and he cupped his hand under her chin and lifted it firmly until he met her eyes. His voice grew louder again. "This is my chance,

The Soul Man

Girl! Not you, not nobody's going to do me this way, give me a harder way to go than I already got!" For a moment, his eyes darkened, grew blank and inward turning like a dull whirlpool of color.

She did not answer. She walked into the bedroom and shut the door. For a long time he stood, fists tight, legs taut from the anger and fear that still jabbed in his bowels and stomach. "Girl, Girl!" he thought in panic, "I been knowing you such a short time and loving you so long! Don't blow it now, Donny! Let her have the damn kid!"

He took a step toward the closed bedroom door, and then, as if from an eternity of city corners, a sound skirted the railroad signs, the rusty fire escapes, the abandoned grocery store at the back window, and came up to him, breathless, from the street outside. "You forgotten me, Baby?" it seemed to say. "Without me, you gonna burn, Man! But with me you got the whole world by the balls. You can take the shit they've given you and throw it back in their faces! Your old wino daddy's face! That redneck principal that threw you out of high school! The cop that jabs your prick while he frisks you for being Black and on the right street at the wrong time . . . Man, listen to me!"

He leaned again at the window, his forehead on the cold steamy pane, and listened to the sound of drums, of congas massive and tall, some almost as tall as the men who raped them with palms and fingers, and of flutes that wandered like a birdsong, free, improvisational and clear over the steady staccato beat of the drums. He stood for a long time listening before he went into the dark living room, lay down on the couch, and slept.

Rehearsal the next day was bad from start to finish. The amplifier on the electric organ shorted out, and Crazy John went into a tirade and put his foot through one of his drums. It was weird to see him after he did it, Donny thought. He was a golden-skinned boy, sixteen or seventeen at most, with thin rimmed glasses, sweat and tears pouring down his face, his reddish-blond hair fuzzy and disheveled. "Donny," he whimpered, "look at my drum! Man, what made me break my drum?" and he was still crying and rumpling the kinky down on his shining head when Donny left the Jazz Box.

Jesus, am I glad to split out of here, he thought, as he started home. *I better take a nap before the show tonight. Never been this tired yet!*

The walk across town to Athens Street where he lived seemed to take hours, and as he moved slowly and with an almost agonized effort down the sidewalk outside his flat, he recognized the peculiar stir and motion, the clumps of faces that were the remnants of a street crowd, the signal to a ghetto event.

New Perspectives

Young Black children, their hair braided close to their heads or fluffed into naturals, danced up and down the steps of Donny's place in excitement. "Get on outa here!" he cried angrily, pushing past them. An old woman stood, her hands on her ponderous hips, her dress barely closed at the breast by a safety pin, and stared at him curiously.

"They took out a lady what passed!" a boy shouted to his friends, who were racing up the street. Donny stopped, one foot on the rotted step, and stared at the child. He was about seven or eight, with one tooth broken in the front, and animal-scared darting eyes that scanned Donny's face eagerly.

"Mister!" he said. "Mister! Look at the blood on the steps! She came out here like this!" He clutched his taut little belly with both grimy hands, and staggered in an exaggerated gait. "Down to the sidewalk, on her knees, bam!" He sank to his knees on the concrete. The other children watched him silently. "I seen it all! Oh, Man! Blood come out," he threw out his arms, "all over!"

A hand was on Donny's shoulder then, an excited voice harsh in his ear. "Donny, we all tried to find you, Baby! They said you left the club! It's Della! She at Highland Hospital! The cops come and called the amb'lance . . . "

The frightened tones of his friend faded into a jabbering he thought was strangely like the calling of parrots and macaws in the rain forest, a sound he had never heard but often imagined.

The little boy was silent now, frightened by the tall man's expression. Donny turned, and moving very slowly, got into his friend's car at the curb. He did not look up or around him until they reached the hospital. And during the long wait, while the doctors did their job to restore her life, and then gave her over to the nurses who would guide her back to consciousness, he stared unceasingly at the patterns in the floor, until he was told that she was out of the place called Recovery, and in her own bed, and awake to the world again.

When he first saw her at one end of the long ward, his heart was startled into a spasm of relief, for she lay covered only to her chin with a sheet, and the sheet rose and fell gently with her breathing. Della's breaths were long, sweet, and somehow jubilant, the lungs working eagerly and steadily. The sound of her breathing moved in him like a pain and he thought, *Oh Lord, they weren't jivin' me! She's hurt bad, but not gone. She isn't gone.* Until that moment, he hadn't believed that he would ever see her again.

She opened her eyes and the stricture in his throat was washed away in a gush of anger. "What motherfucking bastard did this to you!" Her eyes were like oil-slicked pools, and as she turned her face toward him, one side of her mouth twitched upward in a dim smile. Her voice was quiet, so quiet that he had to lean over the bed to hear her.

"I did it, Donny. . . . I did it for you. . . . I couldn't get it no other way. . . you know that, Donny. . . . I did it for you." And she stopped then because he had turned his back to her, had pounded his fist once against the wall. He wanted to scream at her, to punish her for the wondering softness of her voice, to shout, "You stupid little bitch!" and he wanted to cry, "You messed yourself up for me, Della, for me and I know it and I love you!"

But when he turned back to the bed, he did neither. Instead he sat on a chair by her side and not looking at her, he began to talk. He wanted to talk for hours so that he would not have to hear that soft voice just yet, and he built up momentum until the words became almost a song, melodious and vibrant.

"I'll get a part-time job. No trip to L.A. till I save up some money. Eddie's big-time friend can wait, but we can't!" Her lips parted to speak but he was not watching her, and he rushed on. "And you can get pregnant again, Della. Maybe we'll move out to the country. . . . " He heard her voice, trying to penetrate the warm layer of words that he was folding around himself, but he would not let her, not yet. "Get a house with a yard for the baby. . . . "

Suddenly he was aware at once of several things, of a high-pitched sound in his ears, of a nurse coming into the room with a needle in her hand, of Della screaming, screaming at him: "No baby, Donny! I heard the doctors say it! They thought I couldn't hear them, but I was awake. . . . I hurt myself too bad. I can't ever have a baby now. . . . " She raised herself in the bed as the nurse took her arm. "Not your baby, not with me, Donny, never!" Her voice subsided into a long keening wail, as the needle found her vein, and the cool liquid rushed in. Donny stood by the white bed and stared at her. His face was shiny with tears and sweat.

Somewhere on the ward a radio blared out for a brief moment and a man's voice flashed through the dead, stale air. "Oh, Honey, let's boogie tonight!" the singer's voice shouted in pain and longing, and the music filled the white spaces of the rooms, empty spaces between gray beds and walls and curtains, until a nurse's hand must have snapped off the sound.

In the silence, the woman in the bed lay moaning faintly, and the man heard the rain outside begin to sound wetly against the windows, beating on the glass like a quiet, insistent drummer.

Ages Past

Grant Lowther

Young eyes transfixed
On heavens vast
Burn with a longing
To venture far

Distant stars
Hold wondrous things
That youthful eyes,
Only, can see

With advancing years
Comes daily toil
And former desires
Fade quickly away

As Death's long arm
Advances near
To one whose body
Seems spent and creaking

Those long ago yearnings
Return to the fore
Seen now through eyes
Made knowingly clear

The dreams of youth
The wisdom of age
Worlds apart
Or one in the same?

Good Bye, Minnie

Lola Curtis

The droning of a male voice brought Charlie slowly out of his deep sleep. "Tuesday, June 8th, a beautiful sunny day. Temperatures expected to be in the mid 70s."

Yawning, Charlie reached over to the night table and switched off the annoyance. As he lay down to catch a few more winks, the announcer's voice suddenly came back to him. June 8th! My God, it was seven years ago today that Minnie died. Seven years! Boy, back then I didn't think I had any life left either, Minnie. Those last five years with you being so sick sort of made me go stale. I had a real bad time realizing you wouldn't be here no more. Aah, Minnie, we had us a good life. And weren't you the jealous one! Sure didn't go for me sweet-talking all the girls. You never could understand it was just in fun, Minnie. You just never could understand. Guess it's a good thing you can't see me now. I'm getting to be quite a sport. Yup, a real sport. Ain't bad looking for 67, if I do say so myself, and Dory and Junie think I'm real handsome. Don't guess I'll ever marry again, but maybe one of these years I'll ask some woman to move in with me. Well, no use laying here gathering wool. Best get up and see what the day's going to bring.

Charlie eased himself out of the warm bed, washed, put on a clean pair of jeans and a yellow sweat shirt. He glanced into the mirror and appraised his 180 pounds. Not much fat, he mused—five foot nine and in my prime! He chuckled at that and ambled into the large, sunny kitchen. Turning on the radio, he made sure his favorite country-western station was tuned in. Johnny Cash was singing "Folsom Prison," and Charlie hummed along as he opened the fridge and carefully pried three strips of bacon from the pack. Squatting down to reach the bottom shelf of the cupboard, he pulled out a frying pan, unmindful of the racket caused by the clatter of falling pan lids. When the bacon was carefully laid in the pan and the gas flame adjusted, Charlie set about making some coffee. The song ended and, mentally blocking out the commercials, he started thinking about Minnie again.

I sure never had to do no cooking while she was able to get around. She took a real pride in "doin' for her man," as she liked to say. Boy, how she loved this house, and this kitchen was just about her reason for living. When she couldn't make it out to the kitchen no more, she just sort of give up. Charlie shrugged, funny how my mind is so filled with Minnie today. Haven't had thoughts like this for a long time. Must be the date and I'm just lonesome. Guess I'd better think serious about taking in a housemate.

The smell of the frying bacon brought Charlie out of his reverie. He took two eggs out of the refrigerator and deftly cracked them on the edge of a bowl and let them plop inside it as he had seen Minnie do countless times. He put the bacon on a paper towel to drain, poured some of the extra fat into an old cup and slid the eggs into the pan.

Minnie would be proud of me for learning to do so well for myself. I sure haven't missed any meals. Not that I've had to fix all of them! He smiled, remembering Dory. Hadn't she been the one! Wouldn't have thought one of Minnie's best friends would be so quick to want to take over, but maybe that sparkle was in her eye for longer than I'd noticed. Minnie would have scratched her eyes out, best friend or no. Dory sure helped me over those first months, bringing me food and all. Wasn't sorry when my friend Jake came along and swept her off her feet though, he gave her someone to look out for instead of me.

This time it was a smell of feathers that brought Charlie back to reality and he put the eggs on his plate, leaving the burned part of the white in the skillet. Better watch it, Tiger, you have to eat your cooking, so no use ruining it by letting your mind wander off. He poured a cup of coffee, brought it and his plate over to the table and set it down on the blue Formica top. Sure glad I remembered to get bread yesterday, he thought as he put a slice in the toaster. Breakfast ain't right without toast. Hummph, another of Minnie's sayings. She sure had everything figured out. Except her sickness. I'm sure she didn't ever figure to get sick and leave me. Nope, I don't think she ever counted on that. Chrp. What the hell is that—must be static on the radio. He turned it off and went out to get the morning paper. CHRP. Guess I'd better oil these door hinges. He went back into the kitchen and finished his meal as he read through the paper, letting pages drop to the floor.

Suddenly he remembered, by golly, I've got to get a move on—I've got to be at Junie's by nine! Junie, now isn't she something. A might plump maybe, but her get-up-and-go and smiling face made you wish there was more of her.

Good Bye, Minnie

Now Junie was one gal Minnie never knew about. It was a good day for me when she started working at the coffee shop. Liked her right off, I did. She never worries about nothin'. Says worry is a waste of time. Damned if she ain't right. Not much was ever solved by worrying. She sure has some crazy ideas, though, like the one about dead people's spirits coming back to haunt you if you don't act right. Rubbish. When you're dead, you're dead, and there's nothing you can do about it.

Chrp. Dang it, that's getting to be annoying. Wonder if a cricket found its way in here. Minnie would have had a fit if she'd found a critter in her kitchen. No time to look for it now, better put these dishes to soak and get on over to Junie's. Hot dog, we're going to the zoo, just like a couple of kids. Took Junie to think that up. Wonder how many monkeys they've got. Well, there will be two more when we get there.

CHRP. Man alive, now the back door is screeching at me too. Guess one of these says I'll have to give up my social life for some home fixing. Slamming the door shut, he made sure the lock caught. Junie, here comes Romeo!

The day at the zoo passed quickly. Charlie and Junie took in all the sights, and Charlie even bought tickets for the merry-go-round. They had a little fuss when Junie wanted to ride on the horse, but Charlie finally convinced her that people their age would be better off on the seats that looked like big swans. He told her it would be more romantic that way—and boy, did she like that. After their ride they went back to the car to get the lunch basket Junie had packed. A short walk to the park, and they spread a blanket on the grass and eased themselves down on it. Junie had brought the works—fried chicken, lemonade, salad, and chocolate cake.

As Charlie was about to bite into a chicken leg, a cricket jumped on the blanket. He brushed it off, but he remembered the one in the house and told Junie about it.

"Have you seen it, Charlie?" she asked.

"No, but I keep hearing it, so it must be someplace. Unless its something else, of course."

"Something else like what, Charlie?" Junie was entranced.

"Oh, something like a squeaking door hinge or static on the radio."

"But, Charlie, if you heard it when you were eating, then it couldn't have been the door hinge, now could it?"

"No, guess not." Charlie agreed.

New Perspectives

"And if you heard it when you were going out the door, it couldn't have been the radio, could it?" June persisted.

"No, you're right there–guess it must be a cricket."

"Yeah," said Junie, "must be a cricket, . . . unless . . . "

"Unless what, woman–now don't go getting spooky on me. If I said it was a cricket, it's a cricket, and I'll find it when I get home and that will be the end of it."

"Okay, okay, Charlie, don't get mad. It probably is just a cricket. Anyway, they're supposed to bring good luck, so maybe you should just leave it alone."

"Yeah, well, we'll see. Now let's get this mess cleaned up and head out–it's past three and I want to beat the traffic going home. You sure do know how to fix a picnic, Junie! You're one helluva gal."

It was about four o'clock when Charlie let himself in his front door. He was tired, but it was happy tired. Always like that with Junie. Maybe I should think more seriously about her, he mused. Right now, though, that sofa looks pretty good for a nap before supper. Chrp. Damn, there it goes again. He fluffed the pillows on the sofa and sank down into them and closed his eyes.

As he drifted off to sleep a faint chirp sounded in the distance. In some other distance, Minnie was bustling around and seemed to come closer. Then she was in the kitchen, muttering about leaving dirty dishes in the sink and not cleaning the crumbs off the table, and some hussy living in her house. She picked up the newspaper, folded it and put it in the paper box by the door and floated away. Charlie stirred a bit and then, half awake, cocked his head to hear better.

Chrp. Chrp. That was it!! It wasn't no cricket. It was Minnie! Junie probably knew it, that's why she was so interested. She knew! Junie knew about those things. Do you suppose . . .

Charlie got up off the sofa and walked into the kitchen half expecting to see everything shipshape. Whew–guess that part was a dream, but Minnie has sure as heck come back to watch me.

CHRP. See, now she's really letting me know it. Dag nab it woman, give me some peace. CHRP. No, don't go getting mad, just go back to wherever you came from and leave me be. CHRP. Oh, my word, I'll never have another restful minute. Wonder if she found out about Junie. CHRP. Yep, now she's answering me. Minnie, don't you understand? You're dead and I'm not

Good Bye, Minnie

dead. CHRP. Minnie, let me finish. Listen good, now—you're dead. CHRP. Minnie, stop it for God's sake. CHRP.

Charlie grabbed his car keys and ran out of the house, slamming the door, not caring if it was locked or not. In five minutes he was knocking on Junie's door.

"Land sakes, Charlie, come on in and quit scaring me with that pounding. What on earth's the matter with you? Have you gone plumb crazy?"

"Junie, you gotta help me."

"Help you, what's the matter? You're a big strapping man, why do you need help?"

"Junie, you gotta, you know all about such things."

"All about what things, Charlie, what are you talking about?"

"Those things, Junie, those ghosts."

"Ghosts? Charlie, where did you go after dropping me off? Sounds like someone snuck a funny pill in your beer."

"Junie, listen to me, I'm serous. I didn't go for no beer. I went right home and took a nap on the sofa and there she was."

"Who was, Charlie? You're sounding mighty strange."

"She was, Junie, it was Minnie—she cleaned up the kitchen, no, that was in the dream, but she's there. She's there. She's there and she chirps at me!"

"Oh, my land, Charlie, you must be getting senile. Calm down and try to talk sensible."

"There ain't nothing to say, Junie, except Minnie's mad cuz I'm seeing you and she's come back from the dead to haunt me and she chirps. She follows me around the house and she chirps. You gotta come over and get her out of there. I'll go plumb crazy if I have to spend the rest of my life with dead Minnie chirping at me all the time. It just ain't fair, Junie. You gotta help me."

"Okay, Charlie. Just calm down and I'll go. Boy, I've heard everything now!"

The sun was just setting when Charlie and Junie arrived at Charlie's house. Charlie paled at the thought of night coming on with a real ghost inside his house, even if it was Minnie. But maybe Junie could do something. Maybe make Minnie mad enough to leave. Fat chance, Junie was so friendly Minnie would probably take right to her and make me leave.

He slowly opened the door and peeked in. CHRP.

New Perspectives

"Hear it, Junie, hear it?" CHRP.

Junie's eyes opened wide in astonishment as she said, "Yaah, Charlie, I do." CHRP. "Get out of here, Minnie, you're dead." CHRP. "Go on now, go back where you belong." CHRP. Junie walked from the kitchen to the living room. "Go back, Minnie." Chrp. "Go on back, Minnie. You don't live here any more and you're scaring Charlie." The chirp was fainter. She yelled back to Charlie, who seemed stuck in his tracks inside the kitchen door.

"I think she's leaving now, Charlie, her voice is getting weaker."

CHRP. "Not in here, it ain't," croaked Charlie. CHRP. "She's staying right here in her kitchen and I'll never be able to eat again."

"Nonsense, Charlie." CHRP. "Whoops, guess you're right. We'll just have to reason with her. Why don't you go outside and I'll just have a little woman-to-woman talk with her and we'll get things straightened out. She ain't going to agree to nothing with you standing there rooted to the floor."

"Okay, Junie, but be careful. Minnie used to be pretty easygoing, but I don't know what's happened to her in the last seven years." CHRP. "I'm going now," he hollered, and in a hoarse whisper, "I won't let anyone move in here, Minnie."

Junie stared around the kitchen looking for her opponent. She knew if she didn't do something, Charlie would probably move out of town and she'd never see him again. "I'd sure miss that old Coot—let's see now." CHRP. "Since it don't do no good talking to you, Minnie, the next best thing is to find out where you're hiding. Guess the only way I can do that is to follow the . . . " CHRP. "There it goes again. Let's see now. When I went into the living room before, it was real faint." CHRP. "So, if I go back there and trace it getting louder, it should put me on the right track."

Junie gingerly tiptoed into the living room, looking like she expected to be struck down at any moment. Chrp. Sure enough, as she passed the doorway, the sound got fainter. So she turned around and tiptoed back into the kitchen.

"Boy, old Minnie must have really liked this kitchen. Bet she don't cotton much to the idea of me being here." CHRP. "Hey, you don't have to yell at me, I ain't deaf."

As she tiptoed past the refrigerator and past the sink the sound seemed to get louder.

"Hell, what am I doing tiptoeing around here like I'm the criminal. Minnie, you get right out of here—get out, I say, or I'll go get a priest to wave

---
16

Good Bye, Minnie

his cross at you. That will get you in trouble with the boss up there." CHRP. "Boy, she didn't like that, she's getting louder."

Junie looked up as if to heaven for divine guidance, and that's when she found Minnie.

"Charlie," she yelled, "Charlie, you get right back in here this minute."

Charlie's head came peeking through the door and he slowly pulled his body in after it.

"What'd you find, Junie?" he asked, trembling.

"What did I find, Charlie? I'll tell you what I found. When was the last time you put a new battery in that smoke alarm over the door there?"

"Jesus Christ, Junie, I plumb forgot about that. Do you really think . . .?"

"Think, you fool, of course I think—a sight more than you do. Now get that thing down from there and take out that old battery. That's what's been talking to you, not Minnie!"

Charlie reached up and gingerly took the alarm from the wall. Carefully removing the battery, he tossed it away with a sigh of relief and a sheepish grin, saying, "Good Bye, Minnie!"

Jubilation?

Frank Bette

Sandpipers and sanderlings
Tarry on the beach.
Then a swift rush,
The whir and whiz,
Maneuvering up and down,
Now showing dark tops of wings
Or again light silver flashes
From the undersides.
Such alluring precision.
Directly all return
Busy adjusting,
Brightly chirping.
A flush of jubilation?

Water Borne

Cecil Fox

It was no place for folks in our circumstances to be living, but it was the only housing available. Our home was in a three-room house built on piles on the edge of Puget Sound in Washington State, and located thirty-five steps down from the street. It was wartime, and we were a young married couple with an infant child.

When a high tide was in, the water was six feet deep under the house, and at low tide there was a sandy strip of beach (not too clean). Both events provided us with many unusual situations, from the ridiculous, to helpful, to distressing.

One day my wife was in dire need of some elastic for a sewing project, and there was none available. What to do? While gazing out a front window at the incoming tide she spotted an intriguing object. I hurried to the boat dock and fished in the item with a boat hook from the landlord's rowboat. What joy! It was a new pink corset with four garters–just the elastic that was needed. I wondered what the wearer was like.

On one occasion we saw a wooden casket float by. Strange, but we had fun speculating. Was it empty? Did it fall out of a hearse? Was it tossed into the water as a prank? Perhaps it was a prop from a lodge ceremony and had inadvertently floated away from its storage place.

Another time an overstuffed chair went by on the waves, floating as serenely as though someone was sitting in it.

New Perspectives

A rewarding incident occurred one day when the tide was out. I was lazily walking around on the beach when my shoe uncovered a glittering "something" in the sand. Eureka! It was a gold wedding ring, which soon netted us $10 from a local jeweler.

On an outgoing tide we frequently performed a useful ritual that, today, would quickly bring environmentalists to the scene, perhaps even a city official. We would lean out one of the front windows, facing the Sound, and empty our wastebaskets. Nowadays neither of us would so much as drop a gum wrapper outside of a proper receptacle.

Weather-wise, winter was the most difficult time. The house was heated by a monstrous kitchen range, converted to oil from wood and coal. We could not afford to heat the bedroom and living room, only the kitchen. Because of climatic dampness there were times when the floor and rugs would mildew beneath the furniture. During freezing weather one's frosty footprints from the front door to the kitchen would remain all day on the living room carpet.

The water pipes under the house were another cold-weather casualty. On one occasion I found myself pajama-clad, anxiously straddling the support boards between the pilings over the water, and striving to thaw out the frozen plumbing with a blowtorch.

The most frightening experience took place one moonless night after we returned from visiting friends. Glancing down the stairs I spotted an intruder on the roof. Seeing us, he jumped down to the boat landing by the back door, ran up the other stairs, turned, and then started toward me. I braced myself in front of my wife and the baby buggy, and when he rushed me I instinctively kicked him in the stomach. Gasping for breath, he momentarily backed off.

In the meantime my wife was hollering "Help, help, call the police."

A man in a nearby apartment building leaned out of a third floor window and yelled at her, "Aw, call 'em yourself."

The assailant ran at me again, so I repeated the body blow. That did it. He took off at a wobbly pace. I was both scared and angry. Fortunately, he did not show a weapon.

After a year of living at Washington Beach we finally qualified for Navy housing. Although we had experienced plenty of fun and excitement in our home on pilings, we were glad to have a better place in which to live.

In 1984 we made our first return visit to the area in twenty-seven years. We were surprised that not a vestige of our former waterside cottage remained. On the bluff where the apartment building had stood there now was a parking lot, and the row of beach houses was only a memory.

The Company President

Delbert B. Campbell

I took my trusty tool bag
And I went out to see
If I could fix a computer
At good ol' PT&T.

I pondered probable causes
As I drove in through the mist.
Not knowing that this "call out"
Was to relieve a specialist.

Well, parking's rough on Folsom
But I found a place on Howard.
So entered through the rear door
Where the computer room is powered.

As I passed along the power bank
Where the computer room gets "juice"
I noticed that the ground wire
Was hanging precariously loose.

But not to disturb the problem,
If that (by chance) was it,
I went on in to relieve my man
Who, by now, was short of wit.

It was readily understandable
Why the specialist was spent.
Standing over his shoulder
Was the company president!

New Perspectives

"Well," I gasped. I breathed my name out.
I smiled as best I could.
Still, he shook my hand with gusto,
As such a great man would.

I told him of a principle
To which all engineers adhere.
You have a cup of coffee first,
Just to get the problem clear.

He agreed to this idea.
A good one, he had thought.
And when we reached the vendor,
The son-of-a-gun, he bought!

He told me that this problem
Had come and gone for days.
It had set no failing pattern.
Not by job, by batch, by phase.

I told him that these symptoms
Were difficult to trace,
But faulty wiring could do it
Anywhere on the interface.

Well, I fixed his problem at the power box,
With help from the electrician resident.
And you never saw a happier guy
Than that company president.

He pulled me into his office
And he took his pen to write.
The adjectives and adverbs flowed
'Til my head was out of sight.

"You need not," I said, "have written
All those accolades so dear.
To have them simply spoken
Gives me purpose, pride, and cheer."

The Company President

"Forgive me, Del," he countered,
"But a letter I insist.
For truth is only truth, you know,
So long as it exists."

To paraphrase the meaning
Of those words spoke so profound:
Facts are only fantasies
Unless they're written down!

A Man Tonight

Helen Cannon

I am sitting at the end of the bar nearest the door. I don't know why, I just feel better there, close to the door. I've got my skirt pulled down over my knees, and my legs aren't crossed. I'm only there for a drink. I don't hang out in bars; I just like one drink sometimes, before I go home.

I don't like this bartender. He's too cool, putting a lot of flourishes in his mixing, lining up the bottles just so. He comes over and stands in front of me without even saying hello. I order a vodka gimlet. Usually I don't ask for mixed drinks, but this fellow gets under my skin. He brings the gimlet and goes back to the register without speaking, doesn't look at me when he slaps my change down.

Some bartenders don't like women coming in alone, but it's really not their business. This is San Francisco, after all, not some backwoods junction.

I wasn't born here. I was born in Ames, Iowa. My father had a piece of ground he called a farm, but he never made anything out of it. I left when I turned sixteen, went out to Seattle and a lot of other places. But San Francisco's it, as far as I'm concerned. I love this city—it seems to be humming to itself all the time. So what if it took me two husbands and twenty years of drudgery to get here? I've been here a long time; that's all dead history.

I've finished my drink and I'd like another one, but I can't catch his eye. I fold a five lengthwise and hold it between two fingers so he can see it if he looks this way. After a while one of the men says something to him and points toward me, and he comes down to where I'm sitting.

I say, "You make a good gimlet." I don't like him, but I have to say something to make him look at me.

A Man Tonight

He does, just barely, and says, "Another one?"

Then I start thinking; I can't help it. I wonder if he figures me for a lush. Or if he thinks I just came in here to pick somebody up. Does he for God's sake think I'm trying to pick *him* up? I say, "I guess so, one more," trying to sound as if it didn't matter all that much.

Because I'm getting on, and I know it. I don't kid myself—it's more years than I care to think about since I was young. But that doesn't mean I'm dead; I still like to go places and talk to people. And I like a drink now and then. Bars are supposed to be warm and friendly; you're supposed to feel welcome.

I'm drinking the second drink when this guy at the far end stands up. Even in the dim light I can see he's young. His hair looks black or dark brown, and he wears it a little long in back. He walks toward me as if he wasn't going anywhere in particular, but I've already seen that smiling, not-smiling look and the way he hitches his shoulders to shake his sleeves down. I know that look. I've been around some since Ames, Iowa.

He stops beside me and smiles. He leans on the next stool, resting his elbow on the bar, and says, "Can I get you another one of those?"

I say, "No, I guess not." But I don't freeze up, and he sits down.

He says his name is Bill. That's good enough for me; I'm not asking for his ID. And then he asks my name and I say, "Janice."

"Janice—that fits you perfectly," he says. "It's got class, like you." I want to laugh, but it's no use hurting his feelings. So I just smile. He asks if I'm from out of town, and I tell him no; then he wants to know if I'm married, and I say, "Not any more." I feel as if I was never married, really married.

"Do you play tennis?" he asks. Next he's going to say how trim and athletic I look—I've heard that before. I say no, I don't play tennis or golf, I don't jog or lift weights. I read a lot and watch TV, I tell him. That's a lie—I read a little, but I hate TV.

He says he runs every morning, and he has that look—lean but solid. Then he says he likes to dance, too. That's my cue; I'm supposed to say I just adore dancing.

"I just adore dancing," I say. I feel like a fool.

"Tell you what." He's trying to sound as if the idea had just popped into his mind. "Why don't we go dancing somewhere? Maybe even get a decent drink."

New Perspectives

There's not a thing wrong with my gimlet, but he's trying to be friendly. So I say, "A good drink would be a nice change." And then I say, "But I don't think I'd better."

"Aw, why not? Look, I'm a nice guy." He smiles to prove it, all sincerity and even, white teeth. "I'm not trying to put the make on you; I just like to dance."

I laugh politely—he expects me to—and tell him again that I'd better not. His schoolboy grin doesn't change; he says at least I ought to let him buy me another drink. "We can talk, anyway," he says. "It's hard to find people you can really talk to."

So after a while we go out together, and I'm careful to keep my head down when we walk under a streetlight. He has a car, a little white soft-top. He stands behind me while I get in. "You've got a really great figure," he says. "I sure had you picked for a tennis player or something like that."

He starts the engine and asks where I'd like to go. I'd like to suggest some place dark, but I laugh and say it doesn't make any difference.

"Let's just drive around while we think about it," he says. We go out Geary, all the way to the ocean, and turn down along the beach. He slows down and says, "Want to stop and watch the waves awhile?"

I say, "I've got high heels on; I can't walk on the sand." I say it quickly; I don't intend to walk on that dark beach with a stranger.

"We'll just stand at the wall then, how's that?"

We get out and walk over to the wall. The tide is going out; it has that tired sound, a little sad that it's wasted all that effort. I know it's silly, but I always feel that way about an outgoing tide. When I try to explain that to Bill, he reaches out and takes hold of my hand. I feel warm and happy, holding hands and watching the black waves roll in.

For years I used to buy those Sierra Club calendars and keep them turned to the pictures of the ocean. People would come up to my desk and say why don't you wake up, it's October; but I wouldn't change the page. That was in Yakima, after Steve and I got divorced.

Bill keeps my hand in his and leans on the wall. He doesn't talk now, and I like that. I just want to look and listen and not think. I try to spell out the sound of the waves, but it keeps changing.

Finally Bill turns his head toward me and says, "Does it make you feel small, or bigger than God?"

A Man Tonight

"Safe," I say. "It's so strong it could kill us in two seconds, but it hasn't—so maybe it won't."

He laughs a little. "That's a funny kind of safe."

I shake my head. "It's safe for right now—that's enough."

He says yes, and then a minute later he says, "Janice . . . "

If it was in a movie, I would catch my breath and let my voice go soft and say, "Ye-es-s, Bill?" But I don't say anything. Then he does something I'm not expecting. He puts his arm around me and gives me a hard, tight squeeze—the way a kid does when he's so happy he can't stand it. I want to cry.

"You didn't want to go dancing, did you?" he says. I didn't, of course, and I tell him so.

I say, "I only came with you because you seemed to want somebody to talk to."

"That's what it was," he says, and then he shivers. "God, the wind's cold. I'll bet you're cold in that light coat."

I haven't felt the cold, but I hug my arms together as if I did. He says, "Let's go get some coffee, want to?"

He hasn't said anything about his apartment, and I'm glad. I know the kind of place he lives in—a "studio" with the bed made up to look like a couch and a folding screen hiding a combination kitchen. I feel suddenly tender toward him, as if we had been dear friends for a long, long time.

I suppose that's why I'm not upset when he picks a place with glaring white ceiling lights. I don't even think about ducking my head as we go in. Anyway, he's walking in front of me, so it's only when we sit down that he looks at me. I know I must look awful; I haven't done a thing to my face and hair since I left home.

"Feels good in here," he says. "I was cold too."

I nod and shiver again, to be agreeable. A boy brings our coffee. I excuse myself and go to the restroom, touch up my makeup and comb my hair so the roots don't show. I don't look too bad, I think—but then, I'm used to myself.

After a while the boy comes again and we let him refill our cups. Bill tells me about his job, and I think he's telling the truth. I tell him about my job—but I don't tell him I got laid off two years ago and I'm living on Ed Bauer's

New Perspectives

charity now. I don't tell him I'm afraid to go looking for work because I'm too old.

He tells me about his cat. I like men who like cats; it shows confidence. I tell him about Howl, the cat I used to have. A plumber accidentally let him out last April, and he ran away. I looked all over but I never found him. I tell this to Bill, and he looks as sad as if it had been his own cat.

We've been sitting there over an hour when he reaches across the table and pats my hand and says, "Janice, you're a nice person."

I study his face. He has a kindly expression; he means exactly what he said. But he's stopped looking at me now. His eyes are aimed at me, but they're not focussed on anything. My stomach knots up. I'm not young, and I don't meet many men. . . . I never meet men like Bill.

I remember when he walked up to me in the dark bar. I knew what he wanted then, and I think he still wants it. Only we've got acquainted now, and it's different. I smile brightly, as brightly as I can, and say, "You're a neat person too, Bill. Really."

A quick little frown crosses his face, and now I'm scared. I keep my voice bright. "Well, what would you like to do now?" I ask. I want to sound ready for anything, dancing or more ocean—anything.

He smiles again—he smiles a lot—but this time there's a little tic at the back of his jaw and I know he's fighting a yawn. I can't ask him if he's tired; it would be like asking him if he wants to go to bed. "Did you have something in mind?" I ask. It sounds terrible; I want to sink through the floor.

He shakes his head and I feel guilty—I should be prettier, younger, the way he thought I was.

"That's not very subtle," he says in a flat voice.

There it is, right out in the open. I'm not sure for a minute that I heard it right. Then I'm angry; I didn't ask him to pick me up.

"Are you gay?" I ask. I hope he is; then it won't be my fault. But he says no, and I wonder if I can kill myself. I know I can't; I've thought about it before and I don't know how. People get pills; I wouldn't know where to buy them.

When I lived in Iowa I hated the flat fields that never varied. I tried to run away with a bass guitar player from Vancouver when I was fifteen, but my father caught up with the band a few miles down the road the next morning. Afterward, I wished I could die. But I didn't; it's hard to die.

A Man Tonight

I was young then; now I'm not. I've got little sagged places under my jaw, as if part of my face has slid down there and was getting ready to fall off. I tell Bill, "It's okay if you don't want me."

"That's not it," he lies. "I'm just not in the mood."

I laugh, or try to; it doesn't come off very well. I even reach over and try to pat his hand, but he pulls it away. That's all right. I'm tough; I can take it.

"Sometimes it's like that," I say stupidly. I start putting my coat on, and he doesn't offer to help me. "Want to go, then?"

But I've scared him, and he won't move. He says, "I think I'll stay here for a while, if you don't mind going by yourself. Do you need cab fare?"

Well, I can take that, too. I say no, I've got it, and I hold my head up high while I walk to the door. There's no cab outside, naturally; it doesn't look like the kind of street where there's going to be a cab. I start walking, a little nervous on the empty street.

I walk a long way before I see Cirro's bar up ahead. My feet are tired, and I think about stopping there and calling a taxi. But I don't; I walk all the way home. I can't help it if I'm crying. Anyway, there's nobody to see me.

Full Circle

Grant Lowther

I knew a man once
Tall and lean,
He played a game,
The game called war.

"Where's my daddy,"
The little boy asked;
"I don't know,"
His mother replied.

One fine summer day
That dread news came.
The game Daddy played
Had been lost, forever.

I know a young man,
Strong, well built.
"I want to be a soldier,"
The young man said.

"That's all well and good,"
His mother returned,
"But one thing you shouldn't forget,
Your father played, too."

Druid's Eve

Marilyn K. Dickerson

Ellen knew that she would be dead soon. She'd already accepted that reality with numb resignation. She was beyond terror, beyond the mindless panic and pleading tears. The girl merely waited now to be claimed by the evil energy that had invaded her home. She was a prisoner in a jail of ruffled curtains and chintz covers, but a prisoner just the same—awaiting execution.

Numbly she stared down at her hands, lying palm upward in her lap. The fingers were bloodied; the nails ripped to the flesh. Trying to escape, she'd clawed first at the front door and then had raced to each of the windows in the small cottage. But the storm's icy drifts had sealed them shut, and she was entombed. How carefully Tom had nailed closed each shuttered window. Suspended in time, she could hear again the determined rap of his hammer.

Finished with his task, her fiance had stomped into the kitchen, brushing snow from the khaki jacket with its silver sheriff's badge. He sauntered to the stove where Ellen stirred a pot of bubbling stew. His eyes glinted with a boyish twinkle as he bent to kiss the tip of her nose. "How's that for service, pretty thing," he quipped. "All the windows shuttered tight. With that nor'easter coming on tonight you'll be as snug as a fat lady in a cheap girdle."

Ellen smiled up at the rugged young man, loving him with her eyes. He was trying so hard to cheer her up. Sighing, the corners of her mouth tightened and she sniffed, blinking back tears. "Damn that storm!" she fumed, damply.

New Perspectives

"This is the first time in five years that Mom and Dad could come during my Christmas vacation, and the Bangor airport is snowed in!" Head bent, Ellen jabbed at the meat in the pot. Turning off the burner, she sat down at the kitchen table, her chin propped on one hand.

Tom slid easily into the chair opposite and leaned across to raise her chin with the tips of two fingers. "I know you're disappointed, Honey," he soothed, the dark eyes gentle. "I was looking forward to meeting your folks, too. I was beginning to think we'd never get them up here to the Maine woods. But let's not make a Greek tragedy out of it. Besides. . . " a smug smile broadened into a grin, "I've got a surprise for you."

Ellen's eyes brightened. "A surprise. . . ? What kind of surprise? Tell me!" She didn't have the heart to spoil his fun. When he'd come in she'd noticed the bulge in his jacket and the way he'd kept one hand protectively over it. As he slowly unzipped his windbreaker a small furry head with two bright yellow eyes peeped out at her.

"Oh, a *kitten*, Tom!" she squealed. "It's adorable!" She cupped her hands to receive the little gray striped animal. A red ribbon around its neck secured a tiny silver bell. "Oh, I just love it, Darling." Ellen fingered the little bell, smiling up at him. "In fact, I'm going to *call* it Tinker Bell." She set the kitten on the table and threw her arms around him. "She's. . . he's. . . just what I wanted, Tom." Her voice softened as he held her close and she met his warm, steady gaze. "You always know what I need, don't you, my love."

Tom cleared his throat and thrust her away with a gentle shove. "I think I know what we both need, my little tease, but I've got to get back to the station. I don't think we can get the tree into the house and manage a little hanky-panky, too. I'm good, my dear," he leered cheerfully, "but not *that* good."

Ellen straightened with an exclamation. "You found a tree, too, you marvelous man? It's Christmas Eve and I must have a tree this very minute."

With light steps, Ellen followed Tom as he strode towards the blue El Camino parked in the snow-banked driveway. An eight-foot spruce lay in the truck bed. In moments, the tree had been lugged into the cottage and set on its crossties next to the fireplace.

"Oh, Tom," she breathed in awe. "That's the most perfect tree I've ever seen! Wherever did you find it? Hanrahan's lot never had the likes of this beauty!"

Ellen was still admiring the symmetry of the snow-dusted branches when Tom's silence registered. She turned towards him with an enquiring look, sensing his disquiet.

Druid's Eve

"I... I found it at the Morbeous place, Ellen. It was growing out of the charred wreckage of the barn. Nothing's grown there since... since the fire. I don't really know why I cut it down... except it's such a perfect tree. I... I wanted you to have the best."

The girl frowned, the exuberance fading. "The Morbeous place, Tom...?" She drew a quick, anxious breath. "Oh, *no*!"

"Oh, come on, now, Ellen." The young man reproved, forcing a light tone. "Stop being so superstitious. Morbeous has been dead for five years. You can't still believe in that old fraud's stupid curse! He was a fake! Just a charlatan fortuneteller who painted weird symbols on his barn to impress the country yokels!"

Ellen shook her head, remembering the newspaper account of the dreadful fire. Four drunken woodsmen armed with torches had stormed out of the village saloon, intent on harassing the strange old man. The rowdy prank had turned into a ghastly nightmare. Morbeous, trapped among his occult symbols and paraphernalia, had died screaming his curses from the loft of the burning barn.

Ellen shivered with a sudden dread. "And now they're all dead, Tom. All four of the men who did it. Zeb Hollister's own hunting dogs mauled him. Roscoe was bitten by some weird African snake no one had ever heard of. Nate and Joe Barney froze to death in a freak snowstorm in August!" The girl drew in a long, ragged breath, fighting her rising fear. "But what's even worse, Tom, he blamed *you*!" She hurried on breathlessly. "He knew you could have stopped it... and *didn't*!"

With a sudden rush of emotion, Tom took her in his arms, holding her tightly. He sighed heavily. "Oh, Hell, Ellen. I know you're right. I could have stopped that crazy bunch! How can I explain it? I was an overzealous young deputy. I thought Morbeous was a menace to the community... fleecing people with his spooky predictions and mysterious cards. OK... OK. I admit I made a stupid mistake about someone I didn't know. It just got out of hand. And because I was such..." Held closely in his arms, Ellen could hear his tight swallow, "such a judgmental fool, a man died, and died horribly."

He clung to her, desperately seeking some solace, and then he gave a hoarse little laugh, looking down into her upturned face. "But you know what, Ellen? He can't hurt me. Not as long as I have you. You're my whole life... my past, present, *and* future. As long as I have you I'm indestructible." He laughed again, his voice strong, his laughter ringing out with an eerie clarity. "So, let's decorate that damned tree and see if we can't domesticate its infernal creator..."

New Perspectives

Powerful in their youth, Ellen and Tom dragged out the Christmas tree decorations from the basement. Soon lights, red, green, and yellow, were strung on the strong green branches and a piney scent filled the cottage.

Ellen perched on the stepladder adjusting the silver star on the top of the tree. A gray, sticky matter clung to her fingers. She brushed it away, noticing a silvery substance that webbed the upper branches. As the tree lights flashed on, she saw a faint, gauzy wisp hovering in the muted glow. It was a minute, probing tentacle. At first, she thought it was a spider web, but instinctively she knew that no spider had spun the diaphanous network that her mind could give no name.

A tinkling bell and the patter of tiny feet heralded Tinker as he skittered across the hardwood floor. Sliding under the tree, the kitten batted at a low hanging ornament, sending it crashing to the floor in a hundred gleaming shards.

Laughing, Ellen hurried down the ladder steps to scoop the kitten up into her arms. It snuggled against her breast and then wriggled free of her and worked its way upward to nestle under her chin. "Tinker," she accused with a chuckle, "you're cute, but I can see that you're *not* to be trusted."

Tom moved from behind the tree where he'd been adjusting the lights. "And it might also be a good idea to cover the fish tank or Tinker Terror here may just have a fish sandwich for breakfast."

Next to Tom's height and width of shoulder, Ellen felt small and fragile. Idly she stroked the kitten's soft fur. "Am I really going to be Mrs. Tom Jarrit in three weeks, Darling?" she asked with a hint of wonder.

He slid his arm around her waist. "Yup," he said. "That's when the loving and obeying really gets serious." He cast a quick glance at his watch. "But if this public servant doesn't get himself to the courthouse pretty quick, he's going to be in the unemployment line before he's in a receiving line."

Tom reached for his jacket, draped over a chair. Thrusting long arms into the sleeves, he zipped up the front. With his trooper's hat in hand, he paused, his eyes serious. "I love you, Cat Lady. Very much," he said simply. "Not because you're a gorgeous blonde or have nice legs and a great tush, but. . . but because of what I am when I'm with you. With you I'm taller and smarter, more perceptive. . . maybe even kinder, I don't know. I can't explain it. I just want to be good enough to be your husband."

Ellen caught her breath, filled with quick emotion. A smile quivered at the corners of her mouth. "Do you mean, Wonderful Person, that a third grade teacher on Christmas vacation really can find everlasting happiness with the town's handsomest, most eligible bachelor?"

"You nut," he muttered, a laugh low in this throat. "But don't worry. Another three weeks and I'll have you whipped into shape." He gave her a quick, fierce hug. With the spicy scent of his aftershave lingering behind, Ellen watched him go out the door. Standing beside the El Camino, he turned to wave.

She cupped a hand around her mouth. "Hurry back—I miss you already!"

He nodded, grinning. "Go talk to your goldfish. I'll be back as soon as I can!"

Dark clouds bunched on the horizon, wind driven over the snow-covered fields. As the small truck disappeared around an icy hedge, a cold gust stung the girl's cheeks and she turned away, shivering. Inside the cottage she stood by the closed door. Without Tom the room seemed empty and lifeless, more so when the howling impact of the storm hurled itself at the small house. The rush of freezing air rattled the windows and roared down the chimney.

The kitten's purr rumbled against the side of her neck, "OK, cat," she said in an effort to comfort herself. "It's a good thing I didn't build a fire. We'd better close the chimney flue before the storm sucks up all of the heat."

Again in the living room, Ellen found herself fascinated with the tree. The lights glowed with a throbbing intensity that magnetically drew her to it. Leaning nearer, she glimpsed her reflection in one golden ball. The face returning her gaze was a shriveled caricature, the eyes wild, the mouth twisted in a mad, silent laugh. Startled, she gasped, stepping back.

Tinker meowed uneasily and Ellen winced as his claw kneaded her shoulder. Nervously the girl turned her back to the tree. "I . . . I must need to have my eyes checked, Tinker," she told the kitten breathlessly. "Twenty-four years old and my eyes are going already." She tried to laugh away the twinge of fear knotting her stomach. "I think what we both need is some nice warm milk. How does that sound? And after I take care of you, I'll feed the goldfish and water the African violets. OK?" Tinker blinked his smug approval.

In the kitchen, Ellen relaxed, her pulse returning to normal as she performed the simple task. She sipped at a glass of warmed milk, while under the table Tinker applied himself to his own dish, head bent, the pink tongue lapping in rapid contentment.

When they'd both finished, Ellen filled a copper watering can. "Time to water the violets, Tinker."

New Perspectives

Re-entering the living room, Ellen found the tree blazing with an unnerving energy. She blinked, mesmerized by the multicolored lights diffused through an unnatural veil enshrouding the branches. Stopping abruptly, she frowned, reluctant to go nearer. And then with a self-deprecating shake of her head, she gave a relieved gasp of a laugh. "Of course!" she told herself, sighing with understanding. "The spruce must have some kind of tree fungus. Inside, with the heat and moisture. . . . " The girl dismissed her fear with another chuckle.

Still laughing, she went to the library table to the right of the fireplace. Switching on the light, she moaned in despair. "Oh, no!" The six African violets she'd so carefully nursed through the past three winters were dried and shriveled in their clay pots, masked in a gray webbing. Only this morning they'd been green and blooming. Impulsively, she touched a finger to the alien network of finely woven threads. With a frightened whimper she snatched her hand away. At first cool and sticky, the substance suddenly burned her fingers. "My God! What is this stuff?" Hysteria choked her words. "What is it?" Ellen backed away, dragging the palms of her hands slowly against her Levi-clad thighs, trying to wipe away the nerve-searing sensation.

The tinkle of a bell cast her glance downward. Tinker bounded across the floor, his little rear pumping up and down, the tiny ringed tail pointed skyward. Padding straight for the tree, the kitten reared back on his hind legs, his right paw swinging in a quick arc. This time a shiny blue globe burst on the floor in a hundred pieces.

Jolted out of her fixation by Tinker's fearless audacity, Ellen burst out laughing. Grabbing up the kitten, she sank down on the couch with him on her lap. She stroked the small, furry head. "Tinker," she said, "You seem to be the only sane mind in a totally insane world. What would I do without you?" In response, he nipped playfully at her finger and then settled down for a nap. Ellen continued stroking the sleeping kitten until, overcome with drowsiness, she laid her head back against the cushion and slept.

Ellen awoke in the darkness, cold and shivering. A deep silence lay heavily over the cottage. Even the storm that she knew still raged outside was muted and distant, held unnaturally at bay. Wanting desperately to hear Tom's voice, she reached for the telephone on the end table. Silence. "Damn!" she said. "The power's off."

Fumbling for a candle and match in the table drawer, she lit a taper with shaking fingers, lifting it to survey the room. The meager glow lighted a familiar place, but seen now as if through a tarnished mirror. The mounting silence made her afraid again. "Tinker...?" Her voice rose. Jumping to her feet, Ellen stood indecisively. "Tinker...? Where are you?"

She lifted the candle, glimpsing the fish tank. "Oh, the fish," she whispered in dismay. Gazing down at the glass cubicle, Ellen's knees began to tremble. Already a mild stench of decay rose from the spoiled surface. Dead fish floated aimlessly, their golden eyes blank. A gray web, intricately lethal, spread upon the dank waters, corroding the lifeless bodies.

It was then that panic erupted in Ellen's brain and she raced to the front door, fumbling, clawing to thrust it open. With a sinking heart she found a wall of ice blocking the exit. Terror driven, she flew to each of the boarded windows, pounding, scratching, and screaming to be let out—discovering with each parted drape that there was no escape....

Now, gasping and weak with fright, she uttered Tinker's name again. She spoke with a child's wavering voice, the sound high-pitched and reed-like, verging on madness. "Tinker...," she sang frailly. "Tinker, my little love. Where are you?" The words hung in the silence, etched in the last traces of hope.

When the tree lights flashed on of their own accord, Ellen cringed, shrinking back as though physically assaulted. She blinked against the brilliant glare, desperately trying to focus on the web-shrouded boughs that had grown in size and breadth, nearly touching the ceiling. The tree pulsated with a self-generating life—imposing, consuming. The girl sucked in a breath on a half scream, fear paralyzing her senses as she discovered Tinker. Suspended from the lower branches, encased in a deadly cocoon, swung the kitten's tiny body. Through the strangling scum she could see the wide yellow eyes and the small sharp teeth bared in a final frozen scream.

Out of nowhere rose a low, compelling chuckle, small in its inception, but once unleashed swelling into a deep-throated, demonic laugh. Magnifying a hundredfold, the guttural voice echoed over and over its ghastly litany of death. Unable to bear its awful message, Ellen doubled over, covering her ears with her hands.

And then from some distant place she heard a quiet sobbing, steeped in a terrible pain, and she knew what it was. It was Tom grieving—grieving for her.

Camels Are for Eating

From the unpublished manuscript "Letters from Saudi Arabia"

Petey Brown

Dear Daddy,

I've been nursing in Saudi Arabia for three months now. It seems like three years. It's hard to know what to write people back home. I wrote one of your sisters about shopping for gold in the souk in Old Jeddah, and she wrote back that she hoped I wasn't going to be a materialistic person. I wrote your other sister about how all the Saudi men keep the finger of one hand up their nose and the other hand in their crotch, and she replied that I was undoubtedly suffering from culture shock.

Your brother, in response to my letter detailing the latest attempted coup against the throne, wrote that it's fortunate I am working in such a stable country. I'm not sure how he arrived at that conclusion, but far be it from me to try to change his views.

I can't compose endless letters about the weather, which almost never changes: sunshine, gross humidity, and perpetual wind bringing us bouquets of grit that gets in our hair and between our teeth. I'm told it does occasionally rain. Westerners who've been out here for several years have repeatedly mentioned the rain that fell last year. An event of great drama, I gather. At any rate, you can see that discussing the weather is pointless.

That being the case, and as I am reluctant to disturb anyone's preconceived notions, I have decided to write to you about camels. I was sure you would be interested. You may read this to all your friends. Afterward, you have my permission to submit it to the Library of Congress, to repose in their archives.

Camels Are for Eating

First of all, modern Saudis do not ride camels any more. They prefer to eat them. For riding, the Maserati and the Rolls Royce are considered infinitely superior. These are driven with maximum speed and minimum skill. They are hurtled through the center of the road monuments (of which there are many) with abandon, and at least ten Yemeni workers are squashed each week by them. In Jeddah. I'm not sure of the Yemeni death toll in other parts of the country. All in all, I wish the Saudis still rode their camels.

It is not against the law to eat camels, only to kill them. I have not worked it out to my satisfaction just how one can manage the former without doing the latter, but as the Saudis are no respecters of logic, I'm sure they've come up with an acceptable method. Camel meat is very expensive, and a Westerner is very favored to be offered any.

I was so favored once, and am taking pains to avoid that status in the future. It is a slimy, purplish-red meat, and very gamey. Also very tough. I was told that baby camels are more tender, but I wasn't favored enough to be offered any. Too bad. I always wanted to eat a baby camel.

The Saudis have outdoor barbecues called "goat grabs" by the Westerners. The much rarer camel-eating events are referred to as "camel clutches." Most Westerners aspire to be invited to such a barbecue. Once. Anyone wanting to go twice is considered brain-damaged.

I saw my first live camels in this country on my way to snorkel in the Red Sea. The people on the Recreation Office bus—all newcomers, like me—were quite excited, and insisted on being driven closer to take their pictures. The driver refused to let anyone out, so the photographs had to be made through open windows. He said camels didn't like having their pictures taken and had been known to kill their would-be photographer. My companions didn't believe that. Some of the women wanted to pet them. I believed the driver.

The camel is incredibly ugly. Mark Twain once said they were beasts plainly designed by a committee. They have harelips and squashed noses. Their knees are obviously the product of rickets, and they have the most hideous feet in the animal kingdom. They are forever chomping sideways with their huge, yellow teeth. They also bite, spit, and stomp.

They have voices—they make a honking, braying sound which only another camel could like. Considering how much they kick and bite each other, perhaps even other camels don't much care for the sound. Or, maybe even camels hate the way other camels smell.

New Perspectives

In the past, when viewing them in a zoo, I supposed they were scruffy looking because they were prisoners, and this had affected their appearance. It is not so. In their native environment, they are naturally mangy and moth-eaten.

They come in three colors: black, white, and yellow. The black ones are found in the northeastern part of the country and are not very prolific. The white ones are very rare and the exclusive property of the Royal Family, who use them for ceremonial occasions. When the ritual is over, rumor has it that they eat the camels.

The dingy yellow ones are the sort found in the desert lying between Jeddah and the Red Sea. They reproduce with alarming ease and dismaying frequency. Finding food is no problem. Once, they ate desert grasses and shrubs, but the Saudis have done away with those things, replacing them with junked cars, construction debris, and household garbage. If the garbage runs out, I imagine they'll start in on the junked cars.

While at the Red Sea recently, I was sitting beneath our Bedouin tent, minding my own business, when three camels came to call. A wife, a husband, and their child. They just walked up under the open-sided tent and made themselves at home. The child-camel ate my peanut butter sandwich. Without being invited to. The three of them bared their nasty teeth at me and spit and hissed. I had to retreat to the water. Then, they knocked down the center pole of the tent and stomped on the fallen remains.

The Arabian camel is the one-hump kind, but whether a camel is the one-hump or two-hump sort, it is not lovely. Even one hump is disfiguring. Quasimodo only had one hump, and no one thought he was lovely either. The Saudis, as usual, have things backwards. It should be against the law to eat camels, but okay to kill them.

This is all I have to say about camels. I've tried to be unbiased and objective on the subject, and I hope you'll agree there's nothing controversial in this letter. If you feel I've succeeded in coming up with a subject that's both neutral and informative, let me know, and I'll write about camels to all my relatives. I expect they would like hearing about camels as much as you have.

          Your loving daughter,

          Supernurse

Dorothy Richardson
Delbert B. Campbell

Your muscles are hard, your body is lean.
Your senses are sharp, your thoughts are clean.

You wrestle as well as the next young man.
You hit a ball like the others can,

You stand your ground when a challenge is made.
A friend, not helped, is a friend betrayed.

But you fall in love with the girl at school.
And, by consequence, you act like a fool.

You let her go first through the classroom door.
You carry her books, yet it's only one floor.

You race to the bench you know she'll be at.
You lend her your coat to use as a mat.

You write for her love. You needn't have asked it.
You find the note in the teacher's wastebasket.

Your heart collapses and your stomach churns.
Your elbows itch and your forehead burns.

Your arms are weak. Your legs are like jelly.
You could walk under a snake and not touch its belly.

Love's not God's work. It must come from Satan.
You do lots of meetin', but not that much datin'.

You promise yourself from this one sin,
You will never, ever, fall in love again.

New Perspectives

Dorothy Richardson sat in one of the front seats in our fourth grade class. Whenever it came time to read a story that had hard words or a poem that had weird words, the teacher would always call her to the front of the class to do it. The same was true in geography. The teacher always called her to find way-out places like Spain or Holland or California on the map. She was always able to point right at the spot. Every time you looked on the chalk board, there would be one of her reports, circled in red, with a gold star stuck on it. I remember once when the teacher broke down and put two gold stars on one of them!

Mother keeps reminding me not to use "so" so much. But, when that's the perfect word, what else can you do? Dorothy Richardson was "so" pretty—not only pretty, she was beautiful. Her hair was long and silky. It was not like the girl's hair in front of me, or any of the other girls' in the class. It flowed with her motion. It hung down to her waistline and moved softly across her shoulders when she turned her head from side to side. It didn't hide her face. It lay there against her ears and shoulders, and down her back. I'll bet it was softer than rabbit's fur. And her eyelashes, if you were to put paint on the tips of them, for sure she could redo the front wall with just one blink.

When the teacher put her up front to recite something, I couldn't help but lean forward in my seat to listen. Her voice was sweet, soft and delicate. She made the words in the book sound real. Some of the things she recited I had been able to sift through at home, because of rained-out chores. But the way she put it; the way her voice went up and down at certain places; the way she sighed when the prince met the princess; the way she quivered when the ship hit the rock; the way she told us those things, it made your Adam's apple hurt.

It so happened that a thunderstorm hit just before the noon bell. Normally, during lunch hour the girls would gather on the sunny side of the schoolhouse and the boys would get together out past the playground. But the rain kept all of us in the "recreation room." Everybody sat wherever they could with their lunch between their legs. It provided me the chance I had been looking for. I moved in as close as I could to Dorothy Richardson without letting her know I was there. I could tell she wasn't paying close attention, because she kept on chatting with a girl next to her. I started to open my brown paper sack to eat my lunch when I noticed the multi-colored, tin container in her lap. She opened it with gentle fingers. She took out a thermos and set it aside. She took out an orange and put it between her ankles. She took out a sandwich that had square, white bread that was wrapped in wax paper. She put it in the lid of her lunch box. She took out cookies that were

Dorothy Richardson

also wrapped in wax paper and lay them in her lap for later. I opened my paper sack. I knew what was in there before I even opened it. I turned my body away from her. In my sack was a biscuit with jowl bacon, a biscuit with jelly, and a fruit jar of room-warm milk.

As I looked at her "store-bought" sandwich and all the perfection of her meal, something went wrong with me. I closed my sack, got up from my seat, and ran to the outhouse. There, I threw the whole works into the wicker basket behind the door. My heart moaned until I was at the point of tears. I sat there by the empty stool.

"Deb, get your marbles!"

When I heard the call, my hand went up to my shirt pocket to insure that my "steely" was still where I had put it. That steely fit best between my thumb and forefinger and had won me many a game of marbles against most foes. I threw the outhouse door open to see my best buddy waving me toward the playground. "One sec!" I yelled, as I lifted my lunch from the basket. I gulped down the bacon sandwich and the jelly biscuit, then I finished it off with the milk before I had even caught up with my friend.

Unbeknownst to me, I had overcome the agony of love in one fell swoop on that singular day.

Where is Dorothy Richardson? I bet she married that tall smart aleck who shot paper wads at her. You know, the one who sat in the back row over by the window. We'll probably never know.

Passing Through

Joe King

Being young, I always thought
The world abounded with everything we sought.
And a certain magic might be found
To satisfy those wishes, *every* wish; why not?

Being young, I cried somewhat
Over things I tried and yet did not
Gain or gather to my frail web—
Time consumed and lost, and all for what?

Being old, I prod the past
For pleasant roles where I was cast
As one who claimed the loves of pretty faces
With soft voices that warmed, then cooled too fast.

Being old, I dream and doze
And speak quite earnestly with those
Who listen kindly about a life behind me,
Yet, it's all some story-tale of truth and fiction that I chose.

Being gone, I'm talked about;
Not often, but enough, no doubt,
To give my momentary stay extended life.
That's all that's left of me—and it will dwindle out.

Second Chance

M. L. Archer

Published in "Horror Show"

Till death do us part he had promised Mary, and he had meant it; no one could ever question that.

"Thank God, they didn't buy it," Rod Wilson stated to Tom. "They would have been careless with it, maybe wrecked it." Rod ran a loving hand over the Lincoln's sleek, warm hood. They're like me, these cars. The thought mused through him. Enjoying their second time around as I enjoy my second family of children. The thought surprised him; he was rarely given to dismembered thoughts.

He looked out over the lot, a place of dreams, with the red and white pennants flying, the cars shined as if for royalty. A sense of satisfaction danced a polka in him. There were joys in second-time-arounds, the joy of helping people with little more than the jingle of change in their pockets, helping them to own their very own car. For the cars, too, it was a reprieve, a second time around, a time for picnics again, days at the beach again.

Maybe the assurances of spring in the air, the breeze flapping the pennants, the green, festive smells of spring, which even above cement helped sell a car, had broken open his thoughts.

He fingered the slightest of dents in a cream-colored Cadillac. The Cads and Lincolns they handled so often were near perfect. But in life nothing seemed to achieve perfection. Certainly not his own life. After the shock had

New Perspectives

worn off, and Mary had been committed, he had discovered a tolerance for imperfection that he had never realized was a part of him.

Of course, his children approached perfection. How could they not? *My Frank's six now*, he reminded himself, *and Margaret, she's four, and then there's the baby. I never thought I could be so happy again.* One of these days he would compare their photos with the others, the family of children who lived only in the past now. There was a resemblance, wasn't there? But perhaps it was better to let sleeping dogs lie.

That was where Mary sometimes made her mistakes. If this set resembled their first three children, with their lungs choked with bathtub water, she would be the one to dwell on it. But she enjoyed their new set as much as he did. A man didn't really have much time for children; lack of time alone made them the mother's, in the end.

He started his New Yorker and backed out of the lot. He could almost imagine, even as it gave him a chill, that his new family was buried beneath the gravestones, like the others. How old had the first ones been? *Six years, four years, and six months old*, if he considered the dates on the stones. He couldn't even think of their names without trembling. Better to forget, he reasoned. They were children drowned so many years before. "A tragic thing," mourners had whispered at the funeral. All but unhearing, he had nodded. And after the spillage of words, of questions in autopsies and hearings—words enough to last till eternity—and the snick of the institutional lock, after all that, his Mary's face had snapped the tragedy home to him. He had cried then.

But, miracles did happen.

The fear of life, of forging ahead, he had none of that. For a while, he'd wanted to go back in time—what really was wrong with that?—to go on picnics again, to take his son to baseball games, to sit in the chaise lounge on his day off and gaze at the children running like puppy dogs about the green lawn; the children neat and clean, the house a modest, suburban tract home.

He could have afforded a better house. After the "accident" he had gone so far as to study the ads. But he had realized that Mary knew her way about the familiar rooms. And when she was released from the institution—he had never admitted for a second that she would not be cured—if a moment should arise when her mind was confused, she would feel safe there; she would know where the sugar and coffee were stored.

Eventually the confused days had relinquished her, as a stubborn fever might finally break and relinquish a sick child. "I think she's ready to go home,"

Second Chance

the director of the institution had told him. "There seems to be little chance of a recurrence."

Afterward, in the car, laughter had bubbled in Rod's throat. Chance of recurrence—how could there be? He had hugged and kissed his Mary. They had no children. He and Mary could be taken for newlyweds, just starting in on life together. You can't—

And she had been cured, cured like the scars on the graves now green with lawn.

A wild happiness had danced in her eyes when she'd found she was expecting. She had been even happier with their very first child, and her new pregnancies had followed the pattern of her being not quite so happy with the second pregnancy and even less happy with the third pregnancy.

Now driving toward home, he saw Gabe Mecham and slowed to offer him a ride. But Gabe waved him on, apparently preferring to walk. Hell, he ought to know his own preferences, Rod mused. The man was a know-it-all. He'd been the first to shake his head when Rod had announced, "I plan to start a second family."

"Childless women are often happy," Gabe had asserted. "There could be an alternative."

"Alternative, hell," Rod had answered. "What can take the place of a family? Why shouldn't a completely cured women be given a chance at all of life again? Motherhood, that's the life to keep a woman's mind off the past. A woman isn't anything without a runny nose to wipe, lunches to fix, or a sick child to care for." He remembered his own mother at his bedside, caring for him endless, sleepless nights, when he'd been sick with nothing worse than the chicken pox.

"That's how I kept my sanity," he added. "I stayed busy. I didn't dwell on the nonessentials. Only the facts. Only what mattered at the moment. That's why I like selling used buggies. They're tangible. I can kick the tires if I have a mind to; I can rub a finger over the paint. The customers get something for their money."

"Sounds good," Gabe had replied. "But you're tempting fate, my man. You're tempting fate."

Fate? He had laughed at his neighbor; now he looked back at him in his side-view mirror. Let him walk. Who believed in fate? Or Freud, for that matter? From what he'd read, mental breakdown could be triggered by associations and patterns. Well, Freud should see her now. By all accounts Mary should have. . . No, she was better now. She'd given birth to more

New Perspectives

children. Some people, worrywarts, small-minded nit-pickers, liked to complicate elemental matters. Why, a woman was made for babies.

He laughed aloud. *Fate is the hunter.* A chill quavered him. *Yes, the hunter.* That long ago time, in a panic of dread, he'd hunted the house, before finding Marlene in his bed, where Mary lay when he made love to her, found Marlene with the blue electric blanket arranged over her drowned body. While sirens had screamed from somewhere else, he had discovered Jeffy under the bed, with a blue blanket tucked over his lungs too, lungs filled with bathwater. And the baby—

That dusk he had found the house stagnated in quiet—with no dinner on the table. He had shrugged and gone to the bathroom. He'd washed his hands and turned. His glance had fallen inside the tub. The baby's hair had been floating in the filled tub, like a blond mask over her. A man shouldn't scream, but he had. Mary had left the baby in the tub a second and she had drowned! Anguish had cut him to the bone; it was a wonder he hadn't bled. Now he would hardly glance in a tub, ever.

And then he had found Mary, unconscious, dribbling from the mouth. He had phoned the fire department, his mother, the police. . . .

He shuddered.

From all appearances, Mary looked about to die from the jumble she had gulped down from the medicine chest. Across the mirror, she had written *God told me to do it. They are safe from evil now.* Mary had been a quietly religious person. Each Sunday, she had dressed those three children for Sunday School. *As she did these three.*

He stopped at the stoplight. The mounting tension of workers driving home with frayed, day's-end nerves, seemed almost an infection about him. Ahead the next right led to his children, to his Mary. She had always been his Mary, even then, even as she was unconscious and struggling to die. That long-ago day, his street had suddenly quieted, silenced with the decorum owed the dead and the obviously insane.

The light changed and he forged ahead. Hell, he hadn't meant to mull over the past. A man should never over-think. Grab life by its nape and forge ahead. Perhaps it was the fresh scents perfuming the air that had forced the memories back into his life. Spring had just exploded into greenery that day.

He turned onto his street. So they were back where they had started, when they were fairly young marrieds. *Back where they had started.* A curious shudder grabbed him. That other day—with the acacia in goldish bloom, the one Mary had complained about because the seeds blew about too

Second Chance

much—had been horrible. He had felt its horror, even with the love, every time he'd visited Mary at the institution. But what else was there to do with horror but not to dwell in it?

Three long years she had languished in that institution, with Dad and Mother and his friends—God damn them—almost begging him to divorce her. But those years had been long enough for Mary to forget. Maybe psychosis wiped out memory, so even the institution was a blear. She never spoke of it. The neighbors, who had recently joined the block, surely couldn't see the institution in her appearance, in her family. Their family looked average. Hadn't he read somewhere that three children was the average?

Yes, they both had been granted a second chance. A second chance. They were back where they had started. A family once again. Maybe on his next day off he would take the kids and Mary to Chabot Lake and rent a boat. The water, ominous, blackish, clutching, stretched below him. No. A picnic would be better. Mt. Diablo was strewn with wildflowers in the spring.

He parked in the driveway. He'd always liked this stucco and brick house. Odd how Mary had assumed he would have sold it. Somehow she'd expected his life to crumble because hers had. Women were queer creatures. Sometimes he must admit Mary had some unfathomableness in her. Just now, he could have been coming home that other time. The chestnut trees ten feet taller. The acacia in goldish bloom.

Happiness filled him like one of Mary's special teriyaki steak dinners. If he had a drum he would beat it to announce his arrival home. That was one thing he liked, how with the snick of the front door, the children came running.

Everyone deserves a second chance, he thought. No need really to hold anything against anyone, even murder. What was murder, after all, but something which, like every minute past, could never be undone. No use to hold it against anyone. Momentarily he had, but in hours he had felt the futility of that. Mary too had had her second chance. *We are back where we started. Till death do us part.*

He ran toward the house. When he thrust open the door, he heard the water running over the bathtub.

Genesis

Lucile Bogue

I was an offbeat experiment from the very start. I have no record of my conception, but it was probably not the usual run-of-the-bed kind, as my father was an ex-Mormon with all the leanings, and my mother was a divine musician, a saint, and a Gentile.

But judging from the subsequent form which my corporeal body took, it is easy to reconstruct the scenario of that sweltering night of July 19 in Salt Lake City.

The creating angels were gathering up the spare parts, ready to knock off for the day, when a call came from the Lord.

"Hold it! One more creation."

"But God, it's quitting time!"

"Sorry, gang. But this is a rush order."

"Good Lord," said another, "we're almost out of parts."

"Use whatever you have left."

"They're not going to match, Lord."

"Oh, well. You'll think of something. You always have. Be innovative."

"God," said the youngest angel, "are you paying us overtime? The whistle blew ten minutes ago."

"Well," hesitated the Father.

"My feet hurt," said the oldest angel. "I want to stretch out on a fleecy cloud somewhere."

Genesis

"Okay," granted God. "Overtime pay. *If* you come up with something that resembles a human."

They set to work, but without much enthusiasm.

"Here. Here's a pear-shaped body we've tossed into the trash can. Would it do?"

"Pear shapes went out with the Italian painters."

"I know. That's why we dumped it."

"Fashion is irrelevant," snapped another angel. "Let's get on with it."

"Okay. Narrow shoulders. Good wide bottom."

"At least good for childbearing."

"Girl-child, then?"

"Haven't found the right parts, yet. Don't know."

"Here's a vivid imagination. Let's toss that in. It'll fit, regardless of sex."

"Let's get the body, first. Here are a couple of outsized bosoms we couldn't use anywhere else."

"Okay. Put 'em on the assembly line."

"Here's a beautiful skeleton. Nice fine bones."

"How come it's in the leftovers, then?"

"Well, it's pretty small, I guess. A little over five feet long."

"Good grief!" said another. "No wonder it's surplus. It's all out of proportion. Look at the hip bones . . . clear up under the ribs. No waistline at all!"

"I have a pair of very small feet here," called another. "Can you use 'em?"

"And here are some tiny hands. At least these would match."

"And guts. Here are some that go on forever. Must have been designed for a giant. Could we stuff 'em in, do you think?"

"Sure. That immense hip basket would hold a whale."

"Look. Here's a slightly damaged liver. Shall we risk it?"

"Sure," one said, glancing at her watch.

"And here's a stomach not even fit for tripe. I found it in yesterday's garbage. It had been condemned when we discovered it was allergic to milk. And it quivered when we walked past it with our lunch pails."

New Perspectives

"God just said, 'Be innovative.' He didn't ask us to perform any miracles."

"I'd hate to use a stomach like that, though. The poor little devil."

"Don't be so noble," said the watch-watcher. "We haven't time to be choosy."

"How are we going to fasten this conglomeration together? The pot of collagen is empty."

"Here's some bubble gum we can use."

"And here's a little baling wire. That ought to hold."

"Oh-oh! We forgot a heart. See what you can find."

There was a long, noisy interval while they clattered about among the trash cans. At last the oldest angel held up something that looked like what was left after Eve took a bite out of the apple.

"Do we dare try this?" she asked.

"Sure. Why not?" said another carelessly.

The old angel held it up to her ear. "But it has a distinct murmur."

"What does it say?" asked the youngest angel, with some sarcasm.

"Don't be flippant. It needs a new valve job. It sort of clatters."

"Come on! Quit quibbling! I'm ready to zip it all up."

"Okay." She laid the organ tenderly in the chest cavity. "At least I'll make sure that the heart is in the right place."

After a time the angels backed off to survey their creation, wiping their hands on their flowing robes.

"All done?"

"Yep."

"It's a girl, then?"

"What else, with those bulging boobs?"

And thus endeth the story of my creation.

A School for Madina

(A Personal Experience)

Sybil McCabe

Edwin's request shocked me. I was at a loss to know how to answer him.

Only a week ago we had buried my husband, Mac, here in Madina, this small remote village in Liberia, West Africa. I still felt the strain of coping with his long illness, and now from losing him entirely. Today, still numb, I sat in Madina's palaver hut, the community meeting place, with Honorable Edwin Fahnbulleh, unofficial village leader. I hoped to find a way to repay him and his tribal people for their kindness in allowing me to make my husband's last wish come true.

"I want burial in beautiful, peaceful Madina," Mac had said, and Edwin helped me make all arrangements.

Not anticipating that Edwin might have an agenda of his own, I began by inquiring whether or not I might buy a new pump in Mac's memory to replace the defective one in the village center.

"Aunt Sybil," Edwin's wife, Mamusu, said before Edwin had a chance to speak, "our people possibly can manage to buy a pump for themselves, but there is something they need much more."

I turned toward her, feeling a special affection. Mamusu, a school principal in Monrovia, was actually one of the main reasons my husband and I had realized a special relationship in this village. We had known Mamusu long before we came to live in Liberia's capital city, where she and Edwin lived.

New Perspectives

Mac and I were school administrators, and Mamusu had stayed with us in California while she earned a college degree. We became part of her extended family, "Aunt Sybil" and "Uncle Mac." It was only natural that, when we arrived in Monrovia as members of a team from San Francisco State College working on an educational project, our relationship continued and also included her husband.

Edwin was a highly respected member of the nation's legislature, but enjoyed spending weekends on his farm upcountry. Besides acquainting us with Madina, Mamusu and Edwin amazed us with the number of doors they opened for us—official city doors as well as tribal country doors—some which otherwise would have remained closed to white Americans.

Now this tall, handsome man with chocolate-colored skin and sprinkles of white in his close-cropped black hair sat across a small table from me, ready to speak. Edwin's Western jeans and T-shirt were in sharp cultural contrast to the long robes of the elders and the tattered shorts worn by village men. I was not prepared, despite our close relationship, for the magnitude of his request.

"A school." Edwin stood up very straight and looked directly at me the first time he said it. "A school would be a fitting memorial for Uncle Mac. I beg you to help us get one."

"Yes, Aunt Sybil," Mamusu urged, "we want the children here in the country to 'have book' like city children do. Madina people are wise in the ways of their tribal world but, with nationalism our government's goal, such knowledge is not enough. English is our nation's official language, and all our people should be able to speak it. The twenty-eight tribes throughout our country must know English to communicate with one another. Everywhere education is our greatest need. That's why we must have our own school in Madina, a school for all children. You will help us, won't you? We want a great future for Madina."

Overwhelmed, I heard little more either said. Instead, I gazed at Mamusu, her petite figure almost hidden in a long gown of bright African print. I thought of Mac and wished he were here to deal with this impossible request without alienating the goodwill of our African friends.

"Aunt Sybil," Edwin said again, more loudly, as if to rouse me from my lethargy, "both children and their parents long for a school, but the government cannot accommodate our small village."

"A school!" I choked out the words which, now spoken, took on a new reality. I could manage a pump, but I didn't have money for a school, even with

A School for Madina

the memorial contributions family and friends were sending. The villagers had less. Their average family income was something like fifty dollars a year.

Mamusu looked at me appealingly. "Yes, Aunt Sybil, a school." She smiled confidently. "Remember how Uncle Mac, who was usually joking, would say seriously, 'The way to help people is to show them how to help themselves.' The children need a school to better learn how they can help themselves. Not so?"

"But a school costs an enormous amount of money," I blurted out, then tried to compose myself.

The palaver hut where we sat stood open from floor to ceiling, and it seemed that in the course of the conversation all the people in the village passed by to look in. While they could not understand English, they evinced keen interest in our conversation. I recognized Jusu Fahnbulleh, hard-working headman, and some of the women in their ankle-length wraparound skirts of indigo tie-dye designs. Most of them carried babies on their backs and led another small child by the hand. Bright, eager-looking children of all ages, scantily dressed, quietly joined the grownups looking in on us.

Yes, I thought, these children do need a school, but there is no way I can provide one! For a moment anger flared inside me. How could Mac do this? Why had he requested burial here and left me with an impossible problem to handle on my own?

Mac and I had been in Monrovia almost three years when he developed cancer. During those years he had made many trips to Madina, first to visit Edwin's small pineapple plantation and to learn something of upcountry life, and later to help the villagers improve their gardens and groves with special seeds, encouragement, and irrigation. They returned his help with affection and respect.

That evening I thought about those many visits of Mac's as I watched some of the village elders squatting beside this white man's tomb, discussing with him life in Madina and life hereafter, as if he were still able to hear them. I wished that Mac could see this tribute. I wished, too, that I could build a school, but of course I knew that it was impossible.

When I returned to Monrovia, I mentioned Edwin's request to members of my team. Few were enthusiastic. With their own lists of obstacles, they further discouraged the idea.

"I doubt that many children would attend. Boys have bush school in their secret Poro Society in the jungle, and the girls have an equivalent in their secret Sande Society."

New Perspectives

"Building materials cost too much!"

"Everything would have to come from Monrovia and be hauled a hundred and twenty miles over a dirt road full of potholes to Madina. Besides, no one has a truck."

"It's far too complicated a project."

And yet, somehow, something about Edwin's request would not let me rest, and, as the days went by, seemed to affect our educational team in much the same way. Objections and problems gave way to ideas. Before I had a chance to completely talk myself out of this impossible dream, several teammates volunteered their time on weekends to help in any way they could.

"It just might be possible," our leader said, "if we can get the Madina people to make this a do-it-yourself project and work without pay, and if someone on our team could supervise . . . "

"Why not? Especially if we can get the villagers to use free local materials," Al, our blond, broad-shouldered building contractor agreed. "Count me in."

Enthusiasm spread quickly, and soon ideas began changing into plans. Edwin Fahnbulleh joined our team members in discussions.

"I'll give six acres of my farm land for a school campus," Edwin announced when a group of us met as a committee. "And, in addition, I am donating the palm grove to the school. Oil from the nuts should pay teachers' salaries and more."

I could only add a grateful "thank you" as Edwin continued. "We must get started at once. This is March, near the end of the dries and the best time for outdoor work. Later, the wets will slow us down."

Within days our committee of villagers and Americans decided not only on curriculum but also on facilities. Classrooms, an office for a nurse, a vegetable garden, a chicken shed, a pigpen, and a soccer field were only some of the amenities which met with instant approval. The big question remaining was what sort of local material to use for building.

"My people do not want their school of mud daub walls and thatched roof like their huts," Edwin explained. "They want something finer, and they suggest concrete blocks."

"Concrete blocks are out," Al said immediately. "They're not local material."

But it turned out he was not quite correct. Although none of our committee members realized it, the soil in the huge termite ant hills which

A School for Madina

dotted the entire landscape had an adhesive, concrete-like quality. Builder ants chewed the dirt and mixed it with their saliva to get this result. Headman Jusu explained the process while Edwin translated his Vai dialect into English.

"Bug-a-bug dirt," Jusu said with great enthusiasm. "Everywhere. Ants use like concrete to make tiny rooms for queen termite eggs to hatch. No more life in mounds. Army ants invade. Eat eggs, termites, everything. Everything finished. Now fine for school."

"Well, he hardly could have come up with a more native material," Al agreed.

After several tests in a laboratory in Monrovia, Al developed a formula using the bug-a-bug dirt in a block which would resist the heaviest of tropical rains. To cap his efforts he devised a press which made one block at a time.

When Al demonstrated the formula in Madina, everyone wanted to mix and mold a block. The crowd cheered with each success. Six parts bug-a-bug dirt, mixed with one part cement and water, produced perfect results. After every man had a turn, block making became a serious business. More tools and presses were needed and were somehow acquired. Sooner than I had expected, the villagers pressed enough blocks for the walls. What had seemed like an insurmountable task a short time ago now looked more and more like a reality.

Though my work in Monrovia kept me from going to Madina as frequently as I wished, Al and Edwin regularly reported that in spite of a few minor problems things moved along almost too easily.

Then the wets and a malaria epidemic hit Madina, both at the same time! The workers had the reinforcement rods in and were ready to start building when torrential rains came. Roads flooded, so that Al and Edwin could not get to the village for six weekends straight. When they finally succeeded, they found the village deep in water and the school compound standing in the middle of a lake.

"All our people were lying on cots in their huts, feverish with malaria," Edwin reported. "No one was able to work." He paused and his face brightened. "When the school is built and can provide malaria depressant tablets to take regularly, everyone's life will improve."

As soon as things returned to normal, nothing could stop the school's progress. Even though men had to take time off for the necessary seasonal work, the school was ready for a roof by the end of February.

"Roofing material is expensive and we don't have the money," Edwin worried. "What can we do, Aunt Sybil?"

New Perspectives

I thought of the Memorial Fund Mac's family and friends had established. Why not use that to pay for a roof? The school was surely a memorial. Mac would have been delighted in the growth in skills and independence among the villagers during the many challenges this project presented.

I knew I had made the right decision as I stood with the crowd at the dedication in April. The roof, a soft gray, covered the gleaming whitewashed walls. The school looked beautiful. Over the entryway hung an artfully crafted sign proclaiming it the "Madina-McCabe Memorial School."

A lump formed in my throat and I brushed away a few tears as I thought of all the love, efforts, and teamwork that had gone into the building of the school. Every village man, woman, and child past kindergarten age had involved themselves in one way or another to make an impossible dream come true. My tears gave way to smiles as I greeted Madina people and their friends of the Fahnbulleh clan from neighboring villages. Some of these visitors had walked as far as twenty miles to see and admire.

The images of that day blur together in a special collage of memories: blond, lanky Al, resplendent in a long tribal chief's robe of hand-woven country cloth and matching cap, his wife explaining proudly that the Madina citizens had made Al an honorary chief of their village; Jusu beaming as he showed me the classroom furnishings and proudly emphasizing "desks and chairs my people make!"; Vai-educated faculty members—two male teachers and a nurse—waxing enthusiastic about the school's possibilities; and mothers cutting and sewing school uniforms on a treadle sewing machine someone had donated.

The last image of that day is the dedication ceremony itself. Members of my San Francisco team and others had gathered under a shaded area. I began walking toward them when Mamusu motioned me to sit with her. As Edwin addressed the suddenly quiet gathering in Vai, she softly translated his words. "Edwin is saying that this school for Madina should give other villages new hope. They can do what we have done."

Honorable Fahnbullah then addressed the crowd in English, with a Vai teacher translating. "While the school is a gift from Uncle Mac and from others on the San Francisco team, it also is a gift from the Madina people to themselves, especially to their children."

The ceremony progressed, but my thoughts strayed to the changes the school already had brought to the village and to what it would mean in the future. If only Mac knew! I could almost hear him commenting, "Well, that's the way it is when you help people help themselves. One idea leads to another." With a chuckle he might add, "But who would have thought our friends would utilize the work of termite ants to build the school they wanted for Madina!"

The Bagman

D. Leah Miller

"Come on, ya gonna sleep all day?" Pete teased as he shook Mike's shoulder.

"Get lost!" Mike mumbled, burying his head under the pillow.

"Throw some clothes on and get your bat. I got a game set up with some guys up on Main Street," Pete insisted.

"It's too early," Mike groaned, but sat up anyway, trying to rub the sleep out of his eyes.

"Hurry up! I'll meet you at the hoop," Pete called over his shoulder as he slammed the bedroom door and thundered down the stairs.

Mike pulled on his jeans and a T-shirt and began rummaging in the closet for his bat. His hand found the hard wood and he gave a sharp tug, freeing it from beneath some camping gear. Mike slid his fingers over the smooth surface, remembering that Christmas morning just four years ago when he was nine and still had his family.

Mike had unwrapped the long package, parting the frothy folds of red tissue paper to reveal the Louisville Slugger. Dad had laughed and winked at Mom as Mike had flung his arms around his neck in a tight hug. They had been happy then. But that's all over, now, Mike thought, and it's all Shirley's fault. If it hadn't been for her, they would still be a family. He wished she'd drop dead.

In the kitchen, Mike grabbed a cold Pop Tart and crammed it into his mouth while searching the refrigerator for some milk to wash it down.

The Bagman

"How come you're up so early?" Shirley, asked, leaning against the kitchen doorframe and folding her arms across her breasts.

"Ball game," Mike mumbled around the Pop Tart as he continued surveying the contents of the refrigerator. Great! This is all I need, Mike thought, she's probably going to stand here bumping her gums at me all morning.

"At least take time to have a decent breakfast," she was saying, her bedroom slippers making scuffing noises on the linoleum as she headed for the stove.

Mike slipped out of the kitchen and made for the front door.

"Can't, Pete's waiting for me," he shouted as he banged out of the house. She's always trying to be nice to me—trying to "win me over," Mike thought angrily. But it won't work—I'll always hate her.

Opposite the unpaved parking area lay a small square of asphalt, and midway along one edge was a pole supporting a rusty basketball hoop. The net had long since disappeared, but the hoop continued to function as the apartments' "recreational area" and the usual meeting place for Mike and his friends.

Mike had met Pete and the other guys the same afternoon he had arrived to spend the summer with his dad and stepmother. He had joined them at the hoop and they had shot a few together. The five seemed to hit it off well and over the next few weeks discovered they had a lot of things in common—including a great dissatisfaction with their home lives.

Billy's mom had a houseful of kids and no husband—most of the time—although a lot of guys "came and went." Billy disliked them all and stayed away from home as much as possible. Billy was short and rather chubby, with long, coal-black hair that he wore tied back "Indian fashion" with a rawhide thong. He had never met his father, but claimed he was part Cherokee.

Phil's dad knocked him around a lot, so Phil stayed out of the way—and out of reach. Phil looked a little like Steve McQueen, except for the thin white jagged scar that ran from beneath his left nostril to the top of his lip. It lifted the lip slightly and gave him the appearance of having a perpetual sneer. Mike thought it looked pretty cool.

Pete was the tallest, and rather good looking—at least girls seemed to think so. He'd been blessed with thick reddish-brown curls, hazel eyes, and perfectly even, white teeth, which he flashed at the drop of a good joke. His

New Perspectives

easygoing nature put him on everybody's "Okay Dudes" list. Everyone's except his dad's, that is. Pete's dad spent his time slurping up the suds at the Turf Club since his mom had up and died of cancer a couple of years back, leaving Pete on his own most of the time.

Eddie had a thick mop of whitish hair that fringed the top of his horn-rimmed glasses. He always wore cut-offs that revealed two skinny legs punctuated by the knobbiest knees Mike had ever seen. Phil said they looked like a couple of peas speared with toothpicks. Eddie was an okay guy, though. You could talk to him about things and he was smart—not "street smart" like Phil and Billy, but smart in other ways. Eddie's folks were kind of weird, but otherwise not too bad.

When Mike met Pete at the hoop, Phil and Billy were waiting with him.

"Hey, what's happening?" Mike asked.

"We got a problem, man!" Billy whispered excitedly.

"Yeah, " Phil agreed, "Me and Billy was up ta the fort and guess who was there!"

"Who?" Mike asked.

"The Bagman!" Phil and Billy both exclaimed.

"The Bagman?" Mike repeated, not understanding what they were talking about.

"Yeah, you know, the old guy that walks up and down Route One with the trashbag," Billy reminded him.

The Bagman was a common sight to anyone traveling between Beltsville and Laurel. He was out there every day walking toward one town or the other with a large trashbag slung over his shoulder. The Bagman's face was browned from the sun and covered by a heavy growth of black beard, making it almost impossible to tell what he looked like. He wore the same dark green pants, shirt, and old, tattered Army jacket—no matter how hot the weather.

"What's he doing in our fort?" Mike asked, his brain searching for some rational explanation. He glanced over at Pete but saw only a reflection of his own surprise and confusion.

"Sleepin', last time we looked—just layin' there sleepin'!" Phil responded with obvious amusement.

"Come on, we'll show ya!" Billy said and headed toward the woods.

No one waited for a second invitation.

The Bagman

On the way to the fort, Mike's mind was a whirl of confusion and anger. It seemed the unimaginable had happened. Their sanctuary had been violated —invaded by enemy forces! Everything was spoiled—again.

Soon after the five boys had become friends, the idea of building the fort had come up. They had been discussing for the hundredth time how much they hated living at home. They decided they needed a place to hang out.

"You can't talk about stuff at home with your folks always snooping around," Phil had said, "besides, in your own fort you can put your feet on the furniture, smoke, cuss—hell, you can do just about anything you want to if the other guys don't mind."

For several weeks they had devoted themselves to building the fort. Mike's dad had let them have some lumber and nails and even some good roofing shingles. Eddie had come up with a "hardly used" mattress that had been a hell of a chore to drag the mile or so through the dense woods—as had the old electrical spool they had found and were using for a table. But they had worked together as a team and had managed it. Pete had borrowed his dad's kerosene lantern and they were then able to stay up at the fort until late in the evening. The fort had become a second home to them.

Even though the fort was sheltered beneath a heavy canopy of shade trees, by mid-morning it would become unbearably hot and sticky. Then they would head for the air-conditioned comfort of the shopping mall and the video arcade until late afternoon, when the day's swelter had settled into just plain miserable mugginess.

On the way to the mall they would stop and try to talk Eddie into coming along, but usually he wouldn't.

Eddie was always dreaming up some new way to make a buck, and his latest scheme was to hang around McDonald's with a roll of paper towels and a bottle of Windex tucked under his arm. He'd catch the customers as they parked their cars and talk them into letting him clean their windshields for fifty cents.

Eddie did even better in the early evening when he caught the cars lined up to get into the Route 1 Drive-in. Most of the teenage couples didn't much care if they could see the movie or not, so he always did better on the nights when they were showing a Disney flick.

When they reached the fort Phil put his finger to his lips, signalling them not to make any noise. They stepped into the darkness, unable to see after the strong glare of the sunlight, but as their eyes adjusted they were able to make out the form on the mattress.

New Perspectives

The Bagman lay on his side, knees drawn up slightly, his head resting on one bent elbow, the torn and soiled Army jacket blanketing his legs. His mouth was slightly open, a thin line of spittle running from the corner of his parted lips, and he was breathing deeply.

Phil motioned for them to follow him outside.

They followed Phil through the doorway, then back along the path, this time cutting off to the left, hopping a narrow, brown stream and finally stopping beside a large fallen tree.

Phil swung a leg over, straddling the tree trunk, and fished a pack of Marlboros from his boot.

"Well, what are we going to do?" Mike asked, "I mean, we can't just let that old bagman *have* our fort, can we? If we let him sleep there today, he'll probably come back again!"

"Sure, he'll just move in *permanently*!" Pete said.

"We gotta get him outta there, and make sure he don't come back!" Billy stated vehemently, his black eyes glittering.

"How can we do that?" Mike asked.

"Maybe if we just wake him up and explain that it's *our* fort and all . . . " Phil offered.

"Are you nuts!" exclaimed Phil, "The guy's probably a mental defective—probably one of those weirded-out Viet Nam vets. Didn't'cha see the old Army jacket he wears?"

"Maybe we could call the cops," Mike suggested

"Oh, sure!" Phil replied sarcastically. "Tell them we have this little place here where we come to smoke and get high sometimes, or look at Penthouse and down a few brews, and we'd appreciate it if they'd run the old guy off for us!"

"Yeah, then we could go down to Hyattsville courthouse and swear out a restraining warrant—Ha!" Billy sneered.

Phil lit a cigarette, snapping his lighter closed with a sharp metallic click.

"I know how we can get rid of him so he'll never come back here," Phil snickered.

They all looked at Phil expectantly.

"How?" Pete asked.

The Bagman

"We just sneak back in there and give the old bum an old fashioned hotfoot, that's what! My uncle Joe and his buddies in the Navy used to do it all the time! Old Bagman jumps up yellin' and stompin' his boot out, see, and takes off like a bat outta hell while we laugh our asses off!" Phil explained matter-of-factly.

Billy, of course, thought it was a great idea, but Pete and Mike weren't so sure.

"How do you know he'll leave after he stomps the fire out?" Mike questioned.

"Don't be such a jerk!" Billy groaned, "Would you stick around someplace where a bunch of guys set your foot on fire?"

"Yeah, we'll tell the ol' bum he'd better split or next time we'll burn his balls off!" Phil laughed.

They all laughed at that, and it was generally decided that the hotfoot operation was a "go."

Back in the fort, they found the Bagman still sleeping soundly. Mike noticed a faint smell of whiskey, and underneath that the musky scent of stale sweat and urine.

Phil held the lighter under the toe of Bagman's shoe until it began to smoulder. When the flame finally caught, they quickly backed toward the doorway, four pairs of eyes riveted to the smoking foot.

Outside, they hurried for cover from which to observe the show, Billy following Phil behind a huge oak, while Mike and Pete ducked behind a thicket of laurel bushes.

They held their breath and listened, expecting the Bagman's surprised shout of realization at any moment. Sweat trickled behind Mike's ears and began to gather in tiny beads on his forehead and upper lip. Why didn't the guy yell? Mike wondered. You'd have to be dead or something not to feel your feet on fire! Maybe the flame had gone out, Mike was thinking, when he heard a rustling sound and realized someone was coming up the path.

Eddie was just stepping from the path into the clearing in front of the fort when the first scream tore the humid morning air. It was followed by several more panicky shrieks and accompanied by slapping sounds—as if someone was beating a dusty carpet.

Eddie froze, his brows knitting together in puzzlement.

Suddenly, the Bagman appeared in the doorway, feet and legs blackened and still smoldering, his eyes wild, the white showing all around like

New Perspectives

a dog ready to fight. In the next second he was barrelling across the clearing toward Eddie, his burned and blackened hands stretched in front of him in a weird parody of a sleepwalker.

Eddie was still standing there trying to comprehend what was happening. The Bagman was almost on top of him before he came to his senses and spun on his heel to run—only slightly too late.

Bagman grabbed for Eddie's throat but missed as Eddie turned. He managed to catch Eddie's ankle as he fell, pulling him to the ground. Eddie screamed.

The scream jolted Mike into action and he dashed across the clearing to Eddie's aid.

The Bagman had a vice-like grip on Eddie's ankle and was scrabbling with the other hand to secure a grip on Eddie's bare, bony knee. Eddie saw Mike and began yelling for help, his voice a high screech of terror.

Mike swung the Louisville Slugger, and Bagman screamed as his wrist bones snapped under the smashing blow. He yanked the hand between his knees to protect it as he rolled over, moaning hoarsely. Mike swung the bat again, hitting the Bagman's shoulders and back, the bat making a thick, satisfying thud with each blow.

Several blows landed on Bagman's head, cracking it open with the soft, moist sound of a ripe watermelon, and Bagman's groans ceased. Still, Mike couldn't stop. A dark, deep fury fueled the raining blows as waves of anger and bitterness spilled over to wash away the Bagman.

Then Mike's feet were flying into the air as Pete and Billy wrestled him to the ground and Phil pried the bat from his hands.

They lay there panting for several minutes—a tangle of arms and blue-jeaned legs, until somewhere, high in the trees, a squirrel chattered his discontent and reality began to assert its authority.

"Holy shit," Billy whispered.

Later, Mike lay on his bed, hands folded behind his head, eyes staring at the ceiling—not seeing the water stains and cracked plaster, but the events of the day flickering across the screen of his mind like images from some low-budget horror movie.

Mike had watched, as in a trance, while Phil and Billy had dragged the Bagman's body back into the fort and deposited it on the mattress along with the gruesome bat. Billy took the kerosene lantern off the table and poured the

The Bagman

kerosene over them. Mike had stared at the bat, suddenly remembering how it had looked lying in the red froth of tissue paper on that long-ago Christmas morning, all shiny and new. It was lying in a red froth now, but it sure wasn't tissue paper, and it was shiny too . . . No! He had jerked his mind back from the direction it had been heading, clamping it down tightly—like the lid on a jar of bees.

Standing on the path, they had watched Phil light the lantern's wick and toss it through the doorway onto the mattress.

Mike kept seeing Bagman's face, wild with terror, the bat, bloody and terrible, and the flames—the flames that had consumed the evidence of his insanity. He kept hearing the screams—Eddie's and the Bagman's and the thudding of the bat as it . . . or was it knocking? Yes, knocking. Someone was knocking on the door.

"Mike, are you okay?" Shirley asked as she tapped lightly on the bedroom door.

"Yeah, I'm okay," Mike answered.

"Can I come in? I'd like to talk to you," she said.

"Yeah, I guess so," Mike replied.

Shirley stepped into the room and closed the door softly behind her.

She had seen him slipping quietly up the stairs earlier and had noticed he didn't have his bat, which she knew was his prized possession. Also, he hadn't seemed interested in the fire trucks or the fire up in the woods, and dinner had been passed up, even though it had been burgers on the grill—his favorite.

"What's happened? Where is your bat?" she asked.

Mike looked at his stepmother, her forehead creased with concern, and tried to gulp back the flood of tears struggling to erupt. Suddenly the tears were slipping down his cheeks in hot streams. Mike was humiliated, but unable to stop them—any more than he had been able to stop hitting the Bagman.

Shirley sat on the bed and gathered him into her arms. She had longed to be close to him, to be a friend, if not a mother, but there had always been an angry wall there. Now the wall had been breached by tears, the whole terrible story pouring out along with them.

When the tears and the story were finished, they sat there in silence for a long time, Shirley brushing the hair back from his damp face.

New Perspectives

Mike pulled away from her and sat up, feeling foolish and scared.

"Are you going to call the cops?" he asked, his voice trembling.

"No," she answered quietly.

"Why not?"

"Because that's a decision you will have to make for yourself," she answered.

"I don't get you," Mike said. "Why are you being so nice to me? You know I've always hated you for stealing my dad and wrecking my family."

"I know," Shirley said, "I always hoped some day you'd understand that you can't 'steal' a person, and that a family is more than certain people in a certain house—a family is just people who care about each other. It doesn't mean they have to be living together or even related to each other. Mike, you didn't lose your family—it just changed. Actually, you could say you have two families now," Shirley explained.

"Well, if that's true about people caring about each other, then, counting the guys, I guess I have three families," Mike said.

"Yeah, I guess so," Shirley said.

"But what are we going to do?" Mike asked, still frightened.

"Why don't you call the guys over and we'll talk about it?" Shirley suggested.

"Yeah," Mike agreed, wiping his cheeks with the back of his hand. "Maybe together we'll be able to figure out the best thing to do."

"I'm sure you'll make the right decision," Shirley said, as she hugged him and stood up to leave. "After all," she smiled, "you've got a lot of 'family' to help you."

Promised

From the novel, *Another Part of Town*

Betty Matulovich

Chapter 19

    If somebody ever decided to give out a prize for the mother who could think up the most jobs for a kid to do all at once, I figured Mama would be right there first in line. For the last week all I'd heard was her saying, "Johnny, do this! Johnny, do that!" Then, when I got all those "this and thats" done, she went right ahead and found some more. My head was spinning, my back was aching, and I was wondering hard why people wanted to go and get married for anyways. What was wrong with just being good friends? I moved back from the window I was washing to stretch my back. I knew Mama needed help getting the house and yard ready for the party after Melissa and Mr. Charlie's wedding tomorrow. But expecting two kids—she'd been giving my brother Seb a lot of "this and that" stuff, too—to do the work of maybe about twenty guys was hard to understand.

    Seb moved a ladder over to the outside of the window I was washing on the inside. He stuck his tongue out at me. I stuck mine back. I don't know why, but it made us laugh. I guess because we were both silly tired. I'd already figured I was probably going to sleep through the whole wedding. I got to thinking about my brother, watching him swing the rag back and forth across the glass. Seemed to me we were getting to be better friends—I decided maybe he was finally growing up . . .

New Perspectives

From the parlor, or from that direction anyways, I heard a gosh awful squawking sound. I quit wiping on the window to listen. Seb had stopped working; I could tell he had heard the sound, too. We looked at each other. I shrugged my shoulders, then I saw Seb was pointing. He wanted me to go and find out what it was. I got down off of my orange crate and went looking.

Sure enough, the parlor door was standing open and more weird sounds were coming through the opening. Cautiously, I peeked around the door into the room. Mama and Aunt Clara sat on two chairs, half facing away from where I stood. My mouth fell open as I looked at the four guys in front of them. Those guys' hair was all slickered down with some kind of greasy stuff and each one of them was holding a music instrument. I knew a little about music, playing a clarinet pretty good in the school band myself, so my eyes went from one instrument to the other, trying to figure which one it could of been that had sounded so sickly—it beat me. I looked the group over. It was like they were wearing costumes, because they were all dressed the same: red and green plaid, baggy pants, green suspenders with bright brass-looking clip fasteners, red shirts, and green ties. With a few ornaments here and there they would have passed for Christmas trees.

I put my two hands over my mouth to keep from laughing out loud. Seb came up behind me. "What the *heck*?" he half whispered, seeing Mama.

Then the horn was raised to one of the players' lips. Well, I'd seen a newsreel once where guys were big-game hunters, and if what that baggy pants guy was blowing wasn't the mating call of a bull moose I'd eat my window-washing sponge.

Mama's hands flew up to cover her ears. I guess before she could stop them, because she quick, polite-like put them back down in her lap. Aunt Clara couldn't seem to make her head quit shaking, and me and Seb were falling against the wall, hands clapped across our faces to keep the howls of laughter inside. I was thinking that horn blower would make a better foghorn.

Then, as if that wasn't enough, a skinny guy holding a fiddle stepped out in front. He seemed to be the leader. He raised his bow in one hand and placed the fiddle under his receding chin right up against his knobby Adam's apple. "That's enough warming up, fellars—let's hit it!" With a half-circle swing of his bow at the group, he brought it down on the fiddle strings. Then no sounds like I'd ever heard before come pouring out of our front parlor; they might have all been playing the same tune, but one thing was for sure: they weren't playing it together.

Promised

Seb had gone staggering off right at the beginning. I saw him sitting on a kitchen chair with tears streaming from his eyes. He was holding his sides, he was laughing so hard.

"Hold it! Hold it!" cried the skinny leader. I could see his Adam's apple jumping up and down. I guessed he was nervous because his face was as red as his shirt. He turned to Mama. "The boys ain't had much practice together lately, Ma'am. They'll do better next try, you'll see!" He turned to the group, his face determined. "*Play* it this time, fellars!" They did, each in his own way.

Suddenly I was feeling awful sorry for those guys in there because I was remembering a day not too long back when I had been a part of almost the same predicament . . . . It had been assembly day at Prescott Jr. High; not just *any* assembly, but a very important one. It was the day the board of trustees were to be entertained. For weeks Mr. Blume, the music teacher, had drilled the band. Faithfully, in unison, our eyes had followed that magic stick held firmly in his guiding hand. How much we had come to depend on it for our direction, the holding together of our music, none of us knew. Then came the day we had prepared for—and no Mr. Blume. He was home sick with the flu. Panic took over. It was our turn on in fifteen minutes. Finally someone pushed Ernie Newton forward. Seems poor Ernie had had the misfortune to have had three months of private music lessons; therefore, in someone's desperate mind this made him the only chance of leading us to success.

Poor Ernie, he'd given it his best try, standing up there in front of us white-faced, waving that stick, part of the time like he was driving in a home run or rippling over ocean waves, and the rest of the time like he was swatting flies. The sounds that we made, each to our own beat, I was still trying to forget . . .

Mama was standing up; Aunt Clara was, too. I had a quick glimpse of four silly, red-faced smiles, then I took off before Mama saw me. I heard her saying, "You leave your number. I call tonight to let you know if we can use your—ah—music. Later tonight I call." Mama was always polite.

I was back hard at work when Mama and her sister came into the kitchen. I didn't think Mama was paying any attention to me, because she looked like she was thinking about something else, but she said, without looking my way, "When you finish windows, Johnny—go straighten back porch."

What did I say about prizes? Mama turned full around to Aunt Clara. "Clara, what I going to do? I tell Charlie I take care of getting music!" She paused. "*That* is *music*!?"

71

New Perspectives

Aunt Clara laughed. Then it was I discovered my aunt was very kind. "Oh, Maria, the poor boys were maybe nervous. They practice tonight, tomorrow will be fine!"

"I no think so—but what I do? No time now to get some other people—oh that Mrs. Fazio! I wish I no listen; she say these boys make good music two years ago at her Angelina's wedding . . . " Her voice trailed off. I wondered if she was thinking if maybe that was the last time those guys had played together.

I finished the windows and went out onto the back porch and began to shove stuff around on the shelves. Their voices came to me through the screen door. I caught a word here and there, then my ears perked up. I'd heard my own name mentioned. I moved closer to the door.

"I see picture," Aunt Clara was saying. "Oh, my! You should see! She be fine for Johnny. Yes, just right. She come on boat yesterday from Yugoslavia." I heard the sound of my aunt's hands clapping together. She always did that when she got excited, and her round cheeks got redder and her blue eyes squinched up, making her look like a chubby Kewpie doll.

"Just right for *what*?" I muttered under my breath. I guess I was sort of like Papa, thinking Aunt Clara was always fixing into other people's business.

"She should let others do own thinking—not all the time arranging things," I'd heard Papa say that to Mama more than once. Not that Papa didn't think Aunt Clara was well-meaning. I'd heard him say that, too. Now I was edgy. Aunt Clara had never made no plans for me before . . .

"She come to wedding with Cousin Hazel?" Mama asked. I had the feeling I'd missed something somewhere. I wished I'd been listening sooner. But the mystery cleared up quick enough. Too quick.

"Ah, yes, she be there! Hazel say she just right for Johnny, too!"

My gosh, they'd had a regular convention about me. I was straining my ears now, their voices had fallen to a mumble. Then sharp and clear I heard Mama saying, "But, Clara, maybe in America parents no make marriage arrangements for children!" Marriage! My mind went reeling.

"Ach! Foolish Maria! What difference where we are? It is our way. Besides, Johnny will be glad to marry this girl—you wait and see."

Married! Me get married? Had Aunt Clara gone daft? Didn't she know I was only a kid? None of my friends was married at twelve. Fear hit me; I'd have to go to work all day long, like Papa. Now it was me thinking I was too young to do something. Besides, I had sort of made my own plans, mainly to marry Rosita when I grew up and move over to her mother's house where I could eat all the tamales I wanted. I forgot, for the time being, that Rosita was letting some other guy sometimes carry her books. Another thought come shocking to me, that this girl they were talking about probably didn't even know what a tamale was, her from way across the ocean.

They went back to talking about the wedding-party music and I relaxed. Maybe I'd heard them wrong . . . Finally I finished and found Mama had at last run out of things for me to do. Seb went off to deliver his newspapers, and I went over to Sammy's house. We went from there to the vacant lot over on Fifth and Pine streets. A few guys was tossing a ball around. I thought of the marriage talk again. I said to Sammy, "You know what?" I didn't wait for him to answer. "My mama and my aunt is planning to get me married."

Well, Sammy, he darned near choked on the apple he was chewing. "Married!" His eyes went wide and white. "You talkin' married, *married* boy? Why, you jus' a puny kid—that crazy talk!"

I didn't care much for him calling me puny or laughing so hard and jumping around slapping his legs. "Whewee!" he kept saying. "Why, I kin jus' see ol' Johnny here all duded up in a long-tail coat an' a preacher go-to-meetin' hat! Ah, you gonna look jus' fine come your weddin' day. Yes, sirree!"

"Ah, shut up, Sammy!" I was sorry I'd opened my big mouth. Some of the kids were looking over at us. "Maybe I heard wrong." He kept on laughing. Some friend. "Shut up, Sammy!"

"Awright, Awright! I's quittin'!" Then he finally did, him probably seeing as how I was getting mad. "Come on," he said, "I'll race ya over to the pool hall!"

"You're on!" I cried, happy to be off the marriage subject.

"Get ready to lose!" he yelled.

"Not *this* time!" I yelled back.

We both dropped down on one knee, with our two hands, fingers spread apart, touching the ground in front of us. Racing always followed strict rules in our neighborhood, a set pattern that all the guys followed.

"Ready?" Sammy asked.

"Ready!" I replied. Sammy started the countdown. "On your knees!" he yelled. "Raise your cheese!" Our rear ends came up together. "Breeze!" he screamed, and we were off, flying away from the grass-circled lot, turning off of Fifth onto Wood Street, then onto Seventh, panting and straining. Sammy

New Perspectives

pulled away from me. We passed the meat market and Sammy shot across the street and spun around in front of the pool hall to face me as I skidded up.

"I win!" he shouted, "I win!" like it was something new. Sammy always won. I guessed his legs had more stretch in them than mine.

"Yeah, yeah, you win." I had to get home. I had to find out if I'd heard right what I'd heard. "See ya later, Sammy."

"Sure, Johnny." He started to walk away, then he turned back, calling to me. "Jus' don' go gettin' married without ya tellin' your ol' friend Sammy, ya hear?" He was grinning at me like a fool. I waggled my fingers in my ears at him. I could still hear him chuckling as I walked down the street.

I walked into the house to hear Papa saying, "But Maria, they play nice music. I hear when I stop for game of pool sometimes after work."

Mama looked cross. "I no want pool hall music in my house."

Papa gave up. "All right! We have—what you call them?—noisy, off-key boys instead!" He turned and winked at me as I closed the door. "Or maybe I beat on washtub and play harmonica? And Johnny can blow his clarinet!" Mama glared at him. It was Aunt Clara who spoke next.

"Maybe Nick is right, Maria. Maybe pool hall boys is all right." Mama didn't answer.

After supper I helped with the dishes, then went to my bedroom to read. Nobody had said anything else about the girl, so I figured I'd let things ride, too. I was willing to think I'd heard wrong. With the door open I could hear their voices. I'd got into my book though, and I wasn't paying all that much attention until I heard Papa's voice getting a little higher.

"What you mean? Fine for Johnny?" My ears popped wide open. Captain Kidd could raid the English ship without me—I put the book down and tiptoed to where I could peek through the half-open kitchen door.

"Yes, fine for Johnny, have marriage arranged—nice girl—good family. She be American citizen then, too." It was Mama talking. A chill took me; Aunt Clara had done got to her. Mama was sounding like it was all her own idea. Where was the doubt I'd heard in her voice earlier?

Papa was sputtering, "This America—that not done here!"

"No difference; old country, new country. Old ways still good." There was Mama's sister, right in the middle of the planning-for-everybody department. "Seb already pledged," she said. "Remember, Nick?"

"Yes, but we were in *old* country then."

Promised

"No difference!" It was Mama again. "Girl is here, at Cousin Hazel's house. She come long way for this; her family make plans. We no lose face, say no, and send her back!"

My heart beat slow and hurting. I was a goner, cooked and fried. Papa wasn't going to fight for me. I'd probably be married by the middle of next week. Boy, was Sammy ever going to laugh now.

My head plain up and quit working. I couldn't figure no way out of *this* mess. Since I couldn't think, I just sat listening. Papa was back to pushing the pool hall musicians.

"They know lots of tunes—nice dance tunes . . . "

"No!"

"Maria! Listen to Nick! Who knows they come from pool hall? Besides," and here Aunt Clara did a turnaround from her kind words spoken earlier, "*anything* be better than what we hear this morning."

Mama continued to look stubborn. I went out onto the wide front porch, decorated with streamers and balloons, both pink and white, that waved and bobbed in the cool evening breeze. Chairs were lined up along the wall and at the ends of the porch under the honeysuckle vines; the center was kept clear for dancing. Below, under the Ivan tree, a group of chairs had been placed for the musicians, whoever they turned out to be. Another stack of chairs was piled by the low hedge. Everything was ready for Mr. Charlie's and Melissa's wedding day—and the end of my carefree life. How Mama and Aunt Clara could do such a dirty trick on a helpless kid was beyond me . . .

I went to bed early, still hearing the argument of "music" or "noise!" I tossed and flopped around all night; my mind kept waking me up, reaching for a plan of escape, but finding none. Morning finally arrived. Slowly I pulled on my suit pants, my head fuzzy from lack of sleep. It wasn't until I sat picking at my breakfast cereal that a plan began to take shape . . .

City Boy, Oakland 1959

Roque Gutierrez

Standing in holy-white
BVDs at 3 am, rolling
dough balls between honey-brown
hands for the smelt to eat
off black-barbed hooks

half-open windows lay
dull light on curled
wallpaper, purple
faded dreams bared
to the slivered board

he passed beneath apartment
house windows hollow-eyed
and empty, a boy attached
to a paper bag in sneakers

the night
yawned wide
and swal-lowed him whole.

Back to the Bagley

Jean Tucker

Bagley, Wisconsin (pop. 317), is nestled in the bottom lands of the Mississippi River, between the Burlington-Northern railroad track and a county road that leads to nowhere. Looking up the main street of Bagley, you see the post office on your left and, on your right, the bank. After the post office is Scheuerman's Bar and Supper Club. Across the street from Scheuerman's is Oswald's Tavern. Beyond that—next to the little firehouse with an ancient fire engine rusted to the ground—is the Bagley Hotel.

I first came to Bagley for refuge on a rainy night of camping a few miles upriver. The hotel's sign was brightly lit and promised welcome food and warmth. The door opened into a room with a pool table. Most of the activity, though, was off to the left, in a sizeable dining room with Formica-topped tables and a long, mirror-backed mahogany bar. The kitchen produced respectable hamburgers and steaming homemade soup, dished up with side helpings of local chitchat. The food was dispensed by a young woman named Barb with a wry grin and imposing presence, who tended bar at the Bagley when she wasn't driving the local school bus.

In the course of the evening, when I asked for the restroom, Barb pointed me upstairs to the hotel proper. Halfway down the once-elegant corridor was a bathroom with crazed linoleum and a grimy claw-footed tub. On the wall above, a sign crudely lettered in dark crayon said, "DO NOT DRESS DUCKS IN THE BATHTUB." As Barb explained, the hunters could grow unruly, especially if the season was good. In fact, a few years back, the owner had had to crack down on them for letting their muddy dogs sleep on the bedspreads.

New Perspectives

Having been to Bagley, I had no choice but to go back. By now it was deep winter, when the nights were long and the campground frozen over. No one was about except for a few die-hard ice fishermen, and my companion and I had our pick of rooms at ten dollars a night. After inspecting them all, we chose one with a brass bed and a handsome oak dresser. We noticed that, if you turned off the bare bulb hanging from the ceiling and viewed the room in the thin, snowy moonlight, the rainspots blended into the ceiling and the peeling wallpaper was barely visible.

On this sub-zero evening, the soup smelled good and the hamburger was tempting. But my friend, a city-bred person, was bemused by the nightly specials printed on the menu: Thursday—chicken-fried steak with mashed potatoes and gravy; Friday—catfish dinner; Saturday—turtle. Turtle? The Bagley Hotel, as it turned out, had become known for its turtle as far away as Prairie du Chien, some twenty miles to the north. When Barb came to take our order, my friend asked with polite hesitancy, "The—uh—turtle . . . could you tell me how that's served?"

Barb narrowed her eyes and seemed to weigh the legitimacy of the question. Without expression, she replied, "On a plate."

Over a year elapsed before the next visit to Bagley. We arrived hungry, as usual, and our menu choice was straightforward: homemade vegetable soup and Bagley burgers with everything. We were puzzled to see a sixtyish gentleman tending the bar and figured that it must be Barb's night off. A little probing, however, revealed that Barb had left the hotel and was now driving the school bus full time.

Was this a bad omen? The next surprise was that the price of a room at the Bagley Hotel had skyrocketed—to fifteen dollars a night! This, the bartender explained, reflected the renovation that was under way. The owner was installing new walls and ceilings, literally building rooms within rooms because nothing in the old structure was level or plumb.

Once upstairs, we could only admire his handiwork. Two of the rooms had plush carpeting, freshly painted woodwork, and well-chosen wallpaper that was seamed invisibly around the odd-shaped windows. One room even had a shiny doorknob with a push-button lock—an amenity unknown in the Bagley of old.

On the back porch, where overflow duck hunters used to sleep like sardines among their dogs, stood paint pots, ladders, and rolls of variously patterned wallpaper. The hallway smelled musty, and in places the walls

Back to the Bagley

showed exposed lath where chunks of plaster had fallen away. How many duck seasons would come and go before all nine rooms were remodeled and the hotel was restored to its former dignity? And how would the rich royal blue carpeting stand up to hunting boots and dog feet? We felt somewhat relieved that the transformation was gradual, so that we could acclimate ourselves to the new Bagley Hotel.

Before we turned in that evening, we shared a few toasts with the new bartender, a retired meat inspector who drives the local school bus when he isn't working at the hotel. A courteous and friendly soul, he mentioned that—in case you did want turtle some Saturday night—you'd need to call ahead and make arrangements. After all, there isn't that much demand for it any more—even in Bagley.

Bunce Island

Don Donovan

A dozen miles east of Freetown, Sierra Leone, in West Africa, the estuary is dotted by a maze of verdant islands. One of these is called Bunce Island. Sailing past this speck of land measuring a mile in length by a half mile in width, I observed nothing that would set it apart from the other islands in the estuary. But Bunce Island has the distinction of being classified as a Historic National Monument of the Republic of Sierra Leone.

When I visited there, a caretaker, his wife and two children were the only permanent residents. They lived in a small hut with plastered mud walls. The roof was of corrugated iron. The caretaker supported his family by fishing and raising a few vegetables, some chickens, and sheep. This was supplemented with a small stipend he received from the government for his services. As I approached the hut, located in a clearing near the beach, I found the man and his wife working in a vegetable patch in front of their dwelling. Fishing nets hung drying over a long pole that extended between two upright posts. In front of the nets slumbered a half dozen black-headed sheep. As I walked past the animals, my presence disturbed them, and in an instant they were on their feet, running and jumping in all directions. The caretaker, a man of about fifty, was dressed in a loose-fitting toga-like garment that made his body appear rather heavyset. His sparkling black eyes exuded friendliness as he extended his hand to me with a hearty welcome. His bare-breasted wife wore a skirt that extended to her ankles. Though she appeared shy and stood in the background, she, too, welcomed me with a friendly and curious smile.

After a brief visit the caretaker told me of an old cemetery at the east end of the island he was sure I would find interesting. Again we shook hands and I directed my steps towards a trail that led through lush tropic vegetation. In a few minutes I was reading quaint epitaphs of soldiers, sea captains, and

Bunce Island

employees of an English trading company whose bones rest in the soil of Bunce Island. Most of the tombstones bear dates of the eighteenth and nineteenth centuries, and a few go back to the seventeenth.

From the cemetery I walked another trail that skirts the north shore, towards the west end of the island. Soon, the ruins of red brick walls covered with twisted vines loomed before my eyes.

In the late seventeenth century a fort was constructed here by an English trading company. Passing the island in a boat one cannot see the ruins of the fort's crumbling brick buildings because they are hidden by jungle. Facing the fort's walls, lying on a carpet of grass which is speckled with yellow flowers, are a dozen old cannon, their muzzles pointing towards the murky waters of the estuary. For many years these cannon have reposed in silence, but in centuries past they belched their thunder and fire against attacking Portuguese privateers, French men-of-war, and English pirates. Sometimes these assaults were beaten off, but more often they were successful, and the fort's unfortunate garrison found themselves prisoners of the enemy.

It was in 1663, when Charles II chartered the Royal Adventurers of England to trade into Africa, that serious trading operations were started in the vicinity of the Sierra Leone Estuary. Two forts, or trading factories as they were called, were built. One was established on Tasso Island, which is located a short distance to the southeast of Bunce Island, and another on Sherbo Island at the eastern extremity of the estuary. These trading stations carried on a lucrative business with the Tembe tribe and other indigenous people of this part of Africa—the most profitable trade at this time being in ivory and Camwood, a hard timber used in making a red dye.

Hardly had the Tasso Island fort been established than it was captured the following year by the Dutch Admiral De Ruyter. After this fiasco the company's operations were moved to adjoining and more defensible Bunce Island. In 1672 the Royal Adventurers were reconstituted as the Royal African Company, with Sherbo Island as the central depot and Bunce Island as a sub-depot. Two years later both Bunce and Sherbo Islands were plundered by the French. This humiliation led to the abandonment of Bunce Island until 1713, when it was reactivated as a factory. Six years later, it became the company's headquarters.

Robert Plunkett, an excitable and rather tactless Irishman, was in charge of Bunce Island when the English pirate Bartholomew Roberts attacked the settlement in 1720. The feisty Irishman put up a stubborn resistance until his ammunition gave out. When Plunkett was captured trying to escape, Roberts berated him with all the expletives of a pirate vocabulary for his Irish

New Perspectives

impudence in daring to resist. But Plunkett, not to be outdone by his captors, replied with a torrent of profanity which made the language of the pirate seem mild by comparison. This unexpected effrontery raised much laughter among Roberts' men, and they bade their captain to hold his tongue, for he was no match for Plunkett in the respected art of cursing. So it was by his mastery of the skill of swearing that old Plunkett saved his life.

The company became increasingly concerned with the ease with which attackers captured the fort. In 1726, William Smith, a surveyor, was sent to inspect the fortifications and to make recommendations for improving the defenses of the island. The plan which he submitted for the Bunce Island fort shows fifty cannon mounted on a triple bastioned stone wall facing the anchorage. Inside the walls were the houses for the company's employees and the slave quarters. Accompanying Smith was a new and energetic governor determined to suppress all trading rivals. Among these were the Afro-Portuguese, native Africans who had adopted the language and, to some extent, the customs of the Portuguese. The new governor's policy to divide them diplomatically from their African relatives only succeeded in uniting them against him. In October 1728, an Afro-Portuguese by the name of Lopez surprised the fort, burned it, and drove out the governor. The company then abandoned its operations in the Sierra Leone Estuary.

After the departure of the Royal African Company, the fort was purchased by a London firm, Grant, Oswald, and Sargent. Buildings were restored and it was once again fortified. Though its defenses were ill-maintained, it was considered the best English fort on the coast, and its amenities even included a two-hole golf course. But when the French attacked the fort in 1779, during the American War, it fell after only token resistance. When the French destroyed the fort, it was again rebuilt and Bunce Island enjoyed even greater prosperity, with the slave trade becoming the chief source of revenue. During the last two decades of the eighteenth century, thousands of human beings were shipped from Bunce Island as cargo to the New World.

This prosperity, however, was short-lived. In 1808, the properties of the various English trading enterprises in West Africa were transferred to the Crown. Accompanying this change came an act abolishing the slave trade. With the loss of its primary source of revenue, Bunce Island lost its importance. Some trading activities were continued, with timber the alternative for slaves. But the superintendent of the island found it increasingly difficult to maintain authority over the Tembe laborers who now knew that they could not be sold. In October 1809 they rioted. A detachment of troops suppressed the rebellion, and the ringleaders were transported to the Cape Coast. Bunce

Bunce Island

Island's days were numbered as a viable community. Soon after this, the island was abandoned. Like the Mayan temples of tropic America, the stately brick buildings were to be buried under twisted vines and jungle vegetation to await resurrection in the twentieth century when their hoary walls would stimulate the curiosity of an occasional tourist.

Only remnants of what at one time must have been very impressive two-story buildings remain today. The largest structure, the barracks, stands as an empty shell with its four walls intact. I entered this building through a moss-covered doorway and found myself in the main room, which was carpeted with thick grass. The massive foundations are constructed of stone, and above these, the two-foot-thick brick walls reach skyward towards the spreading limbs of huge trees that stand outside the walls, seemingly guarding this sepulcher of man's past. As I peered through the large windows of the second story, I could see chartreuse leaves of the jungle foliage, made translucent by the tropic sun. Beyond them I caught glimpses of blue sky.

After inspecting the ruins of the old buildings, I headed south where the remains of the stone walls of the fortifications still look out towards the anchorage. They, too, are covered with moss and twisted lianas. If the old cannon that lay before them could speak, I thought, what exciting tales they could tell of the soldiers who had manned them against French warships and Portuguese sea dogs and attacking English pirates.

A hundred yards from the old walls, a small hill rises from the jungle floor. At its base is a doorway obscured by vegetation. I stooped as I entered the small aperture. Inside I paused for a minute to give my eyes an opportunity to adjust to the darkness. I then made my way down a short flight of stone steps into a dank room which is illuminated only by the light that filters through the doorway. In this dungeon, which is fifty feet square, as many as three hundred captives had awaited the arrival of slave ships to transport them to the West Indies. My imagination conjured up pictures of the miserable conditions of these unfortunate people. I could almost hear their plaintive moans and cries. The thought of their hopeless plight, of their almost total despair, and of their cruel sufferings depressed me. I stayed only a few minutes in this hellhole. Quickly I ascended the steps to the sunshine and clean air, to the green grass and trees, to the brightly colored flowers and the happy chirping of the colorfully plumaged birds.

God made Bunce Island a beautiful place. Man made it hell.

Grandma's Airplane Ride

Allen J. Pettit

I think it all started when Mama decided to get married again. Mama's marriage and departure from the old home place left Grandma living by herself way out there in the hills. I agreed with all of her children—Mama, Bill, Celia, and Vallie—that that wasn't a good situation, especially since the nearest neighbor was half a mile and two hillsides away. Suppose she slipped or stumbled and fell? Seventy-seven-year-old hips break easy. That had happened just the year before to her old friend and neighbor, Miss Annie Leeman, and she had lain in her front yard and died in the rain during the course of a couple of days before her son, who lived two hundred yards away, got a chance to stop by and see how she was getting along.

Persuasion, arguments and fear won over sentiment, nostalgia, and maybe even common sense. We convinced Grandma to break up her housekeeping of fifty-two years and to go live with her children. Now I wonder why we were dumb enough to do that. But back then it seemed like a good idea to override her weak arguments and easily tiring defenses, even if all of us did have to gang up on her to do it.

She didn't have much to pack up, or store, or give away. Just some chipped pieces of china, some homemade, sweat-stained quilts, an old lady's souvenirs kept from her children's and grandchildren's childhoods, and her own thin wardrobe. There was no filmy, silky lingerie in Grandma's world of calloused hands and wood-burning cookstoves.

It wasn't long before discontent set in on the new arrangement. Role reversals are tough on mothers and daughters. Even from my faraway place in Great Falls, Montana, where I was serving a tour in the U.S. Air Force, I could

Grandma's Airplane Ride

hear the problems as Grandma made the first swing around the circuit of living a few months with each of her children.

She was a true child of the Old South, of Scotch-Irish-English ancestry and descended from the early Virginia settlers who had filtered south and west through the mountains of Appalachia. Her lineage was a tough and hardy breed, refined out of the successive generations that had the courage and strength to keep moving and carve out new places of their own in the wilderness. Andrew Jackson was rewarded with the presidency for showing them how to use the Treaty of Doak's Stand to wrest rich land from the Cherokee, Choctaw, and Chickasaw. Some of the sons and daughters of those pioneers were the ones who, drawn by the westering instinct, went on to Texas and Colorado and got to California in time for the gold rush.

Grandma's folks were the ones who stayed and lost track of the ones who went. She was a late-in-life baby, the fifth of six, born just twenty years after her father walked on crutches and an empty stomach from Pennsylvania to Mississippi. He'd left the front half of his right foot on a battlefield in Gettysburg.

From the stories I heard, it seemed that he raised a tomboy daughter amongst his sons, and then drew a certain criticism from his neighbors for over-educating her by keeping her in school all the way through the eighth grade.

I heard from Uncle Owen how young men would earn the wrath of their fathers for tiring work horses by riding them long miles, and sometimes through most of the night, for the purpose of courting his strong-willed sister with the corn silk blonde hair and the summer sky blue eyes, who was described as ". . . a fine figure of a woman."

As I got older I learned that it wasn't until the tall, curly-haired, gray-eyed stranger came along that any man got a second look from her. Not that a lot hadn't been trying.

One of the first big surprises of my young life was when I heard her tell somebody, "When Fred came into this country he had a full head of the curliest, blackest hair you'd ever want to see." She was talking 'bout Grandpa. I did a double take at him and for the first time realized that he hadn't always been old—and bald as an onion.

What she said about Grandpa had made me think that he came from some faraway, exotic place like Yugoslavia or Japan, or India, or maybe Mexico. But something else I found out as I got older was that he came from Winston County, the second county over to the east. He was an outsider.

New Perspectives

Hell, he had to live there for twenty years before folks trusted him enough to lend him a mule collar or a plant plow.

Grandpa was a timber-cutter, blacksmith, hunter and trapper without a peer in our part of the country. He was born a hundred years too late for the company of Daniel Boone and Jim Bridger, mountain men and beaver trappers. Tying him to a family and a poor-dirt farm was caging a wild child of nature.

He let that cage and the years beat him down and turn him into an antisocial, bitter old man who took his whiskey-drinking rages out on his family. From his deathbed, he looked up at his wife of forty-one years and with his last breath said, "Goddam you, Dora."

I asked my wife what she thought about Grandma coming to live with us for awhile. Her answer was, "That's a good idea. We've got plenty of room and a whole new world might be good for her."

"Okay, we'll give it a try and see how it works."

The scenery would be different for her. Except for the recent two hundred mile trip to her daughter Celia's place just outside of New Orleans, where I was to meet her, Grandma had never been farther from home than the forty miles to Vicksburg. Now I was going to take her on a twenty-three hundred mile drive from Mississippi to Montana, but first I had to go get her.

She was an aged, stooped version of the strong grandmother who used to say, "Son, we're out of stove wood. Git the saw and the axe and let's go cut some more." Seems we always ran out in cold, rainy, misty weather when numbed fingers and slippery footing made sawing and chopping somewhat risky.

To a child any adult is a giant. But now the top of her head is not quite shoulder high to me, and the arms are thinner, frailer, if you will, than when we shoveled snow into the cistern. I remembered how she had wakened me one morning. "Son, go git the shovels, we're gonna put snow in the cistern."

"Huh? How come?"

"So we can have cool water next summer. Now go get the shovels."

I ran through four inches of fresh snow to the stables, cleaned the shovels with my shoe heel, and we started shoveling. She misjudged the amount. Later that afternoon she sent me to draw water. I let the bucket down by free-running the chain over the pulley and klang-klang-klang, the bucket bounced on the ice. We broke ice for a month. But the following

Grandma's Airplane Ride

summer everybody in the neighborhood marvelled at how cool the water was in Miz Dora's cistern.

I spent one night sleeping in Louisiana before we drove on up to central Mississippi for a day's visit with the rest of the family before we set out on Grandma's first big trip.

She settled in on the right side of the front seat for the long ride, put her spit can on the floorboard by her feet, turned a rather expectant look on me, and said, "Yep, I'm ready." Her son, Uncle Bill, stepped back from the side of the car by Grandma's door, and away we went.

Her spit can came by way of her being a dipper of snuff. It was a one pound Folger's Coffee can with the top cut out. She kept some paper wadded in the bottom to reduce slopping around. People with queasy stomachs almost never took a second look into Grandma's spit can.

One winter when I was twelve or thirteen, she forgot to buy snuff when she went to town one Saturday for groceries. She used the Levi Garrett brand that came in a little brown jar. The last of her supply was dipped that night while we listened to the Grand Ol' Opry on the radio. By Sunday noon, tension lay so thick in the air that I volunteered to walk two miles each way on a cold winter day to get her a new bottle of snuff.

Anyway, we then set out on our trip and in quick succession came the old narrow bridge over the Big River at Vicksburg, the raised, levee-like roadway across the swamps of Louisiana, then the winding road of cursed curves through the piney wood hills into the East Texas crop oak country, heading for Dallas and Fort Worth–"Big D" and Cowtown.

Grandma and I had some relatives in Dallas. One of them, a granddaughter and cousin respectively, had some years before finished high school and put on her cotton print dress, packed a cardboard suitcase, counted up the twelve dollars in her purse, boarded a Greyhound Bus, and struck out into the world. Courage was seldom in short supply among Grandma's descendants; judgment, sometimes, but guts–no.

Buried deep in my childhood memories is the commotion and uproar over the time some neighbors decided to fence over the gate and deny us right-of-way access across their property to the public road. While Grandpa counselled caution, it was Grandma who walked to the gate, pistol in hand, and dared them to drive one nail or stay one minute longer than it took them to leave.

New Perspectives

Genie's hospitality gave us some rest after our first day on the road. As a seasoned traveler, Grandma had a ways to go. I wasn't really worried about her physically, because I had had a doctor check her out for the trip, particularly her heart, in anticipation of the high mountain passes.

"Now, Ma, if you get to feelin' tired . . . "

"Son, I'm doin' just fine. This sure is pretty country, and I'm enjoyin' every bit of it."

"Well, if you get tired you just let me know. We'll stop and bed you down in the back seat so you can get some sleep."

"Nah, Son, I'm not going to sleep. I want to see everything there is to see. I have always heard of the West, and now this is my chance to see it. No, I'm not gonna do any sleepin'."

That left me wondering, Why me, Lord? For cryin' out loud. She wants to see everything. And if she won't sleep in the car, I'll have to stop. Which means I can't drive all night. Which means two extra days on the road, and two nights in motels that I can't afford. Damn. Well, at least I'm already five days into the trip, and on the return leg home.

It wasn't the two thousand miles of hard driving ahead that worried me, although I did wish they had finished building the interstate highways instead of just talking about getting started. It was the idea of spending money for sleeping when I could be making more miles down the road that really got to me.

But it was a good trip. She marvelled at the limitless, high plains of North Texas and the snowcapped mountains that give character to Colorado. This, the woman who had taken me in, diapered me, raised me, and schooled me, was an avid listener to my tales of the Oregon and California wagon trails that we crossed.

This was also the woman who had set out one sparkling spring morning, walking down the gravel road carrying her sick child to the doctor. The doctor's office was in town—seven miles away. Immunization for diphtheria was unknown then. The child choked, strangled, turned blue, and died in her arms while she walked and prayed for help. Like the praying, crying didn't help. So she turned around and went home, carrying her dead child wrapped in a blanket. And so it was that I grew up with one uncle instead of two. And so it was that I made sure that my children had their DPT shots.

She saw, wondered at, and loved the vastness and the beauty of this great land of ours, and she looked at the valley of the Crazy Woman Creek in

Grandma's Airplane Ride

Wyoming and liked the story of its naming, and wished there were some buffalo left to see.

After noting that Grandma was born just seven years after General Custer cornered the Sioux warriors of Sitting Bull, Red Cloud, and Crazy Horse right at the place where we stood beside the Little Big Horn River, we crossed the Judith Basin country to the Great Falls of the Missouri and home. I had driven forty-nine hundred miles in nine days. I and mine welcomed Grandma to her new home.

It was three months before I noticed signs of homesickness. Another month went by before she said, "Son, I want to go home. This is nice country and all that, but it ain't home."

"Ma, I hope you don't want to go right now, because I can't afford to take you."

"I'm gonna ride the bus."

"Uh-uh. That's a three-day trip, and that's just too much for you."

Disappointment started edging into her face and voice. "Well, there's a train that . . . "

"No, Ma, these trains are all freight trains up here. The nearest passenger train is in Denver, and that's eight hundred miles south of here. You're either gonna have to fly—which you won't do—or wait until I can get enough money together, and time that I can take off, to drive you back down home."

It took another month for the homesickness to outgrow her fear of airplanes and to prod her into saying, "Son, if you'll make the arrangements, I'll fly home."

To reduce her exposure to something she feared, I suggested, "Why don't you just fly to Dallas, spend the night at Genie's house, and then take the bus home from there? That way it's only 'bout twelve hours on the bus and it won't be so tough on you." She was cheered by that thought, so it became our plan.

She was very brave and calm on the drive to the airport, except for the wadded handkerchief clutched in one hand. The tremors didn't develop in her voice and hands until we checked her bags at the ticket counter. Her knees didn't start shaking until she and I left the rest of the family at the gate and started our walk across the fifty feet of concrete ramp to the airplane.

New Perspectives

Regardless of the fact that I had been flying in the Navy and the Air Force for years, Grandma was convinced that the end was as near as the distance to the airplane. Furthermore, there was no doubt in her mind that when they closed the door it would be the same as lowering the lid on her coffin.

I held her elbow and steadied her across the ramp and up the stairway, through the feared doorway, and up the aisle to an overwing seat. I wanted her to sit there so that when she looked out at least there would be something out there to see.

Since the nice people of Western Airlines had let me put her aboard before the rest of the passengers, I had time to tell the stewardesses that this was my dear old Grandma, scared and in a strange world. Would they give her a little bit of extra attention? I left her in their care.

I rejoined my family and we stood by the fence watching them move the stairway, close the door, and start turning the props. The old DC-6's piston engines coughed and choked to life on puffs of blue smoke before they caught and settled into the low idle roar that would take them to the runway.

We all waved, my youngest daughter Nancy from my shoulders, while Grandma waved the now unclenched handkerchief up and down her window as the airplane started moving forward. It swung a fast wingtip past us, then turned tail and taxied away. The only trace of its leaving was a cloud of foul-smelling engine exhaust, and that too was soon gone. We went home. There was nothing to do now but wait.

I timed my phone call to Dallas to allow for Genie to get Grandma home from the airport, plus a few minutes for unwinding and calming down.

I got Genie on the phone. "Did Grandma make it okay?"

"Oh, yes, she's fine. Do you want to talk to her?"

We had a good connection and Grandma's voice came in loud and clear.

"Hello. Son?"

"Yeah, Ma, I'm here. How you feeling?"

"Oh, I'm feeling just fine, Son." I thought I heard a tone somewhere in there that wondered at my concern.

"How was the airplane ride?"

"Son, them young girls was just as nice to me as they could be. Why one of them set down by me when we first took off. And they kept bringing me

Grandma's Airplane Ride

things. And after we changed planes and left Denver, I met some folks that has got a ranch in Oklahoma, and . . . "

I was pleased, and a little surprised, at the strength and enthusiasm in her voice. After she went on and on telling me about how nice everybody was and how someday she was going to visit her new friends in Oklahoma, I began to worry about the telephone bill. I tried to head her off.

"Ma, I'm sure glad you enjoyed your airplane ride. But wait a minute, tell me when are you gonna catch the bus from Genie's and go home?"

"Bus?" There was a question in her voice.

"Yeah. The bus you're going home on."

"Why, Son," she spoke slowly, kind of like she didn't really understand me or the question. "I'm not going on a bus."

"Well, then, how are you gonna get home?"

"Why, Son, I'm gonna fly."

Her tone jarred me as much or more than her words. It was like, 'have you lost your everlasting? Are you out of your gourd? Take a bus when I can *fly*?'

Stone

Linda Marlow

I look into the crystal clear High Sierra water and see a green stone flecked with red. I reach for it. Water so icy cold–painfully cold–that my hand turns red, but I have the stone. I can see it change in my hand from bright and shiny to dull and colorless.

Feeling the smoothness of it and turning it around in my hand several times, I change my footing, lean to the right a bit, look upstream, and throw the stone with just the right amount of English on it so it will skip many times across the water.

Bavarian Chocolate Fudge

Mary Jo Wold

You're sugar 'n spice,
And all that's nice,
You're the delicious sauce on the rice.

You're precious 'n sweet,
A hint of the elite,
Your smile, always a treat.

You're the top o' the line,
Simple, yet so refine,
How best to describe this friend of mine?

As a mom you're supreme,
Any child's dream,
You're the berries 'n cream.

On the scale of a hundred flavors I'd judge,
And from this notion I'll not budge,
My dear friend, you're BAVARIAN CHOCOLATE FUDGE!

The Glass Bowl

Wanda Giuliano

Valerie Thomas always had excellent taste, a taste for the beautiful and a keen sense for special effects. Therefore, she had arranged things so well that the apartment looked impressive, but cozy. Among all the decorative innovations, she had created an alluring corner. At the right side of the white drainboard that separated the kitchen from the living room, she had combined glimmering lights and leafy plants hanging over a huge glass bowl in which she had placed a green phosphorescent witch's castle, pieces of wood shaped like naked trees, water plants, and a horde of goldfish.

Quite a dramatic scene," had been Jack's comment.

"It may be, but I love it; let's not forget that in my college years I took drama classes and stagecraft."

"That's what you told me at the beginning of our relationship. Your preferred characters were Lady Macbeth and Medea, right?"

Valerie nodded. "Right. I enjoyed acting, and I enjoyed creating the scene's dramatic effects."

"Well, you haven't lost your talent."

Was her husband being sarcastic?

Two years later, Valerie hadn't changed her mind about her favorite corner. Of course, she was not a moody person, and regardless of how the world revolved around her, she hadn't changed at all. The glass bowl was still her delight. Off and on, she had chosen with care and added healthy new fish. There was nothing special about little goldfish, but they were so cute and innocent, not mean and cruel like some of the more celebrated tropical fish.

The Glass Bowl

As she did every morning after Jack was gone about his business, Valerie walked into the kitchen and glanced at the fish. The one with the beautiful fins, so iridescent and large, was now swimming regally round and round. Valerie liked to look at it. Lightly, she tapped on the bowl. The fish darted as if to bite her finger, but, hitting the glass with its open mouth, jerked back, shocked, and retreated behind one of the water plants.

Feeling sorry, Valerie waited for the fish to come out of hiding. After a while, she gave up and went into the bedroom. Stretching lazily on the bed, flat on her stomach, she moved the drapes aside and looked out on the street. It was a windy day, with whirling dead leaves and leafy branches shaking—one of those days in which only flashes of sunlight escape between the clouds.

Valerie liked to live on the first floor. Everything seemed so close to her. The only bothersome matter was the sight of the young woman who lived right across the street. The woman had the unpleasant habit of undressing in front of the window while the lights were on. The flimsy curtains projected her naked body in full. Valerie was sure that the show was for Jack's benefit.

Jack joked about it.

"What's unusual about a naked female body? Venus is glorified naked; statues are naked."

"Yes," she agreed. "But who wants to touch naked statues?"

"I couldn't touch her anyhow. My arms aren't fifty feet long! Also," he added disdainfully, "she doesn't have a great body. Her legs are too skinny."

The subject was dropped, leaving Valerie perplexed, for she thought the girl's best assets were her shapely legs.

The thought of Jack made her long for his presence. The days were getting so empty without him. Jack was an extremely ambitious insurance agent. Handsome and suave, he was acquiring quite a clientele. That was the main reason he didn't spend much of his time with her. He was always so busy, out at odd hours. "An agent has to see people at their convenience," he explained to her on several occasions.

"Birdwatching?"

Startled by Jack's voice, Valerie sprang to her feet, facing her husband.

"Now, now," he said, a mocking light in his eyes. "I didn't mean to frighten you. I had to come back to get some papers."

How good-looking he was. The gold-brown eyes that could be, depending on his mood, so warm and sweet, or could freeze in the most distant and cold stare, so much in contrast with the charming boyish smile.

New Perspectives

She felt a pang in her heart just looking at him and a burning desire to caress that face, but for some obscure reason she had to control the urge. Something was stealing her spontaneity, the old ability to be herself, carefree and happy.

Jack was looking at her curiously. "What are you thinking?"

"I was thinking how good you look in that blue suit."

"Do I?" He smiled, pleased with himself.

Valerie nodded silently. Yes, he did look great. Tall, athletic, handsome. The perfect salesman. With his looks, he could sell a frog for a butterfly, and nobody would notice the difference.

Slowly, she followed him into the living room. Jack was now engrossed in reading papers scattered on the table. Bending slightly, he was unconsciously twisting his moustache.

There he was, so close and yet so far, lost in his own world, from which she felt excluded. If she could only shake him from his indifference! How?

Perhaps she could suddenly disappear from his life . . . maybe she could kill herself . . . to punish him! In her mind's eye, she saw herself lying dead. "What's happened?" someone would ask, bewildered. Someone else would shake his head sorrowfully.

Jack, bending over her, would cry, "Why? Why?" Tears would be streaming down his cheeks, lodging in his thick moustache. The idea of Jack's moustache gleaming with tears shed for her was so funny she giggled.

"What's that?" He looked at her suspiciously. "Something bothering you?"

"No . . . no . . . " Valerie said hurriedly, "I was going to ask if you wanted a cup of coffee."

"I don't have much time, but I'll go for the coffee."

The coffee was ready in a few minutes. Valerie carried the steaming cup and placed it carefully on the table. Jack raised his head from the papers, holding one in his hand.

"See this?" he asked with a laugh. "One of the most expensive policies," he said, snapping his fingers, "sold!"

There was now a sly smile on his face. "Guess who is the buyer."

Valerie shook her head. She wasn't in the mood for guessing.

"Mrs. Scott." He laughed again. "Remember La Belle Restaurant?"

The Glass Bowl

She nodded while Mrs. Scott's face beckoned her mind. No, she thought, the poor woman didn't have a chance at resisting Jack's charm.

She could visualize the scene. Jack would jokingly put his arm around Mrs. Scott's chubby shoulders, bending his tall frame just enough to whisper in her ear how good she looked and what a great restaurateur she was, and then, he would sweetly deliver the favorite line he kept in store for older ladies: "I'm truly fascinated by your maturity . . . expertise. Young girls? Pff! A dime a dozen . . . " And at all times, flashing that irresistible smile, enough to sidetrack the woman from the real purpose of his visit.

Seducer! Valerie didn't know whether to laugh or be disgusted at the thought of Jack seducing the lady. She remembered well the cozy restaurant where she sometimes dined with Jack. The owner, Mrs. Scott, was a widow in her fifties who always blinked her eyes coquettishly at the sight of Jack, touching his arm, doing the little girl's act of "Oh, you . . . you."

Valerie was embarrassed for her; more than once she told her husband that he shouldn't tease the poor woman and if all he had in mind was to have Mrs. Scott as a potential client, why didn't he come to the point? But he would laugh, dismissing her.

Selling is an art—a craft—either you are good at it, or you are not."

Reluctantly, Valerie had to admit he was right.

"Yes," she said. "You are a good salesman."

"The best," he boasted. "I know exactly how to handle people, especially women."

Didn't he! Valerie could hardly control her bitterness. That he charmed Mrs. Scott was nothing to worry about. It was his constant talk about a very special client, a woman of distinction, very much interested in his career, that had her worried. She could see a new fire in his eyes, the same fire that once had burned for her.

His boldness was disquieting. Not too long ago, she had dared to ask him the name of his special client, and why she was so interested in his career. He faced her, his eyes cold. "I don't have to tell you anything about my work. Is that clear?"

Never had he been so rude to her. Valerie had felt the urge to scream.

"I'll be late," he said, gathering his papers. "I have a very important deal to close."

She listened while trying to hide her disturbed and tormented thoughts.

"Yes, dear," she said, casually, perhaps too casually.

New Perspectives

A little surprised, Jack gave her a sharp glance. But he was in a hurry and evidently didn't want to waste any more time. He grabbed the black briefcase from the table and left with a laconic goodbye.

The cozy, inviting room suddenly seemed gloomy and dark. Nervously she turned on the television. An announcer touted a new mascara. She couldn't care less; however, she didn't shut it off. It was like having someone around. There wasn't much to do, everything was in perfect order.

"I'll be late," Jack had said. "Don't wait for me. I'll grab a bite somewhere." The idea of eating alone depressed Valerie.

After a few seconds of indecision, she glanced at the glass bowl. Slowly, she went into the small, neat kitchen and looked closely at the fish. The biggest of all, the one she liked the most, was swimming toward his dinner.

"Now," Valerie murmured, "he will open his mouth bigger and bigger, and swallow his food."

For a moment, the thought of Jack crossed her mind. There was something in common between the two of them; the same strong appetite, the same way of savoring the food.

Gnack ... gnack ... gnack ... the goldfish were gulping down one grain of food after another, without stopping. Gnack ... gnack ... gnack .. Jack would chew the food, his perfect white teeth seizing the chosen bite, savoring it with sensuality, the only interruption being a comment on this or that "delicious dish."

His face invaded her mind again. I should not have married Jack. It isn't his fault that women rave about him. She also raved about him, but with discretion.

She had kept her friendly smiles, never pushing herself on him, avoiding involvement for fear of rejection. What chance could she have with all the pretty girls sticking to him like the proverbial flies on honey? Instead, to her surprise, she had attracted his attention; perhaps he had been challenged by her attitude. Thus, without trying, she had succeeded in inflaming Jack beyond her expectations.

"You are a strange girl," he had said. "I never know what is going on in your mind, but for some reason, I feel very comfortable with you."

Then one day, looking at her almost teasingly, he said, "Say, let's go to Reno, with no regrets afterwards."

The Glass Bowl

She never regretted it. Did he? Moving hastily to dispel unpleasant thoughts, Valerie looked at herself in the mirror across the wall by the entrance; her reflection was reassuring.

Her figure was still slender, supple. She approached the mirror and lingered there. She looked with careful attention at her dense, dark, well-groomed hair and at her creamy complexion. Then she opened her mouth, carefully inspecting her white, even teeth. She appraised herself with her deep, brown eyes. She hadn't changed. Then why . . . ?

"I feel very comfortable with you." His words resounded in the back of her mind.

There was nothing wrong in trying to make him happy, in providing him with all the comforts she could think of. That's why after they married she had quit her job in the art gallery, but not without a sense of loss. It had been more important to be home with him. An insurance agent has to come and go at unpredictable hours, and nothing was greater than fixing delicate morsels for him.

"You cook like my mother," he told her once. "That's why I married you." They both laughed.

That kind of happiness seemed so far away now. Just a while ago the thought of killing herself, to punish him, had crossed her mind. Kill herself? What for? To give Jack a chance to play the disconsolate husband? How silly! If there was a thing that she should do, it was to kill him!

"Bang . . . Bang . . . You're Dead!" Wasn't that the title of a movie? Dear God, what was wrong with her?

With a sigh, Valerie moved away from the mirror and back into the kitchen. The aroma of fresh coffee was inviting. Sipping it with pleasure, she gazed again at her favorite corner, suddenly aware of something unusual.

Small specks were swimming about the fishbowl. Valerie realized at once that the small specks were baby fish! The discovery surprised her. She never paid any attention to the shapes of the fish, and of course she had no experience with pregnant fish. She laughed at her ignorance.

Attentively, she followed the stream of tiny fish, thrilled at the sight. Then, she froze. Her favorite beautiful goldfish was swooping toward the small creatures, the voracious mouth opening and closing, methodically gulping them down.

"Oh no!" Valerie cried. "Stop it! Stop it!"

New Perspectives

Frantically, she looked around, searching for a means to end the slaughter. The clean, neat kitchen didn't offer her any help. Meanwhile the stream of baby fish was growing thinner. There was only one way to stop it. She plunged her hand in the bowl, grabbing the slippery fish that in vain tried to escape. By then, Valerie could no longer control her anger.

"You little cannibal!" Her voice was quivering. "I don't like you any more."

In one last effort to escape, the fish slipped from her grip and darted to the opposite side of the bowl. Looking at him helplessly, she murmured, "What's the use? It's too late now. He's devoured them all."

The fish was now hiding behind the white rock on the left, evidently scared. It couldn't have been hungry, she reasoned. Not too long ago she had fed them all. Maybe the little bastard likes different tender bites, she thought. Jack was right. "Change the food," he had said. "Even fish like variety."

Variety . . . variety. The words drummed in her head. She felt strangely alert, recalling events, parts of conversations involuntarily overheard, the anxious female voices asking for Jack.

" . . . it is extremely important, please tell him to return my call."

"Impatient client." Jack's winning smile had reassured her.

The calls kept coming. "Please, it is an urgent matter . . . "

All the messages she had taken in good faith, for never had a doubt crossed her mind. And now, this new client, this distinguished woman.

The bastard, she thought bitterly.

The car keys were on the counter. She reached for them, grabbed the black blazer from the hall closet, and went for the door. The place where Jack would almost certainly 'grab a bite' was down at Jack London Square. She knew the restaurant very well. Jack used to meet her there during their courtship.

Walking into the familiar place reminded her of happier moments. A carved wooden life-sized figure of a sea captain was standing by the entrance. The large, black wooden chairs, the green leafy hanging plants. Nothing had changed. Breathing hard, Valerie looked around. She could see the tables by the window overlooking the water below. How many times had they admired the beautiful yachts tied to the pier? How many times had he told her, "Some day we will have our own boat tied at one of those piers."

A young, smiling waitress approached her. "Alone?" she asked.

"No," Valerie replied, "I'm waiting for a friend, thank you." Taking advantage of the many customers coming in, she moved with forced nonchalance toward the dining room, glancing at people busy eating or chatting.

Her heart throbbed painfully at the sight of Jack. He was sitting across from a very sophisticated young woman. His hand, the hand that she loved, was now gently caressing the other woman's hand, his eyes completely lost in hers.

Valerie could sense his warm, passionate look, so well known to her, the little smile in the corner of his mouth so captivating. That was his tour de force. Jealousy clawed at her soul.

My God, she thought, how handsome he is! Her eyes were burning. She adored that face. She adored his nice shoulders, his strong arms. She adored everything about him!

There. He was looking around. Swiftly, Valerie moved behind a large plant. She didn't want him to see her. "I can't stand jealous people," he had told her. "Jealousy is insanity."

Again, Jack was right. For at that very moment she felt a savage urge to hit him, to scream, "I hate you. I hate you!" With a violent effort she dominated the impulse and, regaining her composure, she walked out without looking back, her head throbbing with pain.

The apartment was cold. Valerie turned on the heater and fixed herself a cup of tea. Sipping it, she looked at the fishbowl. The large goldfish was chasing the small ones in circles, darting from one side to the other.

"Jack in action," Valerie murmured.

Somehow, she had the funny feeling that the red bulging eyes were looking at her slyly. She had seen that look before. Jack . . . Jack's eyes! It was Jack mocking her!

At once, Valerie plunged her hand into the fishbowl and grabbed the squirming fish.

Uttering, "I got you," she went to the window, opened it with her left hand, and hurled the fish down to the ground.

The quivering fish wriggled, leaped, and gasped in agony until the final dart. Then it lay dead.

Gazing at it one last time, Valerie closed the window, muttering, "Serves him right!" She went to the sink and carefully washed her hands, over and over, muttering.

New Perspectives

There was something else that she wanted to do. What was it? Valerie stood still for a few minutes but couldn't remember. After a few moments of indecision, she walked into the living room and paced up and down to give herself time to collect her thoughts.

Suddenly, her eyes lighted up. Quickly she went to the couch, picked the phone up from the table on the left, and looked intently at the emergency numbers that were always kept at hand by the phone. She dialed. As the male voice answered the call, Valerie sank onto the couch.

"Hello," she said. "I just killed Jack."

I Remember Sousa

Cecil Fox

Mother was an accomplished pianist and church organist, and she encouraged each of us three children to play a musical instrument. On numerous occasions I heard her say, "Music will open doors for you." That it did, but none more lasting than music appreciation and memories of John Philip Sousa.

I started on a small-size second-hand cornet while in the fourth grade, and during four years of junior high I played in the school band. In the eighth grade I also played in the high school band for special occasions when more players were needed.

Sterling, Colorado, a town of 7,000 population, was where I grew up, and the school music programs were exceptional. Many times our high school band won first place in the State Band Contest, which made it eligible for the National High School Band Contest.

During my eighth grade the townsfolk raised the funds to send our band to the national contest, held that year in Joliet, Illinois. I was selected to go. We traveled by train in a sleeper car and were housed in the homes of Joliet citizens. My pal and I shared the entire third floor with the son of a local banker. We were taken everywhere to see the sights.

The highlight of the trip and contest for me was the playing of the massed bands on the high school athletic field. There were over a thousand

New Perspectives

musicians with each band leader trying to keep his players in time with the guest conductor on the high platform—John Philip Sousa. I get a lump in my throat just thinking about it. I was so thrilled that I tried to follow Sousa's baton instead of watching my bandmaster. Because I was not used to Sousa's style of directing I soon discovered that I was not in unison with my fellow bandsmen.

Three years later I really met the famous composer—that is, I was within a few feet of him. He brought his band to our high school gymnasium for a concert in the spring of 1931. Our band met him at the station as the train pulled in and played "The Stars and Stripes Forever" as he stepped down from the pullman. Mr. Sousa gratefully acknowledged our salute.

During the program intermission our high school band assembled on the stage, where John Philip Sousa led us in several pieces. Yes, one of them was "The Stars and Stripes Forever." I felt as though he gazed at me the entire time. I played second chair solo cornet, and was seated about three feet from him.

I have so many associations with Sousa's marches: bands in junior high and two different high schools; in municipal bands; in four U.S. Navy bands, including the U.S.S. Arizona; and in numerous parades on Memorial (Decoration) Day, Veterans (Armistice) Day, and for many community events.

Sousa's talent for composing marches has never been equaled. In fact, he was called "The March King." Many of the marches were written for special occasions and celebrations. My favorite marches were "Semper Fidelis," "Washington Post," "Liberty Bell," "El Capitan," "The Thunderer," and of course "The Stars and Stripes Forever," all composed before the turn of the century.

Whenever I hear a rendition of these marches, tears come to my eyes. With the "Stars and Stripes" I become choked up as I recall Sousa and his special style of directing.

As a dutiful househusband I do the regular dusting in our house, and I have a cassette of his marches (by the John Philip Sousa Ensemble) which I play on the stereo. If my wife is not around I turn up the volume and march from room to room. However, I always have to stop while listening to "The Stars and Stripes Forever." It was Sousa's favorite march, and he wrote several verses to go along with the music. A few lines from his autobiography, *Marching Along*, are as follows:

> Other nations may deem their flags the best

> And cheer them with fervid elation
> But the flag of the North and South and West
> Is the flag of flags, the flag of Freedom's nation.

At times when I need cheering up I play his marches on the stereo, and they never fail to raise my spirits. Today, most people feel better when a band strikes up a Sousa march. John Philip Sousa died just a year after I last played under his direction, but his music continues to add joy to my life.

Fernando Flamingo Can Do the Flamenco

Gail E. Van Amburg

South of the border there once was a bird
By the name of Fernando Flamingo,
Whose ongoing yearning was rather absurd–
He wanted to dance the flamenco.

Tho' 'Nando's obsession was utmost to him,
His feathered friends called him a phoney.
He tried to assure them it wasn't a whim,
"Flamenco?" they giggled, "Baloney!"

Then one summer night by the light of the moon,
As the flock settled down by the pond,
A deafening din filled the tropic commune
And the birds skittered hither and yond.

The noise pierced their eardrums, they let out a shriek,
"*Invasión*, call out the Marines!"
"Ith me," 'Nando lisped through the rose in his beak,
"I wan thoo to thee my routeenth."

The blare from the boombox that hung from his neck
Made the fidgety flock flinch with fright.
He hoped to impress them, to gain their respect,
But, alas, they were far from polite.

Fernando Flamingo Can Do the Flamenco

They started to laugh and the howls turned to hoots
As he practiced his web-footed prance.
"Hey, *pájaro*," they bellowed, "you better buy boots
To bridle those boats when you dance."

He knew they were right, any birdbrain could see
That his footwork was somewhat inept,
And his name up in lights on the downtown marquis
Was the least he had come to expect.

So . . .

He took out a loan from the southernmost branch
Of the bank in the middle of town;
The one where the tellers, Benito and Blanche,
Always hang on their cage upside down.

They gave him the pesos and wished him success,
"Fernando," they said, "you've got pluck,"
Then gave him the Best Birdie Boot Shop address
And ruffled his feathers for luck.

His new leather boots with 11-inch heels
Were crafted by *El Zapatero*,
Who threw in some spurs with precise-balance wheels,
A hat, a silk sash and bolero.

The Heron Club owner asked 'Nando to dance,
To appear on the stage at his place.
Fernando was grateful, he welcomed the chance
To perform (and to also save face).

They spared no expense for the show of all shows,
The limos began to arrive;
They came in tuxedos and high-top chapeaus—
The Heron Club hummed like a hive.

The hostess stepped into the center-stage light
(A drum roll preceded her bow),
"*Amigos*, it is my great pleasure tonight

New Perspectives

To bring you Fernando—RIGHT NOW!"

Poor 'Nando just stood there and molted with fear
'Til guitarist Jose played his cue,
Then slowly he straightened and gave a great cheer
And jumped like a mad kangaroo.

His heels tapped the rhythm, a feverish pitch.
The birds—on their feet—yelled "*OLE*!"
Fernando was happy, his heart gave a twitch,
His friends made him feel that way.

But despite all the raves his peers did impart,
Fernando's debut wasn't sweet;
While the thrill of success was swelling his heart,
The blisters were swelling his feet.

The tall leather boots were returned to the store
(The refund helped pay off the bank).
'Nando knew now there would be no encore
And life wouldn't be very swank.

His career was a short one he couldn't relive,
Poor 'Nando, the pitiful thing . . .
He rejoined the flock, a bit hesitative,
With a castanet under each wing.

The Car Igniteth Not

Mary Jo Wold

The time had come for mine journey to begin and I therefore made haste to mine automobile. After no little tribulation, I found mine keys and straightaway placed the proper one in the ignition and began to count: "10-9-8-7-6-5-4-3-2-1-IGNITE." But behold, it igniteth not!

I hasteneth to mine husband and bade him come quickly, lest I miss mine appointment, for I needeth his help, sorely. As we went forth together he sayeth unto me, "Why art thou distraught, mine wife?"

And I answereth unto him, saying, "I placeth the proper key in the ignition and began to count: 10-9-8-7-6-5-4-3-2-1-IGNITE. But behold, it igniteth not."

His voice explodeth from his throat and he demandeth, "What meanest thou, 'It igniteth not'!!" And he did turn divers colours.

I answereth unto him, saying, "It was not wont to ignite, that is all, mine love."

Now his eyes were aflame and his nostrils did flap. My heart shivereth within me as he did pace to and fro. Striking his head with his fist he shouteth unto me, "To say that it doth not ignite telleth me nothing! When thou didst turn the key in the ignition, what happeneth? Did it grind away, or did it click? It doth make a difference if it grindeth or if it clicketh!"

I pondereth these sayings and I perceiveth that he was sorely troubled and perplexed. Lest I evoke his wrath again, I curbeth my tongue and retreateth unto myself. But lo, his voice like one crying in the wilderness implored me once again, "Wife, dost thou not understand that to say 'it igniteth not' telleth me nothing? Incline thine ear unto me that thou mightest

New Perspectives

truly understand—readest thou my lips—TO SAY IT DOTH NOT IGNITE TELLETH ME NOTHING. WHAT DOST THOU MEAN, 'IT IGNITETH NOT?'"

Remembering that the meek shall inherit the earth, I did reply meekly once more, "Mine love, it simply igniteth not!"

Mine husband therefore fell to his knees and rent his garment and smote upon his breast, saying,

"1-2-3-4-5-6-7-8-9-@#$%&*!!!!".

Go Back! Go Back!

Genevieve Bonato

In the early 1930s, at the age of 89, my grandmother quietly folded her hands and departed this earth. Holding her in high regard, I was convinced that with her final breath a great swooping action occurred, wherewith she was transported directly to heaven.

I remembered her as an alert and curious soul, and speculate that, after fifty-odd years, she might have become restive with the celestial sameness and petitioned a furlough back to her home planet.

If granted, chances are she'd zoom in, landing in the middle of my family room and, after looking around, would center her attention on the always-running television, concluding that it was simply a modern version of the movies she remembered.

She'd watch the picture for a time, then cautiously touch a button and the scene would change. One push and something called a "News Report" would flash on, while a second attempt would bring in a strange looking young woman, with skintight clothing and an outlandish hairdo, screeching out a song of sorts, as she writhed and swayed in complete abandon.

Every few minutes Grandma's attention would be distracted by a sudden change in the program, and during these station breaks she would accumulate some interesting bits of information.

At one point, a harried female with a raspy voice would be calling stridently for The Girdle Lady. "I want the when's-a-girdle-not-a-girdle-lady," she'd yell. This would disconcert our visitor, as the girdles she remembered were nothing like the queer looking little thing this poor soul was waving as she screeched for help.

New Perspectives

But then, Grandma belonged to the laced corset school of thought and remembered it well. A no-nonsense, armor-like affair, it went directly over a knit union suit and was fastened with small grommets and laces, which were backed up by sturdy whalebone stays, strategically placed to whip the reluctant torso into line. After all, she would muse, that was what a corset was for—to hold the body erect. And now this—a girdle not a girdle, if you please.

As if this were not enough, another station break and on came the Cross Your Heart bra commercial.

"Well, I never," Grandma would huff loudly. Cross your heart? Why, this was serious business! You used it while you were still very young, to make a point of absolute truth. It was accompanied by a flourishing, widely executed cross, which started somewhere near your collarbone and ended up just above your navel (not that you ever mentioned *that*).

And this word *bra* undoubtedly came from brassiere. She'd never worn one herself, but she remembered when they first became stylish. Most of her generation was satisfied with the corset, which came up high enough so that the bust rested atop, sort of shored up by the stiff underpinnings. Over this went an embroidered corset-cover or camisole which was long enough to form a union with the petticoat. None of this cross-your-heart business!

Pushing still another button, she saw lovely young women extolling the virtues of something called "Underalls." A voice called to them, "Ladies, show us your "Underalls," and these poor programmed creatures would turn and show their bottoms to the world.

Another change, and young girls, not a year over sixteen, were prancing about in jeans so old and faded they looked ready for the rag bag. And tight ... so tight there wasn't a wrinkle in them. Oh, those poor children, she'd think. Imagine the discomfort ... cut halfway up the middle, they were. No wonder they wiggled and squirmed!

Later, a soothing lullabye would precede a baby commercial. "Your baby's comfort begins with Luvs." Now this was something she could understand ... but wait, what was happening? A picture of a little one, ready to burst into tears and wearing a soggy diaper, flashed on. Another switch would show the same child happily clothed in a tight-fitting arrangement which certainly looked like a diaper, although there were no fasteners. Not a safety pin in sight! Following this came an announcement assuring mother that Luvs disposable diapers were the answer to her baby's problems. Imagine, she

Go Back! Go Back!

thought, no pins, a song about them, the assurance that you didn't even wash them, and they'd even been given a name.

The next channel change brought her face to face with a torrid soap opera love scene. For a moment she'd stare, fascinated with the writhing couple, then gasping, "Oh, my heavens!" she would turn hastily away.

Her mind awhirl, she'd decide she'd had enough of this infernal box and would leave the house immediately. As she soared out the door and up over the rooftops, her interest would settle on a lovely park-like area with many paths winding among the green lawns and trees.

But wait! What was going on! People everywhere, running in all directions. Never stopping to talk, or wave, or even look at each other; just huffing and sweating and going, each intent on his own journey.

Like a bunch of ants in a stick-stirred hill, Grandma thought as she watched. And their clothes . . . nearly as odd as they were. Some so baggy you couldn't tell men from women, and others with britches so tight they resembled a second skin. Many wore bands low on their foreheads; others had big, round contraptions on either side of their heads, and a few had wires running from their ears to little boxes attached to their waistbands.

After watching them for a time, her perplexity gave way to understanding. She knew what was happening! These people were daft! Although she saw no fences, she realized that this was part of a mental institution, and they were allowed to run to quiet them.

At this point, overwhelmed by all she'd seen, Grandma would decide she wanted no more of earthly goings-on. A mental request would instantly remove her from the confusion and transport her back to the heavenly sphere.

Thank goodness she made the decision then. Had she stayed longer, think of the things she would have had to cope with. Jet lag, live-in relationships, the space age, artificial insemination, gay rights, AIDS, and the ever-present threat of atomic destruction. But best of all, she didn't stay long enough to find out that nowadays *buns* aren't something to be cooked, but refer to a part of the human anatomy.

So, my advice, keep the curiosity in check, sweet lady of a bygone day. Please don't come back, because who knows what will happen on this crazy planet in the next half-a-hundred years.

Radio Dispatch (Station KFY207)

Delbert B. Campbell

Titles are not for the masses.
Instead, for the choice and select.
They bring to an otherwise routine job
A feeling of power and respect.

A title reflects a position
No other person deserves.
It is usually reserved for management,
Whose particular purpose it serves.

There are specific uses for titles
For those so inclined in a way
To be thought of as "in charge" of something.
(More effective than upping their pay.)

Each of us yearns for a title
To separate one from the rest.
To indicate who, of the motley crew,
Happens to do something the best.

I, too, have enjoyed the persuasion
Of having a title so dear.
Radio dispatch calls me "Unit Six."
KFY207–Clear.

Eyes

Linda Marlow

    I never know from visit to visit how he will be. Some days he might be sitting up when I get there, smiling and eager to hear what I am doing in my life. Other days, and more frequently now, he will be lying on his Victorian sofa covered with the quilt I gave him last Christmas, unable to speak or move because of the pain. Even on those days I know he likes me there.

    When I visit I bring him flowers and maybe fruit or albums. I have orchids for him today, and a new "Yellow Submarine" album to replace the one he played until it wore out. I hope today he'll be happy and smiling and not in pain, but I know better. Somehow I've got to muster up more strength so I don't cry when I see him.

    I knock on the door and Juanita, his nurse, answers. "He's been sleeping all morning and hasn't been able to eat. He's bad today, senorita. I am glad you are here." She reaches for her coat and purse, pats my hand, and says, "I'll only be gone a short time. I have medication and fruit juices that I must get him."

    Juanita is a real sweetie and treats my friend like her friend, not like a patient. A couple of times I have heard her singing to him, soft melodic Spanish songs while he drifts off to sleep. I'll always love her for that. She reads the hunting and fishing stories from the sports magazines to which he subscribes, holding up the pictures of deer, duck, salmon, or trout for his enjoyment.

    I sit down across from him and look closely. His jet-black hair has strands of silver in it. His sideburns are graying, but then they have been graying for years and make him look distinguished. His walrus moustache is mostly white. It got that way after the sickness had taken hold of him. He hates it. I colored it for him a couple of times, once getting it too black, and the other time I got dye on the skin behind his moustache and he looked like Groucho Marx. We really had a good laugh about that. Poor Juanita was horrified by my efforts and stated that next time she would take charge. There was no next time. The dye made him cough and the coughing made him sick to his stomach. The color of his moustache becomes less important as his illness progresses.

His eyes are beautiful even as he sleeps. I remember when I first met him he told me his middle name meant "beautiful eyes," and it was also his mother's maiden name. His eyes open, and even though the illness has taken so much from him it has not taken the laughing light in his eyes.

He starts to speak, but instead of words he coughs. I go to him and rub his back and assure him that there is no need to speak. His coughing lessens and he relaxes a bit. I leave him for a moment to put the "Yellow Submarine" album on the stereo; side two, the "Pepperland" cut, his favorite. I return to sit by his side. He acknowledges the album with a nod and a smile.

"Is the music OK?"

He nods yes. It seems like he wants to say more.

"Do you need a pain pill?"

He shakes his head no.

"Water? Food?"

He moves his head from side to side.

"Massage?"

No again.

"Do you have to pee?"

He smiles and shakes his head no.

"How about a story?"

Again his head goes from side to side.

"OK, I give up. I'll just sit here and hold your hand and keep you company."

His head goes up and down.

"Is that what you want?"

Yes, he nods.

Eyes

"No problem. You have my undivided attention."

Not until he closes his eyes does my expression change to sadness.

Sitting here looking down at him I remember so much. The time he went to the hospital with me when my dad's lungs were riddled with cancer. That he was the one to tell me Dad had died. I was holding his frail hand and my friend leaned down and whispered in my ear. "He is gone, my dear friend. He is no longer in pain."

I didn't know what to do. I hadn't even known that my own father had died. My friend leaned over my father's contorted face, kissed his forehead, and closed his eyes forever.

He was with me, too, when the rest home in which my mother was staying called to say they could not wake her. I remember we entered her meager room and she was sprawled on the bed in the dress I had given her for her birthday just two days earlier. I couldn't move. I didn't cry. I watched as my friend lifted her up, placed her head on the pillow, straightened her dress, and bent down, kissed her forehead, and closed her startled and lifeless eyes.

He squeezes my hand slightly and my attention is brought back to the present. He smiles sweetly, opens his eyes to look directly into mine. I don't move. I try to tell him with my eyes just what he means to me. He keeps smiling, his eyes are filled with love, understanding, and acceptance of what is about to happen to him. He shivers slightly and becomes rigid; and as I had seen him do twice before, I bend down, kiss his forehead, place my thumb and forefinger on the tips of his eyelids, and ever so gently ease them over his lifeless, beautiful eyes.

Someone Cares!

Ann C. Krauss

The woman in tatters, hair all astray,
Stooped her shoulders while wending her way
Along the sidewalk and across the street,
Nodded a greeting to walkers she'd meet.
This was her turf, she knew many who passed;
They were street people, the city's outcast!
She pushed her old carts, filled to o'erflow . . .
As all her goods went wherever she'd go.
Black plastic bags covered most of her things . . .
Bedding, clothes, papers, and odd balls of strings.
They were ties to the world in which she dwelt,
Where few stopped to talk and fewer who'd helped.
Though old and alone, she held her head high . . .
When she came close, and about to pass by,
I noticed a twinkle in her eyes of blue
As if they held a secret to share with you.
Her smile lightened up her weary, worn face,
And broadened some as she quickened her pace!
The reason . . . a bag-man awaiting her there . . .
As she passed, I saw a red rose in her hair!

Sons of the Valley

Roque Gutierrez

dawn

"... The darkness peeled away and the valley played host to the sun.
The owl, its wings abreadth, flew solitary arcs over deserted fields,
keenly aware of strays.
The birds chased one another, tree to tree,
territories for the new day,
making a racket with their shrieks.
The cock had already crowed ... "

R.G.

Sons of the Valley

An old black panel truck sped down from the hills toward a sharp bend in the road. Its lights were still burning, even in the morning haze. One headlight flickered. Handwritten on the side of the truck was "Lou Chan - Farm Contractor." The lettering, in white paint, had run, so the whole makeshift sign looked as if it were on stilts.

New Perspectives

As it made the curve, a rear tire hit the soft shoulder, spewing up a fountain of dirt and gravel. The truck went into a skid and the three men up front were flung one way, then the other, as the truck righted itself on the asphalt.

"Hey, Raymundo, *que pasa*, man? Why are you driving so fast? You're scaring the hell out of the kid!" said the old man who was seated on the passenger's side of the truck.

In between him and Raymundo sat a thin teenage boy; his jet-black hair was combed straight back and pulled down in front, so the hair spilled down onto his forehead. Both of his hands were firmly planted against the dusty dashboard. "Yeah, let's get there in one piece," said the boy.

There were men riding in the back of the truck, and they too had been thrown around during Raymundo's wild ride down the mountain. Now, after recovering from the thrashing, they began to shout.

"Hey! What the hell you doin' up there!"

"You're killin' us!"

"All right! All right!" shouted Raymundo, slamming his hand against the rear wall a couple of times for emphasis. He jerked a thumb at the two up front. "And you two, *can* it, you're alive, ain't ya?"

"For how long? I don't know," said the old man, wincing and rubbing the shoulder he'd slammed into the truck's door.

Raymundo glanced over at the old man and then did a double take. "Hey, what happened there?"

"Where?" asked the old man, looking down at himself.

"I mean *there*, with your hand, what happened to your fingers?"

The old man held up his right hand, the last two fingers just stumps. "Oh, that." He waved the two stumps back and forth. "You just saw that?"

"Well, what the hell, it's been dark, you know. How'd it happen?" asked Raymundo.

The old man put his hand down. "I lost them during the war."

"How?" asked Raymundo.

"Yeah, how?" said the kid.

The old man looked out the window. They were just passing some almond trees, their trunks painted white. He always wondered why they did that.

Sons of the Valley

"Well, you going to tell us, or is there some deep, dark secret you're carrying around?" sneered Raymundo.

The old man sighed, "Nah, it's no secret, but it ain't important, either."

Raymundo shrugged.

The old man rested his arm on the seat behind the kid. "What's your name, kid?"

"Junior," said the kid, his bright eyes dancing between the old man's face and the arm behind him. "Everybody calls me Junior."

"Junior, eh? I'm a junior, too. Peter Juan Escolante, Junior. You can call me Pete."

"Sure, Pete." The kid squirmed forward on the seat.

"Don't you go to school?" asked the old man.

"In the summertime?" said Junior, arching an eyebrow.

"Well, okay, but why aren't you home, with your mama and papa?" he persisted.

"What is this, Twenty Questions? Leave the kid alone," interrupted Raymundo.

The old man took his arm down and looked over at Raymundo. "Sure," he said, and shifted his gaze out the window.

The countryside whizzed by, the old panel truck creating little wispy whirlpools along the dusty shoulder. They were on the road that ran straight through the valley. At the end of the narrow highway the sun began to peek over the horizon, and all three of them shaded their eyes against the sudden brightness. Raymundo reached up to pull down the visor.

"Hey, Ray, look at that sunrise, eh? *Que bonita, verdad?*" The old man Pete squinted into the brand new sun's light.

Raymundo was busy tugging on the sun visor that was frozen in place. "I got no time for no goddamned sunrise," he said through gritted teeth.

"Aw, take it easy. What's the rush, anyway? Those peaches ain't going nowhere."

Raymundo pulled on the visor a little harder. "Look, I got a schedule to keep. The old Chinese Lou wants us there at a certain time. We gotta be there at a certain time, *comprende?*"

"It's that important?" asked the old man.

"It's business," said Raymundo flatly.

New Perspectives

The old man grinned and looked out the window. "Yeah, okay, business."

Raymundo continued yanking on the visor.

"Goddamn thing, nothing that old Chinaman has works. Damn thing, anyway!"

The old man elbowed the kid, "Tell him to slow down. Maybe he'll listen to you."

"I don't think he's going to listen to anybody," said Junior, his eyes, like slits, glued to the road.

Raymundo finally gave the visor an almighty tug, and the whole thing came away in his hand. "Shit!"

The old man and the kid snickered.

"What the hell you laughing at!" roared Raymundo, glaring at them. He threw the visor at their feet. "Just leave me alone! Mind your own business."

The old man held up his hands. "Okay, okay."

Raymundo looked out the window. His reflection glared back at him, teeth bared, the lines on his face etched even deeper. "Ugly face," he thought. He relaxed his grip on the steering wheel and looked beyond, at the sky. It calmed him. "Pretty," he mused, "the sky, the land, all of it."

Everything had changed for Raymundo after the old Chinese Lou had hired him. The old Chinaman had realized he was getting too old to drive. He had sent out the word that he was looking for someone who knew the fields and the men who worked them So a number of men tried out for the job, but Raymundo turned out to be the best. The old Chinese Lou had considered himself fortunate to find Raymundo, but he had never told him that. He figured that would make his new driver cocky, and maybe, just maybe, out of control.

Raymundo looked over at the old man, who was saying something to the kid. The kid laughed.

Raymundo felt the exuberance from the kid. "Hey, what's the joke? Tell me so I can laugh, too."

The old man sat up. "Sure, okay. It's a riddle. Now listen. Did you know that half the hombres in this country play with themselves in the shower and the other half sing?"

Raymundo shrugged his shoulders and then shook his head. "Yeah, okay?"

"Can you tell me the song they sing?"

Sons of the Valley

Raymundo looked at the old man and then glanced at the kid. "No."

The old man burst out laughing, and so did the kid.

"Then you must be in the half that plays with themselves!" he said, choking with laughter.

Raymundo's brow furrowed for just a second, until he understood the joke. Then he began to laugh. He laughed until tears came to his eyes. Still chuckling, he brought out a pack of chewing gum. He pulled a stick out with his teeth and saw the kid watching him. "You wanna piece of gum, kid?"

The boy nodded his head and reached for the pack. A sudden pounding from the back made them all jump.

"Hey! Hey! How about a piss stop? Some of us gotta take a leak," came a shout.

Ray cupped his mouth with the back of one hand and yelled to the men in the back, "Yeah, well piss in your pocket, because this bus don't stop 'til the fields!"

They all burst out laughing again, as Raymundo pulled off the road.

Ten minutes later they were back on the road. The sun had risen higher and it had gotten hotter. Raymundo rolled his window down and let the warm wind wash over him. It didn't help.

"Damn, it's gonna be a burner today," he said.

"Hey, how long before we're there? There's money in them fields, you know," blurted the old man, as if he had just woken up.

"Well, look who's back and worried. Next time take a cab if you're so worried about time," said Raymundo, "and roll down that damn window. It's 120 degrees in here!"

"But I get earaches real easy if the wind blows in my ears. *Por favor*, eh?" complained the old man, holding his hands out.

"You think I care about that while I'm burning up? No way! Roll it down or ride in the back."

"Have a heart, Ray . . . "

"Or in the back," repeated Raymundo.

"Okay, okay," he said, rolling the window down. The old man put his hands over his ears and hunched down. The kid pulled his T-shirt out and tore a small piece off the bottom of the frayed cloth. Rolling it up, he handed it to the old man. "Here, Pete, stick this in your ear."

Raymundo laughed. "Yeah, Pete, stick it in your ear."

New Perspectives

"Very funny," said the old man, stuffing the cloth ball into his ear and scooting down to nap.

Raymundo wiped at the sweat on his forehead as the temperature continued to rise. He stared at the road ahead and then back at the old man Pete. Ah, he's not a bad old man. He just talks too damned much, he thought. He rubbed the back of his neck, pushing himself up straighter in the seat, and looked over at Pete, trying to sleep.

"Christ, go ahead, roll it back up."

"What? You sure?" asked the old man, sitting up.

"Yeah, go on. I was only bullshittin'."

The old man rolled it up and hunched down to take a nap. He opened one eye toward Raymundo. "Thanks."

Some time later they turned down a rutted dirt lane into a peach grove. Workers were already in the trees tugging on the fruit and filling their buckets.

"You see anybody that looks like they're in charge?" asked the old man.

"They're always at the scales counting buckets. They don't pay by the hour, you know," Raymundo said.

"I know that . . . look, there he is, the one with the clipboard."

Raymundo pulled over and a man wearing khaki work clothes walked up to the truck.

"Whucha got?" he asked, spitting in the dirt.

"I got fifteen in the back and two up here, seventeen in all," said Raymundo, jerking a thumb towards the rear of the truck.

"I can add, mister. Better 'n most out here. Okay, we're paying seven cents a bucket. The more you pick, the more you make. A girl will be around with lunches for sale at noon, and you can buy on credit. I catch you cheatin' or stealin', you forfeit your pay. You get caught drinkin', fightin', or fuckin', you forfeit your pay. Now if you understand all that, I can use everybody, 'ceptin' that cripple, there," he finished, pointing at the old man.

"Asshole! Who you callin' a cripple!" shouted the old man.

Raymundo cut him off with a wave of a hand. "Look, Lou Chan sent me out here with people to pick for you and he guarantees they'll work, including the old man here. Now do we have a deal?"

The man folded his arms, with the clipboard across his chest. "I got to have able-bodied people up in them trees. The rest can stay, but he can't."

Sons of the Valley

The men in the back began pounding the side of the panel truck and yelling to get out. Raymundo flung open the door, making the man in khaki jump back. He went to the back of the truck and opened the doors, letting the men out. Going around to the passenger's side, he leaned in.

"I don't think this guy's going to let you work" Raymundo spoke softly, "and I can't make him."

"I know, I know," said the old man. "Let me out."

"What are you going to do?" asked Raymundo.

"What am I going to do? What can I do. I'm going home."

"Home? We're out in the middle of nowhere. How are you going to get home, on foot?"

"If I have to. What are you worried about, anyway. I've been on my own a long time. I'll manage." The old man turned to walk away. The kid slid out of the truck and ran up next to him.

"Where you going, Junior?"

"With you," said the kid, grinning.

"C'mon, kid, you don't want to do that, do you?" he asked.

"Yeah," said the kid, grabbing the old man by the arm.

Raymundo slammed the truck door and kicked the dirt, cursing under his breath. "You sure you're goin' to survive out there, old man?" Raymundo yelled after them.

The old man walked back to Raymundo. "I know you're only talking crap, but let me tell you something." He held up the hand with the missing fingers. "You wanted to know how I lost these. Well, no enemy soldier did it. Some of my own compatriots decided I didn't need them any more. It was the end of the war. I was in Germany waiting to go home. They pushed me into an alley and held me down. They had my money but they wanted more, so they gave me a choice, these or my balls. It wasn't a hard decision. I survived." He pointed at the man in khaki. "And no piss-ant like that's going to get to me." The old man broke out into a grin and pinched Raymundo's cheek. "Don't be so concerned about the old Chinese Lou, Ray. He's a piss-ant, too."

Raymundo laughed.

The old man took the younger man's hand and shook it. "Thanks for the ride."

Raymundo watched them walk away and then went around to the driver's side of the truck.

New Perspectives

"Hey, you wanta pick, maybe you can take that old man's place," said the man in khaki, looking up from his clipboard.

Raymundo looked at him, then back at the old man and the kid as they turned up the road and disappeared. "Nope, you keep 'em," said Raymundo, getting into the truck.

The man in khaki shrugged. "Your boss ain't gonna like that."

Raymundo turned the engine over. "What's that?" he asked.

"You're just leaving like that."

"You're right, he ain't gonna like it, but he ain't here, and I am."

Raymundo headed the old panel truck toward the highway in a cloud of dust. At the end of the lane he stopped and gazed at the mountains framed against the summer sky. "So pretty," he whispered. The old panel groaned as he turned towards the two figures trudging along the highway.

Let Us Say So

Jean Tucker

So many hands
fretting with empty works
to forget their emptiness,
voices striving with voices
to cover up the silence in their midst.

Moving in their habitual small duties
suddenly my hands remember your hands,
the bones in your thinning face
or your hair's soft texture

and I long for the silence.
I long to open my hands
and let them know the full, terrible weight.
I long for the other hands to open
and know that the weight is more than they can carry.

Wherever your hands once moved, there is a stillness.
The shape of each thing you touched is incomplete.
At the center is a small pool of silence
deep as the earth's core,
deep as the sky,
unmoved and unthinking.

The Briarwood Witch

Marilyn K. Dickerson

Did I ever tell you the story of the Briarwood Witch? No? Well, after tending bar for twenty-five years, a guy pretty much hears and sees everything. But my friend, the witch, she was something special.

Just for the record, my name's Angelo, Angie to my friends. I'm the short, gray-haired barman, senior barman, I might add, at the Briarwood Lounge. We all wear the same short red jackets and black bow ties, but I'm the one with the crew cut and the Roman nose, if you'll pardon a statement of the obvious.

You'll notice I didn't call this place a *bar*. I called it a lounge. So you've probably guessed that it's a swanky joint—no funds spared. Ritzy leather booths, thick, plush carpets, and very genteel (that's spelled gen-TEEL) music pumped in over the Muzak system—the works. Like I say, Briarwood is the kind of drinking spa where the clientele never get drunk. Intoxicated maybe, or inebriated, but drunk just ain't in our vocabulary. Class is the word, and in capital letters.

And probably two of our classiest customers are Mr. and Mrs. Garrison. He's an attorney in the Farraday Building a couple of blocks away, and she's an artist for an uptown advertising agency. Some lady, this Mrs. Garrison—a tall brunette with a great face, and a smile that lights up like someone just threw the switch. Not billboard pretty, but the kind of looks that'll still be there when she's ninety. But like I say, she's the real thing, just like her jewelry and her sharp clothes. Yeah, I know, women's lib frowns on the word "lady," but you forget I'm from the old school, and in my book the term

The Briarwood Witch

still fits Mrs. Garrison. If she were wearin' last year's gunnysack she'd still do it with a flare that would turn every guy's head in the joint . . . uh, place. Come to think of it, maybe that's part of her magic. But whatever you call it, the Briarwood Witch's got style.

On Tuesdays and Thursdays Mrs. Garrrison usually gets off work early, and she comes to the Briarwood about four o'clock to wait for her husband. Business is slow that time of day, so I hold down the fort pretty much on my own until the night staff comes on duty. Mr. Garrison slipped me a fiver once when they first started coming in and asked me to look after his missus. An unescorted woman . . . you know how it is. He didn't want her bothered by any wise guys who might think a lone woman was fair game for a pickup. Of course, once I got to know them, I wouldn't take his money. It's always a pleasure to see Mrs. Garrison swinging up to the counter with her breezy stride, bringing with her a breath of expensive perfume.

This particular day when she came in, the place was empty and she seemed preoccupied, like she had something heavy on her mind. She still greeted me with that big smile that brought the quick warmth to her dark eyes, but once she'd ordered a sherry and asked about my wife and kids she just settled down into a sort of quiet trance, her eyes fixed thoughtfully on her glass. From time to time she'd swirl the sherry gently, studying the tiny ripples. For some screwy reason it reminded me of a Gypsy fortuneteller I'd seen once peering into her crystal ball. Mrs. Garrison had that same concentration, the same intensity as she bent her head, eyes unblinking.

In a few minutes I see this young guy come in. He's probably early thirties, well dressed, and carries himself like a man who knows his own worth. I'm watching him through the back bar mirror while I'm slicing limes. He hesitates at the entrance and gives a quick glance around the place. When he spots Mrs. Garrison he eyes her a moment, and then, smoothing a hand over his sandy hair, he comes across the room with long strides. But when he gets right up to her, he stops uncertainly and just stares down at her like he doesn't know what to do next.

Meanwhile I'm trying to make up my mind what *I* should be doing. But something tells me to stay out of it, at least for now. My instincts tell me this guy's no bum. So, Angie, I tell myself, keep your eyes open and take your cue from Mrs. G. I'm keepin' my head down, but my eyeballs are glued to the mirror.

Finally the young dude gets up enough courage to speak. "I–I'm afraid I don't have a smooth line of chatter," he apologizes with a kind of nervous smile. "It's been a long time since I tried to meet anyone, but since there

New Perspectives

seems to be just two of us . . . would you mind if–if I joined you? I don't much like to drink alone."

Mrs. G. doesn't answer right away, but then she looks up with a sad little smile that broadens into a friendly grin. "I must say your logic is overwhelming. Please do join me."

As he sits down next to her I'm Johnny-on-the-spot to take his order. I give Mrs. G. a long look to make sure everything's O.K., but she just smiles, with a little shake of her head. He orders Scotch and water and I go to fix it, but my ears are standin' out straight, listening.

"I think what you really meant," she says, still smiling, "is that you haven't picked up any women in bars lately. Am I right?"

He smiles sheepishly. "I guess I'm pretty transparent. It's just that . . . well, I was married for twelve years, and now . . . I'm . . . well, I'm trying to adjust to being *un*married." He coughs hoarsely, covering his mouth with his hand as though the word stuck in his throat.

Mrs. G. nods, knowingly, her eyes focusing again on her glass. "I see," she says, quietly sad. "You're divorced?"

I bring this guy his drink and he peels off a couple of bills and I go back to work washing glasses. In the mirror I see him sip his drink and set it down again, his shoulders sagging, dejected like.

"I'm not divorced . . . *yet*," he continues with emphasis . . . "but Beth and I *are* separated. I guess a dissolution of marriage, as they call it these days, *is* the next step." His voice trails away and he bows his head, lost in his own moody thoughts.

Mrs. G. eyes him sympathetically. "On the basis of our longstanding friendship, I would venture to guess that you're not too crazy about the idea," she says.

He hunches his shoulders and gives a bitter little laugh. "I'm afraid I don't really have a great deal to say in the matter. I came home one night and she was gone. There was just a note on the mantel and she was gone . . . "

The guy's voice breaks and he goes quiet. He's pressing his lips together hard, trying to swallow down his feelings.

Mrs. G. sighs heavily, her eyes dark, as though she's sharing his pain. "And you don't understand . . . do you?" she says, in a gentle, probing voice. "You gave her a beautiful house, an expensive car and charge accounts at all of the most exclusive stores. How could she not know how much you cared for her? She *had* everything. Except . . . she began spending exorbitantly. To such an extent that you quarrelled over the bills. And she nagged continuously about the hours you kept at the office, and then one night when you came home late she began accusing you of seeing another woman. She couldn't believe that all those hours you had spent working . . . all those dinners she'd kept heating in the oven until they were inedible weren't attributable to another woman, could she? She didn't believe that all those nights when she crawled into bed with you and you had fallen asleep exhausted, that you hadn't used yourself up with someone else."

By this time the young guy's head has snapped up and he's staring at Mrs. G. with one shocked expression. She's just about bowled him over, and she's not through with him yet. On she goes.

"And then dear, faithful Beth suddenly begins seeing another man. You're not aware of the situation at first, but gradually you sense that your wife's become evasive. She no longer meets your eyes directly. You catch her in little lies. A friend of yours spots her lunching with a man that isn't you, and then . . . the note on the mantelpiece."

Mrs. G.'s little speech has really shaken up this guy. All the color has left his face. "How did you know?" he asked, dazed. "How *could* you know?"

Mrs. G. tilts her head back, her eyes almost closed, sort of darkly teasing. "Why, I'm the Briarwood Witch. Didn't you know?" she says. "I read your fortune in my glass before you walked in the door." She laughs, a nice low sound in her throat, and then looks the young guy straight in the eye. "Don't let her go," she tells him, serious now. "You'll never forgive yourself if you do. Try to understand what she's been going through. You're her whole life, and you tried to replace yourself with things. In her frustration to reach you she did everything wrong just so you'd pay some attention to her existence. She was like a naughty child begging to be noticed, if only to be spanked. At least, for that brief space of time she had your undivided attention. Don't you see? All she really wanted was *you*." Mrs. G. pats his arm, her eyes bright with tears. "Now go find her," she says with a little sniff. "You have her address. Don't let her get away. She loves you . . . !"

The young guy stares at Mrs. G. like he can't believe his ears and then, shaking his head, he gets up and purposefully makes for the door. Halfway there he turns, smiling with an embarrassed question: "Do I cross your palm with silver, or something?" he says. "I . . . I mean just for luck?"

"No, you young idiot," she answers, laughing and dabbing at the corner of her eye with a Kleenex. "That's just for Gypsies. As the resident witch I get paid on a monthly basis." She waves him away. "Now get out of here and get on with your life!"

New Perspectives

Laughing, he strikes off a grateful salute and leaves.

For a minute the place gets quiet and then the Muzak starts booming out Chopin's Polonaise Militaire, and who marches in the front door but Mr. Garrison. He's a big, good-lookin' guy with just a bit of gray at the temples and reminds a lot of folks of Charlton Heston. He sits down next to Mrs. G. and gives her a little peck on the cheek and then thinkin' I'm not watching he gives her another kiss on the mouth. "Hi, Sweet Thing," he says to her, and the way he says it you know he's really glad to see her. He waves at me and I come to take his order.

"The usual for me, Angie," he says. And with a sly smile, he adds, "Well now, Angie, have you been keeping the wolves away from my wife?"

I know he doesn't expect an answer, so I just smile and nod.

Mr. G. glances around the lounge and then turns to his wife. "You haven't by chance seen a young man about thirty . . . sandy haired . . . well dressed . . . ? He's Jim Harley, one of my clients. The one I was telling you about last night. You probably got a glimpse of him this afternoon when you were in the office." Mr. G. shrugs. "Oh, well, he probably changed his mind about the drink."

Mrs. G. keeps quiet, but I can tell that she knows Mr. G. is troubled. His hand is on the bar and she puts hers over it, curling her fingers into his.

Still disturbed, he wants to talk. "Jim and I were discussing the possibility of him and his wife dissolving their marriage. But I can tell that his heart's not really in it, and I don't think she wants it, either. I just wish there was some way I could get those two back together."

I bring Mr. G. his drink and I can tell by the way his shoulders are saggin' that he's depressed. I move away, not botherin' him with the tab. In the mirror I see him sigh and squeeze the missus's hand.

"You know what's really strange, Honey," he says to her, kind of distracted, "is that all the time young Harley was telling me about their problems it was like an instant replay of what nearly happened to us when I was first getting the practice started . . . " Mr. G. shakes his head. "I can't tell you what an odd feeling it gave me . . . "

A mysterious smile is barely turnin' up the corners of Mrs. G.'s mouth, but her eyes are gleamin' like she just won the lottery. She leans sideways and nuzzles her head against her husband's neck. "Relax, Counselor. I have a premonition, Darling," she says gaily, " . . . that fate is about to do you out of an attorney's fee . . . ." She laughs happily at her own private joke and lifts her glass.

Mr. G. looks at her a moment, not understanding, and then, catching her mood, says, "I'll drink to that . . . " and they clink their glasses together.

I pours myself a half glass of ginger ale and lifts it to the Briarwood Witch, catching Mrs. G.'s eye. She gives me a knowing little half wink and I nod and drink to a special lady.

Belge Box

Grant Lowther

I keep my love
In a big beige box
Near me always
And hidden away

Hidden from those
Who don't understand
Its power and beauty
Unfortunate for them

Day by day
Little by little
I let it out
To experience life

But should it stumble
Trip and fall
I'll return it safely
To its solid home

It can never be harmed
Nor ever lost
For, you see
The beige box is me

A Birthday Dare

from *Challenge the Sky*, a biography of jet pilot Terry London

Jean Albrecht Lucken

Chapter 11

A fiery August sun danced across the hood of Terry's small white car as it crunched along the pebbled driveway and through the rustic gate of the riding academy south of Long Beach. She parked beside a golden wall of baled hay and hurried into the large red stable.

Inside, Terry moved slowly, giving her eyes time to adjust to the long dark passageway. On both sides, curious mounts nosed over their slatted stalls, tracking her advance towards a distant silhouetted figure. The only light came from an open door at each end of the building. With each cautious step, the smell of sweet hay and horse thickened. "Kris!" Terry called out to her younger sister.

"Down here!" Kris answered. She looped a feedbag over the head of a chestnut mare, who twitched her ears in delight. "Isn't she a beauty?" Kris asked. Nineteen-year-old Kris loved riding as much as Terry loved flying. After school hours, she worked as a stablehand in exchange for free riding lessons.

Terry had proudly watched her sister become an expert horsewoman. She had leaned against the wooden-fenced riding ring watching Kris sail over a hurdle, her brown eyes flashing with determination, and her long strawberry-blond hair trying to catch up with her.

New Perspectives

"Is she your favorite?" Even in the semi-darkness, Terry now could see the mare's chestnut coat gleam.

"No, Toby is—over there." Kris pointed to a sturdy palomino. "He's a super jumper. When he takes off, I think he's aiming for the moon! It's like—well, it's like flying!"

"Hey, wait a minute! I'm the pilot! I do the flying!"

Kris laughed. "I know, I know. Wasn't I your first passenger?"

"Are you ready to go?" Terry turned to retrace her steps.

Kris nodded and fell into step beside her. "Yeah—But are you sure that jumping from an airplane is the way you want to spend your twenty-first birthday?" Kris slipped into the car next to Terry.

"Absolutely!" Terry replied. "I soloed on my seventeenth birthday, helped to build a plane at Cal State on my eighteenth, and, today, on my twenty-first, I'm making my first parachute jump." Terry threw the stick shift into gear. The small wheels ground into the rocky driveway. "Mom and Dad never set any limits on us—and I'm not setting any on myself. I'm planning a new adventure every year . . . so, jump school, here we come!"

"I never promised to jump with you. Remember that!"

"I wanted you to come along. If you want to jump, fine. If you don't want to," Terry grinned broadly, "I'll save some money."

"Okay, just let me make up my own mind."

"Still—" Terry kept her eyes on the road. "I hope you do go up with me. It's great to have someone share an adventure—know the same thrill—compare notes."

"Yeah, it's too bad none of your close friends can fly," Kris observed. "But what you really need is a steady boyfriend."

"Well, I meet lots of guys at the airport, but we're always going off in opposite directions—and finding *time* to date is hard. During the day I work to pay for my apartment and expenses. At night, I'm at the university, and on weekends, I'm at the airport taking lessons or out on a ferrying job."

"You've got to stick around on weekends!"

"I wouldn't give up ferrying for anything! It's exciting to fly different models over new routes. Each flight is an adventure—and I get to visit different parts of the world."

"But how will you meet Mr. Right, if you don't date lots of men?"

A Birthday Dare

Terry made a sharp turn into the dirt parking lot of the parachute school and parked. "I'm not interested in getting married right now. Someday, but not now. I want to fly–even if I'm not sure where." She tilted the rear view mirror to put on a fresh layer of lipstick. "I have to pile up all the hours and experience I can get. You know, I'll always be competing with guys who've been flying in the armed forces. I've got to be as good as they are."

A white ambulance passed as she and Kris left the car.

"See," Kris laughed, "I bet someone forgot to open his chute!"

Terry laughed with her; but her smile vanished when she learned the truth. A young man *had* jumped without opening his chute. She heard that the victim had tumbled backwards from the plane, thrown his hands up sharply to right himself, and ripped open a recent appendectomy scar.

"He must have blacked out in pain," the ex-Green Beret Marine instructor explained to the group of both new and experienced chutists. He slowly pressed his hand back over his straight ebony hair. "The parachute is blameless," he said; his direct, strong voice did not hide the sadness in his green eyes. "In case any of you are wondering, just watch!" He put on the dead man's chute and made a jump, landing a few feet from where the body had thumped to earth. The delay gave the waiting jumpers a chance to tell their most terrifying mishaps–some with equipment failures.

The accident gnawed at her confidence as she worked through the training session. It confirmed her worst fear: *What if the chute doesn't open?* She hid her doubts and looked for signs of nervousness in the other students. Her hands shook as she buckled on the parachute pack and crossed the brown leather straps over her royal blue jumpsuit.

"All right," the instructor said, loading the small Cessna 172, "if you've lost your guts, you can change your mind now–on the ground–'cause once we're up there, you're gonna jump, if I have to pick you up and throw you out!" He laughed. "Now step aside, you lunkheads. Let our one and only little lady up here."

Terry threw Kris a quick wave and forced a smile. Clumsy in her bulbous silver helmet and heavy boots, she ducked stiffly into the doorless cockpit and sat on the floor. The instructor and another student sat beside her. Crouched behind the pilot, she felt the plane rumble over the dirt runway.

"Before we level off at 3,000 feet," the instructor shouted, "let's see if you remember what I've told you."

Under his ordinary words, Terry sensed an inner tension.

New Perspectives

"How will you leave the plane, London?" he asked.

"I'll leap backwards," she answered.

"Why?"

"So the wind won't knock me flat on my back."

"What else will you do?"

"Stretch out my arms and legs in a spread-eagle position."

"Right. You must be upright when the chute opens. You'll drop like a lead cannonball until it does. After that, you'll drop at fifteen feet per second." He looked at the other student.

"What will you do while you're falling?"

"Start counting to ten."

"Right. By then, the chute should open clear of the plane. If it doesn't open, pull your emergency chute. Whatever you do, don't panic and hug your chute so tight that it can't open!" Over the drop zone, the instructor motioned the student to the doorway. White-knuckled, the student hung onto the door frame.

"Jump!" the instructor shouted.

The student's eyes glazed over; he did not move.

"Jump!" With lightning speed, the instructor karate-chopped the student's paralyzed hold. A shriek filled the sky as the student dropped from sight. "Oh, my God! Not two in one day!" the instructor cried in disbelief. "He's upside down—"

Terry imagined that he saw the picture of a second dead jumper flash before him.

"It opened—" the instructor heaved out the words. "He's tangled in the lines, but he'll make it down okay. If he doesn't free himself, he'll just have a rough landing." He looked back at Terry. "Okay, you're next!"

Terry looked into the instructor's ashen face and gulped. She hesitated—then forced her heavy boot onto the wheel fender. A seventy-mile-an-hour wind pried tears from her eyes. She grabbed a wing strut for support against the onrushing slipstream.

"Jump!" the instructor yelled. "Jump!" His commands whistled past her.

When his arm moved towards her, she screamed to the wind, "Oh, no you don't!" Squeezing her eyes shut, she leaped spread-eagle into space. The air rushed by, almost tearing the helmet from her head. "One— two— three—" she counted to ten through clenched teeth. The chute had not opened. Free-

A Birthday Dare

falling at 150 miles per hour, she grabbed the rip cord of the emergency chute. A cracking jolt knocked her hand away. The main chute had snaked from the pack and ballooned overhead.

With a death grip on the shroud lines, she looked up into a thirty-foot white and orange striped umbrella. Bright sunlight sparkled through the thin nylon canopy. "It's beautiful—oh—it's so beautiful—" Suspended in a brilliant blue sky, she silently floated down. Gently swaying from side to side, she scanned the desert below. "So beautiful—so beautiful—" she nervously repeated to the sky. Pulling down on a suspension line, she guided the chute toward the landing point encircled by spectators. Terry tried to locate Kris, but the windsock distracted her. It indicated a ground wind, and that meant trouble. After landing, the chute could become her enemy. Filled with wind, it would drag and bounce her along the rocky ground like a rag doll. The land rushed up. With no time to worry, she reached up and grabbed a handful of lines. *Bend your knees or break a leg!* Raising her feet, she hunched forward, ready to somersault. She hit, rolled, and got up quickly. She ran behind the billowing chute and pressed to the earth. The air spilled out and she gathered yards of striped nylon into her arms.

"Terry, you did it! You really did it!" Kris reached out to help undo the leather harness.

"Well, that takes care of year twenty-one!" Terry laughed with relief. "Got any suggestions for twenty-two?"

Party Time

Lola Curtis

I prepared a dinner,
For twenty or so,
Had food in the oven,
All burners on go.

The dishes were shining,
The table all set,
When I heard a strange sound,
I'll never forget.

Such bubbling and gurgling,
Then foam all about.
The sink was the culprit—
I gave a great shout.

When I turned on the switch,
The disposal belched,
Then it sputtered and stopped,
My pleas thereby squelched.

I looked up at the clock,
Saw that "guest time" was nigh,
And called to my hubby,
"Bring tools—on the fly!"

Party Time

He turned off the water,
Crawled under the sink,
And had the thing working,
Before I could blink.

So I finished my chores,
And cleaned up the mess,
Then off to the bedroom,
To don my new dress.

I then fixed a quick drink,
To make me serene,
Walked into the kitchen,
And let out a scream!

For water was flowing,
All over the floor,
It came from my washer,
Right over its door.

I turned off the faucets,
Mopped like a swabby,
Soon had it all sparkly,
Just like a grand lobby.

When off in a distance,
A chime I did hear.
Dear Lord, I just made it.
My guests, they are here!

Witch in the Vicarage

Lucile Bogue

"Good heavens!" Martha Treadwell almost choked.

She took a great swig of tea that had long since grown cold in the handpainted china cup at her elbow and closed the book in her lap carefully.

"Dear God!" The hair prickled on the back of her neck and she felt a sudden chill. She got up and placed the book in the center of the brightest blaze in the fireplace. Then she got the lavender afghan from the hall closet and wrapped it around her shoulders as she resumed her seat.

"I must get hold of myself before Harold comes home. I must *never* let him know!"

She brushed up the gray hairs at the back of her neck and repinned them into the motherly bun, smoothing out the electric prickles as she did so.

"So that explains it! That's why people have always done what I told them to. They couldn't help themselves!"

Picking up her roll of soft tweed yarn, she began to knit in something of a frenzy.

"So that's why Gavin Treadwell married me, though we both knew he didn't love me. I always wondered why he gave in without a struggle. And God knows, I never loved him . . . or any man, for that matter."

She dropped the knitting in her lap and closed her eyes in prayer.

"Dear Father, is that why Harold has been such an obedient son all these twenty-eight years? Forgive me if I have done anything wrong. But that was the only way I could get a son. You don't really think it was wrong, do you? Harold is such a wonderful boy, and a credit to the Church! Amen."

Having done suitable penance, she resumed her knitting at a brisk clip. Then she heard her son's key in the lock as he came in out of the Kansas winter.

"Hello, hello!" she cried, with joy bells ringing in her voice. She adored her boy. She hated men in general, but Harold was different. He was her own, and raised to order.

"Hello, Mommie dear!" he called back, hanging up his coat. There was an unusual lilt of happiness in his greeting.

"How is Childe Harold?" she chirped the old familiar phrase. But she was troubled, wondering what had put him in such a cheerful frame of mind all of a sudden. He entered, beaming.

"Whistler's Mother!" he cried. "You are a perfect picture in that shawl!"

And she was. Her silvery hair shone in the wintry sun.

"But why didn't you turn up the furnace if you're cold?" he asked.

"I'm not really cold, I guess. I just had a kind of chill a few minutes ago."

"I'll turn up the heat, Mother." He went into the hall.

"No, don't!'

He returned, some of the glow fading from his face.

"My God!" she thought. "It's true! I have total control of the boy! He is Play Doh in my hands! And it's because I'm a witch!"

"We can't afford the extra heat, Son," she amended softly. "A vicar's salary, you know."

Harold took a stance in the center of the room, facing her, his feet set wide apart and planted with determination. It was a most unusual position for him. In fact, she had never before seen such an attitude in this quiet, handsome young man. A silent pout, petulance, cool withdrawal, perhaps. But never before this attitude of cheerful stubbornness. The nausea of fear struck her innards.

"Mother, I must talk with you," he said, his voice strained and unsteady. "I have an announcement to make."

He looked calm and collected, but she knew he was scared sick. She could see his quick breathing and the white line around his mouth. She wanted to take him on her lap as she had always done, but it was too late.

New Perspectives

"Mother, don't be angry. *Please* listen until I'm through."

"Don't tell me, Harold. I already know. You're planning to be married."

She came near fainting as the unexpected words were uttered in the quiet air. Who had uttered them? How did she know? How *could* she know?

"Mama..." he choked. "How did you know? How *could* you know?"

Sudden beads of sweat popped out on his high white forehead.

"Tell me about it, Son," she said grimly. She couldn't tell him how she knew, for she didn't know herself. The knowledge had just struck her without warning.

"I met Sammy at Church Camp last summer in Colorado. She's from New Jersey." His words came tumbling out in frantic haste, as though he was afraid he wouldn't have time to finish before she stopped him. "We're going to be married this Friday. I'm leaving tomorrow morning for East Orange, for the wedding."

She poured herself a fresh cup of cold tea from the cold pot on the little table. With shaking hands she lifted the cup to her lips.

"Harold," she faltered, "you've... you've always been such a *good* boy."

But *had* he? Or had his spirit only been dominated by the powerful soul of a witch? Her conscience gave a sudden painful stab, like a toothache.

"Mama," he seemed close to collapse, "what's so bad about getting married?"

She wouldn't *let* him make a fool of himself! Gone daft over some floozy tourist from New Jersey. She would soon put a stop to it! Lord only knows how many times in his life she had already saved him from grave error, humiliation, and heartache. She could save him again. But it wouldn't be easy. He was not as malleable as he had once been. He was developing a bit of resistance. She would have to be cautious.

"What's wrong with marriage?" he croaked.

"Nothing, dear. Nothing. I was married once myself," she laughed, shrugging off her terror.

"Mother," he grinned in relief and took out his handkerchief to mop his face, "you're an angel! I was afraid you would be angry."

"Angry? What a silly idea!"

"Then you'll come to the wedding?" he beamed.

Witch in the Vicarage

"Oh, I didn't say that! I'm not sure there'll be a wedding," she said, and upset her cup of tea on the floor.

"Oh . . . your lovely carpet!"

He was on his knees instantly, mopping up the dark pool with his white handkerchief.

Harold backed his old jalopy out of the garage early the next morning for his drive to Kansas City.

He didn't have any new clothes for the trip, so his luggage was light, just one big old suitcase, the same one he'd taken to seminary in St. Louis. But almost everything he owned was in it, even the Bible his mother had given him at ordination. She followed him to the car.

"Good luck, Sonny." She kissed him gently, while a tear slid down the wrinkle of her smile.

"'Bye, Mama." He seemed almost casual this morning as he gave her shoulder a hurried pat. "Wish you were coming."

But she knew he was scared by the way his eyes darted away from her. He was afraid she wouldn't let him go. And she was afraid she couldn't stop him.

She couldn't understand this new resistance in him. It was as though her beautiful dutiful son had been suddenly replaced by a stranger.

"Harold, darling," she burst out, "what in the world *possesses* you?"

"Nothing. I'm getting married, that's all. What's so strange about that?"

"It's so . . . so . . . out of character."

"Mother, I'm going to miss my plane!"

"What's she like, Harold?"

"She's a beautiful girl. You'll see."

"Probably not. I'm not feeling well, Harold. I may not be here when you get back."

"Oh, Mother!" He jumped into the car and slammed the door violently. His coat tail was pinned down, so he had to repeat the process. He looked like a wild rabbit trying to escape. The car roared off in a fog of smoke.

She smiled a watery frozen smile in the Kansas wind and waved a forlorn adieu. Frankly, she was terrified. For the first time in her life she felt

New Perspectives

out of control. Harold had defied her! He had done it "on purple purpose," as he had told her when he was two years old and still defiant.

All she could do now was pray . . . and try. She refused to give up.

She wanted to go to the corner drugstore for a bottle of aspirin. She was developing a frightful headache, but she was afraid to leave the phone. She should make the beds upstairs, but if the phone rang she might slip and fall running down the stairs. Better wait. She stared hard at the African violet. She must concentrate.

At 10:13 A.M. the silence of the vicarage was shattered. Martha leaped to the phone. What would he have to report?

"Hello, Harold?"

"Yes, Mom. How did you know it would be me?"

"Who else would it be?" As there seemed to be no easy answer to the question, there was a moment of silence before she spoke again. "What happened?"

"I wrecked the car."

"Oh, Sweetheart! Did you get hurt?"

"No, but the jalopy is a total loss."

"Oh, Son! Thank God you aren't hurt! Are you sure you're all right?"

"Yes, I'm fine. But I just didn't want you to get a police report or something and worry about me."

"That's sweet, dear. Just like your old self. I'll run down and get a chicken for dinner. You'll be coming home, of course."

"No, I'm on my way to Kansas City! Just caught a ride with a truck driver."

"Oh, no!"

"'Bye, Mama. See you after the wedding. Monday, probably."

He hung up. Just like that. She felt the magic ring of her protection around him smashed. Like a fragile Christmas tree ornament. Where had she gone wrong? For a moment she considered going to bed for the day and crying her eyes out. But then she wouldn't be near the phone for the next call.

At 1:13 P.M. the phone rang sharply. Her heart lunged like a colt at the county fair. The cool, crisp voice of an operator was on the line.

"Will you accept a collect call from Harold Treadwell?"

"Of course."

"Okay. Go ahead, sir."

"Hello, Mama?"

"Harold! Whatever in the world has happened this time?" And she meant it. She didn't know exactly herself.

"I was mugged at the taxi stand here at the Kansas City Airport. The guy took my wallet."

"Oh, darling! What a pity! What are you going to do now?"

"That's it. I wondered if you could wire me some money at Sammy's address."

"Oh, Harold-Baby! I couldn't! I scarcely have enough to pay the milkman and the paperboy." God forgive me for telling a little white lie, she thought, but it's for his own good. "But don't worry, dear. Sammy's rich enough to take care of you both, no doubt."

"Mother, she's not rich at all! She's the oldest of six kids and her father works in a bicycle shop."

"Oh, that's too bad."

There was a long, tense silence.

"Mother, I'm flat broke. I had to beg a dime from the girl at the Avis counter to make this call."

There was a suitable lull.

"Darling, you *could* come home, you know."

The line went dead.

Martha went to the kitchen to make herself a pot of tea. She felt weak and shaken. Perhaps she should relax a bit. She took a small flask of whiskey from behind her spices and poured a healthy shot into the teacup.

For a long while she sat in the gloomy kitchen, her head in her hands. The faucet dripped in the grubby sink. The motor of the ancient refrigerator thumped and kicked spasmodically. The parish apparently could not afford either a new refrigerator or a new gasket for the faucet. At times she even doubted that they could afford a vicar, no matter how modestly salaried.

At 4:13 P.M. the phone rang for the third time. The vicar's mother knocked the rocking chair over backward as she sprinted to answer it.

"Harold?" her voice cracked. "What happened this time?"

"Nothing much. The airline lost my luggage."

"Oh, no! Your Sunday suit!"

"Yes. Tough luck, huh?"

"Oh, Hap dear!" She hadn't called him "Hap" or "Happy" since he was six years old when she decided that he would become an Episcopal priest. "Hap" seemed a rather irreverent name for a priest, somehow. But now her frenzy at the possibility of losing him was mounting. "You must come home! This just wasn't meant to be! Please!"

"Sorry, Mother. Sammy is here at the phone booth with me. Everything is going to be all right."

"Son, I hate to say this, but I must. I think you are in the grips of some evil force."

"Oh, Mother, don't be ridiculous!"

"Good-bye, Son. I won't be bothering you again."

She hung up the phone, although she could still hear his frantic voice. A long while she stood there, giving him a final chance to call back and tell her that he was returning immediately. She twisted the phone cord anxiously, waiting. No call came.

At a quarter of five she called the travel agent down by the post office.

"Hello. Nugent's Travel Service. May I help you?" a pleasant young voice answered.

"I hope so. I'm Mrs. Treadwell."

"Oh, yes! Reverend Treadwell's mother?"

"Yes. I've never done much traveling, but I want to go to Las Vegas. Tonight."

There was a stunned silence.

"Las Vegas? Nevada?" the girl managed to respond.

"Certainly. Do you sell tickets?"

"Are you the minister's . . . mother?" the poor girl seemed more than a bit troubled.

But eventually Martha had her way, and a night flight to Las Vegas was arranged, complete with a taxi ride from Plainsville to Kansas City. This would be an expensive trip, but she had the money tucked under her mattress to handle it. It was for a good cause.

Witch in the Vicarage

She packed her two best church dresses, put on her Sunday hat with the little red feather in the hatband, donned her rather flea-bitten coat, and told the vicarage goodbye. A blizzard was screaming across the Kansas prairies by the time the taxi arrived at the front of the house. Martha had been waiting impatiently at the glass in the front door for some time, peering through the lace curtain. She and her small overnight bag fairly shot down the front walk and into the waiting cab.

"Yer a fool, lady," the driver commented as he got back into the car after scraping the banks of snow and ice off the windshield and the rear window. "A damned fool to ask me to drive to Kansas City on a night like this."

"Never you mind. You have nothing to worry about. God is looking after you."

In Las Vegas a million lights glittered and the blizzard was far behind. She checked in at The Sands, as it sounded more innocent than some of the others. Putting on her navy blue dress, she looked into the mirror and saw her dark eyes twinkling with excitement.

"You don't look like a witch," she laughed. "You look more like a minister's mother. Now let's see what you can do, Martha, old girl!"

Lights blazed and flashed, slot machines clattered with mechanic madness, and the voice of Frank Sinatra floated out on great drifts of cigarette smoke. Martha felt frightened and a bit sick. Everything whirled around her in a vast kaleidoscope of noise and color.

But somehow she arrived at the roulette table and placed her bet. How she did it, she didn't know, for she had never even seen gambling and knew absolutely nothing about it. Blindly, she seemed to move and speak like a robot.

"I'll try a hundred dollars on number one," she said timidly, and pushed out twenty five-dollar chips. Such a lot of money to risk losing! In fact, all she had in the world.

The wheel whirled and the ball finally dropped neatly into the groove marked "one." The croupier shoved a large stack of chips in front of her.

"Rake 'em in, ma'am," he grinned at the white-haired lady from Kansas. "You bet heavy, you win heavy. That's three thousand, six hundred bucks, lady! Rake 'em in!"

"Oh, my goodness! Are those all mine?" She was startled that it could work so soon.

New Perspectives

"All yours, ma'am."

"Another hundred dollars, please," she bet again, "on number thirty-six."

The wheel rolled and the ball dropped on thirty-six. The startled croupier shoved another mountain of chips toward her.

"Well, Grandma!" he quipped. "You're on a winning streak today! Want to try again?"

She did. She bet on thirteen, always her lucky number. The wheel whirred. The ball dropped. The number was thirteen. The croupier had lost his smile.

"Well, for God's sake!" he wheezed. "Not again!"

"Say, what is this?" snarled a gambler from Chicago, a diamond flashing on his finger. "Mother's Day or somethin'?"

A short, fat man in a bright jacket "accidentally" stepped on her foot under the table, the foot with the corn on it.

No use in using her "luck" too long in the same game. She scooped up her growing pile of chips and dumped them into her worn handbag. She would try her luck elsewhere.

"Goodbye, boys. And thanks," she smiled sweetly, walking away with her felt hat on and her head high, as she did after church when people told Harold he had a lovely mother. "I've enjoyed meeting you."

The experiment in Las Vegas was a complete success. By the time Martha Treadwell had packed her bag three days later, paid her hotel bill, and caught a return flight to Kansas, her old purse was bulging.

When she alighted from the taxi back in Plainsville, there were lights in the vicarage.

"They must be home!" She went up the walk and knocked at the door. It was opened by a haggard Harold.

"Mama!" he croaked. "Where in the devil have you been? We've been worried sick!"

"Aren't you going to invite me in?" she smiled pleasantly.

"Why should I 'invite' you? This is your home!"

"Not any more, Son. It's all yours. Yours and your wife's."

A girl with pale Swedish-gold hair and the look of an angel came in from the kitchen. Martha smiled at her and gave her a friendly squeeze.

"You must be Sammy."

"Yes." The girl seemed wary. She stood as stiff as an ironing board.

"I've just come back to get my things." Martha was nonchalant. "I'm moving to Nevada."

"Nevada!" Harold shouted for the first time in this life. He had squeaked before. But shouted? Never.

"Yes. Las Vegas. Sammy, would you like to come upstairs and help me pack my things?" She was being terribly cheery. "You two will no doubt want to move into the big room now, so you can help me get my things out."

The girl followed her up the stairs. In the big bedroom Martha turned and closed the door quietly behind them.

"So!" she smiled knowingly. "You got him."

The pale girl looked even paler now, and more angelic. Her head was held high.

"We're married, if that's what you mean."

"Partly." Martha started pulling open drawers and putting the contents on the bed in neat, folded piles.

"What are you going to do now?" Sammy asked with concern. "How can you live without Harold?"

"Don't worry, dearie," Martha smiled mysteriously. "I'll get by."

"I'm afraid Hap hasn't any extra money to give you right now," she apologized softly. "The trip was a little expensive, with losing all his clothes and the car and everything."

"I'm sorry." She was matter-of-fact. "It was all my doing, you know. I thought I could save him."

The girl's blue eyes widened. "Honestly?"

"Yes. Forgive a doting mother, but I put everything I had into keeping him here." She rummaged in her purse and brought forth a large bundle wrapped in a drugstore bag and tied with a bit of gray tweed yarn. "Here is enough to get another car, and a new suit for Harold. Help him pick it out. He's never bought a suit in his life. I always did it for him. Seven thousand and two hundred and eighty-seven dollars and twenty-nine cents."

She handed it to the startled girl.

"It's all I can spare right now. But there's more where this came from."

She pulled the knitted spread from the steamer trunk at the foot of the bed.

Sammy looked dazed. She stared at the package in her hand.

"You mean . . . that you . . . caused the wreck, and everything?"

"Yes. Isn't it remarkable what the human mind can do?"

"But why . . . " Sammy whispered timidly, "why are you moving out?"

"A wise witch knows when she's licked," Martha answered briskly, removing old Christmas ornaments from the trunk.

"I'm sorry. I didn't mean—"

"Tut-tut, my dear. I knew, after all that trouble that Harold had, when he went on to New Jersey anyway—I knew for sure that you had The Power, too, and that yours was stronger than mine. There's no use in battling one of my own kind." She began packing the trunk with folded clothes.

"But I—"

"Hush! No need to deny it. And Harold's used to it. He doesn't even know. And *never* tell him!"

"But, Mrs. Treadwell— "

"Call me Martha." She started taking her second-best dresses from the hangers in the closet and folding them into the trunk.

"But how will you live?" persisted Sammy.

"Don't fret, Lovey. I've found that roulette and the slots have a certain fascination—if you *know* you can win." She laughed. "And think of the food I can buy for hungry people with all that money! I do believe I'm gong to enjoy it!"

"Please don't go. You needn't move out of your own room. Harold and I are doing fine in his."

"No, thanks, darling child." She kissed Sammy's cheek, and then turned to snap the clasps shut on the large suitcase. "One witch in the vicarage is quite enough. Two would be overdoing it a bit, don't you think?"

In an Ashen Land

Prize-Winning Story Published in *Spectrum*

M. L. Archer

He listened to the whine of the bus wheels over the highway, jeering at him; you're the lowest of the low; the bus knew the truth. He wished he'd had money to go by train, even this short distance, by plane, by–by anything. Only the poorest of the poor and lavendered little old ladies went anywhere by bus, and he was a man, still in his twenties even. But then he was on a fool's errand, anyway. He choked on a snort; all his life had been a fool's errand. Why was he going? What did he hope to find after so many years? There'd be the burned out, blackened space in the hills; a California hill, high, undulating and rounded like a woman, like upturned bowls of gold, in the singing hills, like the burned-out space in him. A man should be singing too, not in ashes.

Factories, houses, freeways and fields lunged by him like the lunge of the days of his life inside his brain; the years in prison, Vacaville Medical Facility–facility, a coy name for a prison–the tortured hours talking to and holding off the jailhouse psychiatrist, release, and now this, the stomach-tight return to the scene of the crime. Did the prison show on him as a stink, a blotch to the other passengers? He shut his eyes and staved that prison back. The smells of the bus lay hot around him, the poor smells, the unwashed smells, the plush upholstery smells, and here and there, the well bathed. Wash me in the Blood of the Lamb, the zany thought barreled up in him. Well, he'd been washed all right, in the red blood of prison life, in the white sweat of the truth, in the frozen perspiration of the famished hours, and now that he was free and feeling freedom like a live taste and could go anywhere, anywhere–he

New Perspectives

was homing back like a mindless pigeon. Maybe it was like psychiatry; one always had to leave by the door one came in by. There was—even hidden—no other exit, though you cursed and begged and cried out for someone to point you the way, unveil another door, kick one in for you or out, and show you where to kick out. The headshrinker hadn't been bad, not really, not when you gave yourself up to him and to it. He counted him among his real friends, along with the officer who'd first come to bust him—burdening someone with one's awful secrets made a friend of anyone. Martin Karlotsky, med school grad, unbroken specialist in broken lives; it was funny when you stopped to think of it, and he, Bud Rogers, truck driver, motorcycle rider and sometime mechanic and . . . He couldn't say the label, not here in this sort-of clean bus; that proved he wasn't cured yet, that he had a few more steps to go.

From the seat beside him he pulled his groceries nearer. Good thing he'd bought some in Oakland on that ten-minute stop, bread and bologna. It wasn't bad; he wasn't used to high living; in fact Vacaville had sort of been a step up, with its laundered sheets, clean lavatories smelling of disinfectant, its art classes, its libraries, but the rolling, dry hills and the road ahead of him were gone and the facility was a cage. Susan had made him bologna sandwiches often for his job, he remembered. Slapped together in the bleary-eyed morning, no lettuce, no pickle, no nothing. *And lucky to get it*, she'd dared him with ocean-blue eyes. "I'm so tired," she'd say. "That job of mine is hell." He could hear his voice still as he reached under her robe and touched her stiff, smooth shoulder. "Why don't you quit then?" Stiffness in a woman was like eggshell in creamed eggs. "I always expected you to quit when we got married."

Maybe if she'd quit and tended the kid it wouldn't have happened. Maybe lots of things wouldn't have been, without her snappish reply. "Yeah, I did that once. Next thing I knew I was looking for a job and them hard to get. I made up my mind, you have a job, hang on to it." She had been right, of course. Damn good thing she had that job the day they'd come for him. Susan would've been pretty in a fuzzy-headed way, if she'd got more rest, taken care of herself, been bathed and perfumed and rested, ready for loving when he got home, but no, damn it, it was off to that hash house job she clung onto as if she was someday going to get the Nobel Prize for being there, just for being there, year after year. He stretched his long legs out straight under the seat ahead of him. He'd never yet learned to sit while someone else drove.

Maybe she was there yet, for all he knew. No, he'd heard she'd left the job too, and sorrow had gnawed at him; she should have stayed, won that prize. Didn't she know she should have guilt only for her own sins, not the sins of others? No, he'd been wholly to blame. No one else. Not her! He wouldn't fall into that trap again. Even then he'd known the full extravagant sin, the wickedness of it and the deadly self-poison of his knowledge. He felt it yet, doing something to his backbone still. He ... He ... He ... only was to blame. And she'd taken Feather with her. There, he'd said her name. He could think of Feather sometimes and remember how sweet she was, how beautiful, how exquisite, how delightful, with dimpled cheeks and fat, satiny legs. Why, if she'd been kept cleaner, her hair brushed, dressed in pretty dresses now and then, she'd have been a birthday-party doll. If he was honest with himself, perhaps that'd been what'd attracted him to Susan, when he'd stopped to eat and joke, usually steak, he remembered—not Susan, but her daughter, Feather, sitterless at the moment, a miniature of her, her grown young again, grown five years old again, all sugar and spice and blue-eyed, sober cuteness. When he'd married Susan and Feather'd climbed onto his lap and wound her arms around his neck, he'd thought he'd have to go load the trucks with tomato lugs in the old-fashioned way, to fence the wonder back.

With the shift of the vibrating bus, a youngish red-haired gal across the aisle crossed her lithe legs and he waited for some upshooting live hunger in him. None! Maybe he'd have to be out a week or two longer. He didn't give a hang if it took a month. But no longer.

The bus clunked to a stop at Livermore, atomic town, egghead brains and ranchers mixed. No wonder they maybe made explosives.

With the bus and its new passenger, somebody's mother-in-law, wheeling on the move again through the heat, the knowledge warned him; Susan, Feather, the house, all were gone now like yesterday's smoke. He neatly tucked the crinkly paper back over the bread, put the bologna back in the sack, listened to the lackadaisical talk around him, glanced out the lurching window at the browned, blurred grass. It wouldn't be long now, fifteen minutes maybe till he asked the driver to stop. It was all gone now; Susan, Feather, the little house in the hills, his garden, his strawberries, even the seedling trees, pines, he'd set out. There had been nobody to tend them, to water them. Funny what a man thought of when the sheriff came. "Who will tend my strawberries?" "Who's to water my trees?" You were supposed to think of your crime, not see your strawberry tendrils drying up, pines dying down to make a graveyard of their own. But Feather'd been part of his planting. Hadn't she tailed after him chattering and laughing when he'd firmed the dirt about the strawberry roots, hadn't she lugged her sandpail, full of water, from the furthest reach of the hose to water the trees, as she'd seen him do it? Hadn't he, while he'd dug and planted and dreamed, thinking that damn, small, nasty house was

New Perspectives

a castle, watched, watched her, and felt happiness like a driving song? And after Susan got home and he threw himself at her, hadn't Feather been part of it all?   So it hadn't been crazy to think when they'd come and he hadn't reached for his hunting rifle, *who's to tend my plants, patch the roof on the house?* Maybe he'd even been glad to see them, to put a final end to it. Maybe those Frenchies had, some, even been glad when they'd seen for the last time the self-satisfied, blood-sucking expressions on the crowd and heard the guillotine drop. Self-satisfied, wasn't that what they always were? They'd been smug, he knew, then they'd burned the house down, thinking the lust, the depravity was purged somehow in the crackling crimson flames. There were Old Testament sacrificial types far beyond Atomic Town. It was a wonder they hadn't burned the whole damn countryside in their zeal. In the hot season and all. But he'd cleared wide around the house. Then all through the gloomy rainy season, the winter of the heart, they could remember those snapping, licking red flames to keep them warm.

The bread and bologna sat like a rock on his stomach and his kidneys felt full. A man shouldn't eat on top of emotion; it hit the stomach and kidneys. But it'd been years. He thought emotion was dead. And now he was come to sift the gray ashes, to sit there in the once-green garden, in the once-spruce yard, and cry like a woman, as he'd cried at last in Karlotsky's office, like a goddamn woman.   Hell, weren't men and women alike, despite their differences? He knew that now. He'd discovered deep in himself a soft spot like a woman's, and accepted it, hugged it even, so maybe, to hell with it, he'd cry. He was a nothing, a nobody, not even a has-been or a would-be, so by God if he felt like bawling, he'd bawl and who was to care? But worse luck, maybe he'd look out at the desolation, at the weeds of his life, as he'd glanced out at the rushing neutral towns today, and feel nothing. Nothing! Maybe Bud Rogers was only capable of strong emotions at times like . . .

He jumped up and grabbed for the paper sack. He was getting near. "I'd like to get off here, please," he said to the driver's pudgy, studious profile. "It's a short hike from here."

The bus driver awarded him with a soured, stiff-mouthed look. "No irregular stops, " he said. Then suddenly he braked, snapped the doors open.

Bud trod down onto the gray gravel shoulder. The doors shut with a wheeze after him. Masked bored faces stared down at him before the bus labored off, with a whirlwind of oil smell. It's fear of his job if he stops here, Bud thought, as the silver and blue bus fumed away; fear, fear, fear, why did people fear so much? He stretched his arms, till his muscles tightened, and arched his back, straightened and swung with long strides up the familiar,

In an Ashen Land

strange-looking gravelly road. Funny the countryside should smell the same, so clean, so baked, so languorous; somehow it should smell different, as old people smelled different from young. Cicadas sang him on his way and gravel crunched. But he was different. He didn't even use the same words he'd used, think the same way. He'd read; he'd studied. After he'd topped the first hill, he urinated, watching the puddle of yellow bubble up, then ooze away. He tucked himself back into his pants.

And then like a bursting sun, as if he'd held it back all it'd hold, the memory of Feather burst over him. Dear sweet Feather. He'd never meant to harm her; her skin was sleek as rose-scented soap when he'd bathed her; she was so innocent; it didn't matter if he touched her; it meant nothing; he was her father, her stepfather anyway, and when he tucked her into bed and kissed her dampish mouth—and his hand crept under her neck—with the sudden sweat prickly on him—and he struggled himself back to his darkened, lonely, stirless bedroom to wait for Susan—

A blurring weakness betrayed him and he sank down onto a hummock of saffron-colored, crackly grass. He wasn't used to hiking any more. He was weak from the sun; he'd forgotten it could bear down so hard, so unmercifully it set your heart to chopping, and yet be life-giving. Forty feet from the highway, and he was bushed. He'd been right to be in the company of little old ladies. He looked around him. This was God's country, the boundless uplifting hills and the sweep of true-white clouds. The sweat wept on him. What day, what year could he remember without this rumpus emotion, this surprise weakness? He'd walked like a sleepwalker toward her, toward Feather, through the darkening, becalmed house toward her—toward her—pulled on, seeing her even in the dark, her five-year-old splendor there in the bed clamoring to him, with his heart splitting and pounding in his chest and the hair on the nape of his neck tingling up, up. He'd looked down at her sleeping, her hand curled under her chin, smelling of soap, of blankets, of hair. Yes, he'd fought with himself, by God he'd fought. How many times had he thrust himself back to the doorway while death cried out in him and his loins burned? How could it hurt her? She was so soft, she was unhurtable. With his ache he had to touch her, to run his tongue into her soft mouth, to feel the satiny saliva running over him, to feel the exultation wrung out of him into her. One night—my God—he hadn't turned. He'd swooped her up in his arms, gone beyond their battle, and kissed her so she woke, startled, and he'd whispered as the tumult, the tumescence, beat and raged up in him. "It's okay. I'm your Daddy. Just do what Daddy says."

And she had. Poor innocent little lamb.

New Perspectives

The hot sweat seethed over him like a sweltering river. God damn, that sun was hot. Good thing they'd caught him. Before it was too late. Men often murdered their victims to keep them from telling. "Daddy was nasty to me." Good thing Susan'd got diarrhea from eating some of her yesterday's hash and come home early one night. Good thing they'd burned the house. Luck had been with him, after all. He stood up, shivered in the naked sunshine and hiked on, over gravel, through crunchy beetlings of dried grass and singing cicadas. He was almost at the edge of the once-clearing. He'd see it and go on. On to where? He hadn't paid taxes on it for years, nor had Susan, as best he knew. Wherever she was, poor thing, she was still his wife, as far as he knew, probably done now with marriage forever.

Should he look up Feather, apologize, say "I'm heartbroken I spoiled your life"? Make amends? He snapped that fuzz from his head. No, let her be, don't remind her he'd made a mockery of her innocent beauty; let her be to forget he'd ever lived, to forget she'd watered his trees. People had it all wrong with psychiatrists, thinking they eased your guilt; they made you live it for the first time in all its flagrant horror so then it was a part of you like your arm, like your breathing. A true part like them. To be accepted.

The ashes were overgrown with coarse wild grass. Even the satisfying incense of ashes was replaced with the redolence of hot sun on dried grass. It hadn't been a bad little house, not good either; it'd had a foundation under it, anyway. He kicked the dusty foundation and felt its solidness and heard its thunk. Someone could have rented it, have maybe made love there, ate there and felt full, fell sick there, got well there, taken the stigma from it. Cold ashes crunched where his chair had once sat.

It was hard to even know where his garden had once been. He saw dead, stone-colored stalks, which might have been his pines. He couldn't tell. In full summer there were burned up stalks aplenty. Summer was a tawny lion here. Why had he come? There was nothing here! He wasn't cured yet, no matter what Karlotsky said; he was still playing the fool. Bud Rogers, Fool! "Strawberries won't grow here, nor pines either," Susan'd said, leaning into his arms about her waist. "It's alkaline."

"In the Valley," the rich San Joaquin Valley, he'd meant, where he was from, "you plant anything, it grows." Maybe because he'd expected them to take root, they had.

He'd no one left in the Valley anyway. He ranged down what might have been his boundary line. But he'd been happy here, too. He remembered the delicious scent of Susan's hair, when she'd shampooed it. That's what lasted, not so much the touch as the scent. Feather was probably as dead inside as these gray stalks, taken over by weeds, only standing upright somehow, as they did. He'd killed her after all, molested to death the last spark in her. See, in this wilderness of ashes and stalks he hadn't bawled like a woman after all. He'd only stared around with deserted, deadpan eyes. The land blurred before his peering eyes and his anguish; golden, green, tawny, bronze and brown. Green? He stared before him. A sprig of green recaught his eyes. A tree? His tree? My God, there was something green! Something alive. Only just, but alive. He dropped on his knees before it, pinched its spindly trunk, rubbed it, tweaked it, buried his fingers in its needles, crushed some and sucked the scent, made sure he wasn't just wishing it there. A pine! Goddamn it, it was a pine! How had it lived? Elation burned in him like a sun. Had he accidentally set its roots down near some hidden dampness till it struggled on, found its own deeper source of life? He studied the grass; yes, it was different here, sloped at another olive-colored angle. He touched, as if in prayer, a spiky twist, the pine, his pine, scraggy maybe, fighting, fighting, but still green, still blessedly green. Tears stung in his eyes like nettles.

Sobs like a baby's shook him; the sweet tears bathed his cheeks, ran salt into his mouth and down his chin, sprinkled baptismal wet drops on his prison-made suit. Goddamn it, one of the little bastards had lived, fought the odds, seen the depravity, yes depravity, he could call it by its name, the flames, the crowd, the silence, the long years and had fought on, lived on. He caressed its rough crusty trunk. Didn't they say life began at forty? He was far this side of forty, with maybe more years, different years, ahead of him than behind.

He broke off a clutch of needles, only a bit so the tree wouldn't be further stunted, and stuck it in the lapel of his brown suit. He sucked in a breath of the sun-hot air. How fresh it was, how tranquil, like good, clean grass encroaching over all, obliterating all, and washing clean. It would be solid green here in the spring, stretching and soaring for miles and miles. Ashes made soap; his mother, telling of her own mother, had told him once of making soap from ashes; and soap washed clean. The sun was out. The cicadas sang. He touched the green of the tree again. There was no use watering it, seeing to it; it would make its own adjustment, its own fight; it shouldn't be set back by attention. Water might kill it.

There were other places, other hills, other towns. In Arizona, maybe the hills were tawny too. He turned his back on the ashes. He touched the green in his lapel. The tears on his cheeks felt wet, but the springing sun would dry them.

And he moved on with slow steps, and then surer. On.

Holy Moses

Genevieve Bonato

Music plays an important role in the memories of most of us. Many of my happiest childhood recollections, dating back to the early part of this century, are centered around my grandmother, Janie, and her organ, "Holy Moses."

I don't know how the instrument received its name, but I do know that "Holy" provided great joy for my brother Buddy and me. Buddy especially enjoyed the organ stool and delighted in twisting it to the highest position, climbing aboard and twirling giddily back to floor level. I liked the stops that regulated tone and got pleasure in pulling out the one marked "tremelo," which added a satisfying quaver to Janie's already shaky efforts.

She wasn't the most accomplished organist; but to me she was wonderful. Her fingers, slowed by arthritis, sometimes faltered as she changed chords, but all she had to do to get our full attention was to sit down, open her song book, adjust her glasses, place her feet on the pedals, strike an opening note, and we would run to her side.

Most of her music was slow paced and sad; why I do not know. Perhaps her Gaelic heritage had a bearing on it, but I think being of the Catholic persuasion was a contributing factor. She had sung in the choir, and in those days the music tended toward solemnity, with hosannas and hallelujas being used sparingly. Needless to say, she had never been exposed to the happy Protestant groups that went to camp meetings, visited with old friends, ate wonderful food, sang rousing hymns, and praised the Lord with great gusto.

True, there were joyous songs to be sung: "Polly Wally Doodle," "Oh, Susannah," and with the advent of World War I, numbers like Irving Berlin's

Holy Moses

"Oh, How I Hate to Get Up in the Morning" and "Over There," which promised that ". . . the Yanks are coming, their drums rum-tumming . . . " We, however, stuck to the dolorous.

I remember "Silver Threads Among the Gold," which did nothing for me . . . just someone getting old and having their hair turn gray wasn't very exciting. My very favorite was the story of Nellie Gray, which brought me to tears each time I heard it.

> Oh, my poor Nellie Gray,
> They have taken her away,
> And I'll never see my darling any more.
> They have taken her to Georgia,
> For to wear her life away,
> As she toils in the cotton and the cane.

I knew nothing about toil, had no idea what constituted cotton 'n cane, but I wept bitterly for her plight.

On a more heartening note, Janie usually ended her musical bouts with "In the Sweet Bye and Bye," which held forth the possibility that "we will meet on that beautiful shore." I often visualize this as a lovely body of water, and as we come wading happily in, Janie will be there to greet us, and, by some great omnipotent act, she will be seated at the keyboard of "Holy Moses" as she welcomes us into the Lnd of the Sweet Bye and Bye.

Spring

Joe King

And again a Spring of rushing waters,
Where green on green grows and clings
To ancient, craggy forms of earth and rock
Which mock the temporalness of change.

We see that life gives birth to life
Amid a torrent of ten thousand splashing voices,
Coursing this way, cascading that way,
Plunging t'ward the sea.

The past is covered over by the new,
As the dead and dying will their bodies,
Through some pantheistic plan which links
The burning star and frozen glaciers.

And, like the waters of each Spring,
We tumble, toss, and carom through
The rocks and rushes of our youthful days,
Vibrant in our quest for distant Summer suns.

Tokyo Interlude

Allen J. Pettit

In 1945, the conquering Americans took over operation of the Naval Air Station, Atsugi, Japan. And by the middle fifties, little had changed; the old high-ceiling, gray-painted barracks were still drafty, and winter's chill still overpowered the little steam radiators.

Our enlisted complement of three flight crews, sixty-six men, was housed in one aged wooden barracks' barn-like lower floor. A row of tall gray metal lockers down the middle divided the rows of gray metal-framed double-deck bunks.

Snugged in my lower bunk, I pulled a blanket corner across the top of my head and down over my eyes to protect them against the late Saturday morning sun. It reached for me through the tall uncurtained windows as I daydreamed of distant, desirable things like Wife, Home, and Happiness. A night at the E.M. Club with too many friends, too much Nippon Beer, and a Japanese band rendering their version of American hillbilly music had left my head and stomach not quite up to braving daylight. Hard leather heels thumping through the barracks didn't help my headache or my disposition, either one, particularly when they stopped by my bunk

"On your feet, sailor. Wake up, goddamit!"

New Perspectives

Somebody shoved my legs aside and sat on my bunk. I squinted with sensitive eyes. "Well, I'll be damned. C.B., how are you? You damned civilians, in your fancy suits, got no respect for us hard-working Navy men, do you?"

"Jay, it's like I told you in that letter. These airline people appreciate good flight engineers, and you're missing the best things in life, boy. I'm telling you that this civilian flying is white glove compared to what you're doing."

Slapping me on the rump, he jumped up and stood balancing his stocky body on his toes. His sense of humor faded fast when asked if standing like that was to save wear and tear on shoe heels or to look taller than five-six.

"Get up, boy. Get out of that sack. I'm takin' you to my crew party in Tokyo tonight. Let's hit it."

"Well, hell, why not; maybe I'll feel better. Can't feel much worse. And besides that I've got plenty of time. The old man said, 'No flying 'til Tuesday.' Why don't you go over there and say hello to Frank and his crew while I go shower, shave, and shine."

On my way to the shower room I took a quick body count on my sleeping crew, or rather the ones who hadn't spent the night in town. About half of them were missing.

I hadn't seen C.B. for some six months, when we had landed in Okinawa for some crew rest. We had needed it after a hard week and a hundred hours of flying airborne radar control for the Seventh Fleet's fighters. After they had put us in a quonset hut up on the hill above the airstrip, we dispatched a runner for a dozen cases of beer and settled in for a quiet evening. As it got on into the night, George Gardiner, another flight engineer, had begun spinning a long yarn, ". . . at eleven thousand feet density, I had twenty-two hundred RPM and one-sixty-three BMEP. We was turning out two-one-nine knots with a nautical mile of zero point seven six . . . "

"Couldn't have been. It was closer to zero point eight two," C. B. had cut in.

George hadn't liked C.B.'s butting in on his story, so we had an automatic argument going. We broke out the books, which proved C.B. to be right. He was one sharp young man. It was our loss and the civilian airline's gain when he quit the Navy.

I had already finished dressing when Frank decided to go with us. So while we waited, C.B. had his chance to tell me about his latest adventures. I took with a grain of salt his stories about the pleasures of having mechanics to

Tokyo Interlude

relieve the flight engineer of airplane repair work, and stewardesses to bring coffee to the cockpit.

Before Frank could get his coat on, C.B. was at the door. "Let's hit it, men. I got a taxi waiting. He's gonna take us to the big city of Sagami-o-ska, where I'm gonna buy you guys a drink for old times' sake, collect that bottle that Mama-san still owes me, and then it's on to the train, men."

"Frank, if he's buying, start drinking the good stuff, and we'd better check and see if a new star rises in the east tonight. But then, again, maybe it's because of all that big money he's makin' now."

The gate guard Marines gave C.B.'s civilian I.D. the once-over before they let us out into the gate-side community of cafes, tailor shops, and the like in ramshackle, unpainted buildings. On past these were the fields, rice paddies and vegetable gardens; source of the cloud of stench that covered the island. Nearly every foreigner fought nausea on arrival. On my first trip, I had caught the scent when we were at sixteen thousand feet and still three hundred miles offshore. Early each morning, in those days before modern fertilizer, honey bucket wagons would make the rounds of benjos making collections of "night soil" that were spread in the fields. Few Americans escaped, and fewer yet forgot the stomach sickness caused by eating vegetables fertilized by human dung.

Daylight and a sky darkening with gray overcast clouds riding in on the treetops wasn't as kind to the town's gray mud and grime as were the nighttime neon lights of ninety-six bars, three cafes, one gas station, and one train station.

C.B. was still in charge and riding high. "This is it, driver. Stop here. On to the Wagon Wheel and my bottle of bourbon, men." He led the way in, threading a path between the water-filled mudholes in the alley. It gave Frank and me some time for trading quips with a klatch of girls, in faded off-duty kimonos, standing around the front door of the New York Bar.

Before he got the screen door open, C.B. was yelling, "Mama-san, Mama-san, you old devil, where are you? Your baby boy is back again." When she peeped out of the door inside the back hallway, her round old wrinkled face creased into a big smile and she waddled into a hugging match with him. Over her shoulder he told us, "I sweet-talk her and get the prettiest girls. Ain't that right, ol' gal?"

A few of the girls peeking out doors down the hallway drifted into the bar to join us. Puffiness of recent sleep and hasty application of comb and

New Perspectives

lipstick were subtle aids to their soft sexiness. Their chatter didn't quite drown out some querulous male voices in the back rooms.

Mama-san broke out some of that good Nippon beer, Frank pushed some tables together, and I had just got seated and settled when a tapping on my shoulder turned my head. Sour-faced Bob Harris stood behind me with his hairy belly hanging out over his skivvy shorts, demanding, "What the hell is goin' on out here?"

"What does it look like? We're having a party."

"Well, there's too damn much noise and I don't like it."

"Oh, hell, Bob, go put your clothes on and come out and have a drink with us."

C.B. spoke from across the tables. "Wait just a minute. This is my party." His blue eyes were needle-pointed on Bob. "And friend, if you don't like it, there's the door."

I knew there was ill will between them that went back to the early days when C.B. had worked as a mechanic in Bob's engine build-up shop, but still I didn't expect Bob to start around the tables. C.B. had been sitting with his hand around the neck of his bourbon bottle. He jumped up, chair toppling backwards, and lifted the bottle. Bob ducked; that was a bad move, because C.B. took one quick step and slammed an up-jerked knee into Bob's face. The remembered sound of nose-bone crunching held all of us for a moment as Bob hung suspended, then sprawled face down. He didn't move. There was a few seconds of quiet stillness before Frank turned to Mama-san. "Have a couple of girls dress 'im and put 'im in a taxi back to the base. Here's a thousand yen; that'll be enough to pay for it."

Fueled by cold beer, warm girls, and nervous talk, the party started gaining momentum. That quick, savage fight pushed my memory back to the last winter, or rather, last monsoon, when we had been working out of Subic Bay. C.B., Frank, and I had gotten wetter than hell hiding from the Filipino Police and the Shore Patrol on the roof of the Palace Bar. Our "Escape and Evasion" training had come in handy on our way back to the base. George Gardiner and two of his radarmen had wound up in the Olongapo jail, but that was after we had cleaned up on an unholy alliance of four general-service sailors and two Marines off the mighty U.S.S. Coral Sea.

While I had been woolgathering, the girls had started some music going on the record player. My headache was about gone, and things were getting lively when Mama-san whispered, "You make C.B. go. Harris wake up in taxi. Driver say he say bring back buddies and get C.B."

Tokyo Interlude

"OK, Mama-san, no sweat." I waited and caught a lull in the conversation. "C.B., what the hell are we hangin' around here for? You said you was takin' us to a big party in the big town. That there was round-eyed girls, and free booze. Let's get to it, man!"

"Why not? Let's do it. Mama-san, tell 'em to clear the tracks. That the three best flight engineers in the whole damn world is headin' for Tok-yo. Me and my two helpers."

The train rolled in on the left-side tracks and reminded me of the "first time Japan tripper" electrician on my crew who had gotten on the wrong side of the tracks, wrong train, wrong direction, and instead of going north to Yokohama, he had spent nine hours riding trains around southern Japan.

We boarded for a little less than an hour's ride. "C.B., gimme that bottle. I need some first aid. Frank, you want a shot?"

"Yeah, let me have some of that. I got to get tuned up for C.B.'s big party."

C.B. looked at me with that baby-faced grin. "Jay, this is one helluva lot better'n that Mayday ride last year, ain't it?"

"You better believe it."

Frank hadn't heard the story, so C.B. had an audience. With his ability to take a little story and expand it to a point almost beyond recognition, I had to listen closely just to keep up with him. We had had an attack of the stupids and had gone to Yokohama on the first day of May, when the Communist demonstrators were out in full force. They were going to lynch us from a street light pole when a friendly shopkeeper rescued us in a taxi and put us on the train back to Sagami. We had stood back-to-back, sweating and worrying, until we reached the base. Even then, we had to bluff our way through a threatening mob to get inside the gates.

C.B. made the story last until we changed to the Tokyo train and found seats on the long lattice-slat benches that ran the length of the car.

I looked around to check out the car. "Good lord in heaven! Men, that right there is a beautiful girl. Yellow, white, black, red, or green, she is beautiful."

Frank didn't answer. He just sat and looked, with an expression on his face like some people wear in a cathedral.

C.B. wasn't to be distracted from his goal. "Don't sweat it, men, I've got some round-eyes waiting on us. Never mind the local stuff that . . ."

New Perspectives

"You just hush." Frank's Southern drawl was soft. Ah'm gonna go talk to her, so you don't say nothin'; if you do, keep it clean."

"Jay, it's me an you, boy; Frank's in love. Gimme that bottle so I can kill it."

Listening to him talk about his new life in the world of civilian flying and keeping an eye on Frank in case somebody got jealous made it a short ride.

As the train slowed to a hissing stop in the Tokyo station, Frank and the girl, hanging on to the overhead straps, walked to us.

"Jay, C.B., this is Yoshiko. She's going with me."

"Jesus Christ, Frank, what . . . "

"Let it go, C.B." I cut him off. "You got something lined up, right?"

"Yeah, but . . ."

"C'mon, partner, let's us go get a taxi and find that party-time hotel."

We were again convinced that all surviving kamikaze pilots had been retrained as taxi drivers.

The desk clerk switched C.B. to a two-room suite without any argument, and the fact that he didn't make the rest of us register didn't mean much right then.

It was still early in the evening, and C.B.'s captain's party was quiet, not much of a party, really; just him and one stewardess. He was lying on the bed while she soothed his brow with a damp cloth. We learned that a commode lid had fallen and cut his forehead. He didn't volunteer, and we didn't ask any details. The party didn't brighten up until the honey-blonde stewardess, sitting on the bed beside the captain, held her bare foot out for inspection.

"I hurt my little toe this morning."

Her belt-tied pink silk kimono slid aside, revealing all of the leg she had—on that side, anyway. C.B. leaned forward, cupped her ankle in his hands. "My mother used to kiss my hurts and heal 'em. I will rescue this damsel in distress."

She couldn't, or wouldn't, stop him as he started at the bottom and, slowly working his way up, ran out of leg. The captain sat up. "C.B., damn you, I'll . . . " He didn't finish whatever he intended to say, because the door flew wide open in a fused banging, wood-splintering, nail-screeching racket, and there stood a giant of a man on one leg. The other leg, the one that he used to kick the door in, seemed to be stuck halfway across the room. His entrance did get our attention.

After the shouting died down, the just-arrived copilot was introduced to Frank and me. When he picked me up, by way of greeting, with one arm around my shoulders, I didn't question why he was called "The Bear."

His arrival, three round-eyed American girls in tow, spiced up the party. It wasn't long before the place was packed with flight crew members from various airlines. Some while later, the hotel manager brought a carpenter to fix the door. Later still, he made a wasted trip to tell the captain that the hour was too late for the hubbub. That was when I noticed that Frank and his girl had left.

The noise level was going up, the booze level was going down, and I had to close one eye to keep from seeing double. So I decided that with a bunch of strangers getting lushed up and C.B. occupied nuzzling a young lady's neck, it was bedtime for me.

I shucked down to my skivvies, and that bed felt good; but fragmented whispers from Frank's side of the rice-paper room divider slowed the tide of sleep.

"... you're so pretty ... I wish ... promised myself ... "

"...I like ... you hold ... no talk ... "

In my opinion, Frank deserved some sympathy. For the last two years he had subdued his sex drive with a determination that would have done a Franciscan monk proud.

"... swore ... never touch ... but you ..." His slow, soft voice faded. And I heard enough of her answer, " ... understand ... you sleep ...," to think that she just might be what he needed.

When I first met Frank, he was coming off a busted love affair that had come on the rebound from a wrecked marriage. One night in Guam, sitting outside the barracks with too many cans of beer, he had needed somebody to talk to. I had listened until dawn, and it had all poured out. He had been hard hit; an Alabama boy steeped in the code of "southern gentleman chivalry." He hadn't known of unpedestalled, unprincipled women. And once the rules were broken, he quit the game.

I drifted off to sleep on the hope that, with any luck, she might crack his shell and make him try his wings again.

Morning came too early. I wasn't ready to wake up, much less get up, when Frank briefed me on his plan-of-the-day. "We're going to breakfast and

New Perspectives

then for a walk in the park, then to meet her folks. We'll be back 'bout dark to have supper with you."

C.B.'s bed hadn't been slept in, and he didn't show up even after I had a late breakfast in the hotel's Americanized restaurant.

I killed the slow afternoon by wandering around sightseeing and window-shopping. That soon grew thin, and after deciding to rest the body between parties, I was back in the room and in the midst of a pre-suppertime nap when Frank and Yoshiko came back.

"Jay, I have never in my life seen anything like this. We had a great time; her folks are just wonderful people."

"I'm happy for you, but I'm also hungry. C'mon, I'll buy you—both of you—some supper. Have you seen C.B.?

"Nah. But if I know him, he's prob'ly busy gettin' the party started again."

We lingered long over supper wine. Frank talked of going back to his father's dry-cleaning business in Huntsville. He didn't know that he glowed when Yoshiko talked of her college years and how she had become an American general's secretary at the Tachikawa Air Force Base. By just looking at her, I could easily see that she was a world removed from the bargirls that had left the rice paddy (or were sold by family) to acquire a dowry. I wondered at the ways of Cupid.

Up in the captain's room, we found the renewed party offering the promise of getting wild. It was starting with more people, more refreshments, and louder music than the night before.

Liquor-laughter, milling crowd, partner-changing, floor-dancing, corner-kissing, bed-wrestling; that pace couldn't last past the witching hour. Frank and Yoshiko disappeared early.

Getting up to dance, I had to step over a body; C.B. had crossed his liquor limit line and passed out. "Don't go 'way, partner. Shtay right there 'til I finish this dance." He did.

I needed some volunteer help to get him to his bed, undressed, and tucked in. And since I was in my "one-eye-closed-to-see-single" stage again, I turned in, too.

Once, in the middle of the night, I awoke to hear the bed-creaking primordial rhythm of male and female coupling. Fate had led Frank and Yoshiko to the budding promise of love.

Tokyo Interlude

Morning came with the little drummer boy in my head keeping pulse time. I was quite sure that he hadn't cleaned his feet before walking in on my tongue. C.B. was tossing and mumbling in troubled sleep. Through the wall came the harsh breathing and whimpering sounds of orgasm, then silence.

Some whispers in her barely audible voice, then Frank's whisper, ". . . love you . . . bathroom . . . few minutes." The bathroom door clicked closed. That must have waked C.B. He groaned, rolled over, and sat up on the side of his bed.

"Man, you look bad, real bad. Like death warmed over," I needled. "I've seen better heads on nickel beers."

"Screw you too, fellow. I'm going to the head."

"Wait a minute. Frank's in . . . "

By that time he was up and through the connecting door. I heard him take a few steps, and then knew he had stopped to look at the girl in the bed. The bed squeaked under his weight."

"Okay, honey, I'm next."

"No, you go back to you bed."

"Don't try to hide under that cover from me, gal. You took care of Frank, and now you're gonna take care of me."

Frank roared, "C.B., what the hell are you doing?"

"Don't bother me, boy. I'm gonna get some of this . . . "

"Goddam you, you rotten . . ."

The building shook from a body hitting a solid wall. By that time I was to the door and saw C.B. lunge off the wall for Frank. They bear-hugged and staggered a few steps to fall over a chair and roll away from each other. The girl jumped out of bed and ran to me. "Stop them, Jay, stop them!"

"I wish I could, honey, I wish I could."

Frank yelled, "You bastard!" and charged. C.B. ducked low, caught Frank on his back, turned, took three quick steps to the window, and bent forward from the waist to throw Frank through the glass, off the fourth floor.

It didn't work out that way. Frank saw what was coming, threw his legs up, and body-whipped himself sideways across C.B.'s shoulders, so that his head and hips were hammered into the window frames. C.B.'s head went through the glass and stopped. Frank slipped off C.B.'s back and hit the floor loose, slack, and unconscious as a dropped doll.

New Perspectives

C.B. didn't straighten up. I took a couple of steps toward him with the girl clinging to me, when, still bent over with his face on the windowsill, his knees buckled to a kneel. He fell backward across Frank's body to land sprawling on the floor. His left leg kicked out straight and jerked spasmodically a couple of times as his head turned toward us. Yoshiko made a soft moaning sound and turned her face against me.

The broken glass in the bottom window frame had slashed across C.B.'s face at the eye line and then raked deep bloody ditches up across his forehead as he fell back. His life welled up and escaped around a lone shard of glass jammed through his right eye socket.

C.B. was beyond help. A quick check proved that Frank still had a pulse, but his pupils were slow to contract when I lifted his eyelids.

"Get dressed, girl. Quick. we'll get out the back way."

"But I want to . . ."

"Forget it. That glass hittin' the sidewalk is gonna attract people, so get moving or we're in jail—C.B.'s in the ground, and nobody can help. Get dressed."

She helped get Frank up on my back so I could practice my "fireman's carry," but he was heavier on each flight of stairs. By the time we reached the end of the alley and flagged a cruising taxi, I was almost too weak to put him in the back seat.

The driver objected. "He drunk. He puke in taxi. Get out! Him no ride."

"Shut up and take us to the train. He's not drunk, he's sick. Now get going."

The short taxi ride gave us time to finish buttoning and zipping ourselves and Frank, and to tie his shoes.

Ticketed and holding Frank in a slumped position between us, we waited on a bench for the train.

"Honey," I briefed her on my plan, "when the train gets here, I'm gonna take him back to the base hospital. He got one helluva knock on the head, but I think he'll make it. I hope. Anyway, you take a taxi and you go home and don't tell anybody anything. None of those people know our last names. My crew'll swear we never left the base if anybody comes lookin' for us. So you go home and sit tight."

Tokyo Interlude

"I can't do that." Her face started going soft. "Frank needs help." Then her voice faltered. "And if they send him to a hospital in the States . . . I'll never see him again."

"Now don't you go gettin' all teared up. They won't send him anywhere. Maybe to Yokosuka, but not . . . okay, I'll tell you what. Wait 'til day after tomorrow, and I'll call you. Gimme your phone number, and for Chrissakes don't forget the main thing—we don't want a murder rap hung on us."

The Marines at the base gate had seen lots of drunks, so I didn't have any problems carrying Frank through. But lugging him into the hospital did attract some attention, which was just what he needed. They didn't question my story about his tripping and falling out of the mess hall door.

After the next day's early-morning flight, I went straight from the airplane to the hospital and found Yoshiko sitting by Frank's bed, holding his hand. It took a minute to recognize her because of the well-tailored western-style clothing.

"Girl, what . . . how did you get in here?"

"I'm a general's secretary, Jay, remember?" The steady gaze challenge in her eyes softened into something else as she glanced down at Frank. "He just went back to sleep. But he much better; doctor said he had a severe concussion, but he can get up and walk around tomorrow."

Frank stirred and opened his eyes. She leaned over him, and from their faces I thought it looked like that promise of love might still bloom after all.

The Carrot

Frank Bette

One morning, I was pushing a cart at Safeway. Headed for the produce department, I picked up one carrot sort of indifferently. As I put it on the top tray, something struck me, seeing the lonely carrot there. Would I have the courage to pass through the checker with this one item? Immediately, in a nervous sort of way, I pushed the cart aimlessly around the store and I became more agitated trying to make up my mind. Perhaps I would expose myself to ridicule, and there was really no need to do it. Again, a personal whim or desire urged me on. So, at last, I gripped the handle firmly, pushing the cart toward a woman checker. The carrot at this moment seemed truly the one and only outstanding item in the store. When the eyes of the checker met the carrot, she exploded into a loud burst of laughter. I was glad she understood.

Ribbons Retied

F. "Perky" Peling

We think we have the past all tied up with ribbons or safely tucked away in a photo album, until such time as an event of the past is relived and the memories spring to life with the freshness of the present.

My memories of Joe were neatly labeled "My First Boyfriend," and then "The Young Man I Married" in 1940, when I was eighteen and he twenty-one, just before the Second World War. Three years after our marriage Joe was dead, killed instantly in his B-17 Flying Fortress over Germany. Half the crew bailed out, but Joe and four others were hit by flak and plummeted to earth in the plane. After the grieving years, I was able to set aside that period of my life and move on to remarry and raise two fine sons, with the old memories behind me. They were in the past, all tied up neatly and stored away to be brought out only occasionally and viewed with tenderness.

Such was my intention last summer when my husband and I made a trip to Europe. I wanted to include in our itinerary a visit to the Ardennes American Cemetery in Belgium, where Joe is buried. After the war, I had been given the choice of having Joe's body returned to the States, but I would have no part of it. In addition to having little use for ritual, I was angry with the efforts the government made to picture our men as heroes. I resented the Purple Heart they sent me. What I wanted was Joe—my young, sweet husband who had joined the Air Corps because it had to be done, not because of a flag-waving patriotic fervor. Let them keep him over there; what difference did it make? Neither of his parents were alive, and Joe and his only brother had not been close. It was my decision alone.

New Perspectives

Many times since those early years I have explored my feelings about ritual and have come to understand our human need for ceremony, for a need for closure. Still, in 1966, on my first trip to Europe I felt no great urge to visit the cemetery. Even on this recent trip I was willing to forego the visit if it was too inconvenient. As it turned out, however, our young Belgian friend, Christophe, who picked us up at the train station in Brussels, was more than willing to drive us to the cemetery near Liege that afternoon.

We took a southeasterly route out of Brussels on a highway that ran through the countryside, where cattle grazed in the fields. After about an hour we came to the turnoff just before Liege and crossed over the Meuse River. Here German troops had been thwarted in their attempt to cut off supplies to the rapidly advancing Allied Front after D-Day. We continued south on streets through an area that reminded us of old steel mill towns in Pennsylvania. We followed the signs that led to the village of Neuville-en-Condroz until we reached the road into the cemetery.

It was a warm day early in September, much like the September day when Joe and I had been married. We drove through the open main gate down a straight avenue shaded by tall horse chestnut trees on either side to a broad green mall. We turned into the parking lot at the right where there were only two or three other cars. It was quiet, so quiet, away from the surrounding roads and the traffic. I noticed someone in the distance across the mall, apparently the gardener, but no one else seemed to be around. I felt awkward and wondered why I had come here after all these years.

My husband, with his usual intuition, sensed my hesitancy and said, "Aren't you going to go to the Visitors Building?" A few steps took us inside the well-appointed lounge area. We stood there and looked around until someone in charge came out of the side office.

"Bonjour," he said.

"Bonjour," I replied.

Obviously, he recognized my American accent, because he then said in English with a French accent, "I'm M. Dessente, the Assistant Superintendent. May I help you?"

I told him I would like to visit the grave of Joseph C. Perkins.

"Are you a relative?"

"He was my husband." I showed him the official letter I had received from the government.

He excused himself to check his records. "Ah, yes. Here we are. Will you come with me?"

We had expected to be given a map or directions and then left on our own to find that one cross among so many. But M. Dessente led us from the Visitors Building. He was chatting about the grounds in a way we knew he was proud of being a part of the American Battle Monuments Commission. He also mentioned that he was a Belgian married to an American woman from Connecticut.

We walked past the large, two-story rectangular block that was the Memorial Building and were then standing at the top of a dozen or so stairs looking out over the white markers. I had envisioned a view of the gravestones as far as the eye could see—much like the ones I had seen in the states–but instead I could clearly see the pattern of a Greek Cross divided into four sections by the two intersecting paths, and defined in the near distance by a row of trees and a flagpole.

M. Dessente led us down the steps and along the broad central path between rows of headstones, mostly crosses, but some Stars of David as well. Before we reached the intersecting path, M. Dessente led us to the left at Row 25 to Cross 13. And there was Joe's name. I had a sudden rush of tears, totally unexpected, and sobbing I turned to bury my head in my husband's shoulder. His comforting arms were around me. All the ribbons had come untied.

M. Dessente spoke reassuringly. "This happens to many people, even though it has been over forty years. It is most understandable."

To gain my composure I noted aloud that it was quite a coincidence that Joe's grave was Number 13 in Row 25. His plane had been shot down on his thirteenth mission on the twenty-fifth day of July. M. Dessente then recalled that as a boy of eight he and his family and friends would see the American planes fired upon and count the survivors as they parachuted out. He didn't say, and we didn't ask, if his family was part of the underground that saved the lives of many of those boys after they landed.

"Joe at twenty-four," I mentioned, "was considered the 'old man' of his Group."

"Yes," said M. Dessente, "the average age of the boys buried here is about nineteen."

"Ohhh!" Christophe, our twenty-year-old Belgian friend, was impressed and showed it with this exclamation. Up to that time he had been silently following us around. He was expressing what we all tend to forget, how young are the *men* who go to war. But the architects of the cemetery had not

New Perspectives

forgotten. M. Dessente pointed out that at the east end of the central transverse path is a bronze figure symbolizing American Youth.

We walked back up the steps to the Memorial Building and noted that on the side facing us was engraved an inscription to the Missing Servicemen. M. Dessente invited us inside, where on each of the three walls huge maps of Europe are painted showing the main battles and the flight routes of the planes. His recounting of the battles brought back those years of excitement and fear and tragedy for our world as well as for me, personally.

I was still reliving those years when we returned to the main building, where we signed the Visitors Book, thanked M. Dessente, and departed. It had taken me forty-three years to visit this spot, and I now knew I had made the right decision, no matter what my reasons, to have Joe buried with all the other young boys in this beautiful place with M. Dessente watching over them. I could now say a final "Goodbye" and retie the memory packet with crisp new ribbons.

Can the Sun Melt the Sidewalk?

Roque Gutierrez

the hoot owl sits regally
on the truck seat
next to me, eyes wide
jeaned and toothless

asking me, "where's everyone going?"

and the best answer
i can give cannot break
the image, that all roads lead home,
or to golden arches,
or to hot-dog heaven,
or to any eden his mind conjures

asking me, "why is the moon out in the daytime?"

of course i know
but the explanation is lost
as his mind explodes
in a myriad of directions
spiraling away from what is
the truth
the back of his head faces me

asking me, "can the sun melt the sidewalk?"

i tell him what i know
not to worry, that
"no it can't"
but i save the rest for later
he needn't hear now

that some day it will.

The Day the Piano Arrived

Shirley Johnsen

The arrival of the piano in August 1932 at our mining camp home in Luanshya, Northern Rhodesia, Africa, came as a joyful surprise. We hadn't realized we had been so long without any kind of music, which had been such an important part of our lives back home in California.

I don't know whether or not my father had told Mother about his purchase beforehand. He was a great one for surprises, and she kept secrets equally well. We children learned of the piano only minutes before a truck, with its blanket-covered load, rolled into the driveway.

As soon as the truck stopped, we all gathered around. Two of our houseboys, Sixpence and Philamone, came at my father's call to help unload the rectangular object. They settled the shrouded piano in a corner of the living room (probably a predesignated resting place).

A breathtaking unveiling followed. Saut, one of the garden boys, too shy to come inside, peered through the window. Tommy, my younger brother, described the piano to the cook and the picannin, comparing it to a sort of giant kalimba, a native African instrument. The beauty of the little spinet entranced Mother and me. Curly veins in the wood patterned the reddish-blond wood. Matched whorls, resembling Pekinese faces, enhanced the upper front. We discovered later that these whorls suggested any number of creatures, depending upon one's imagination or the changing light.

We waited impatiently for Daddy to open the lid so we could see the keys and hear their tones. We knew he enjoyed keeping us in suspense. It reminded me of Christmas morning back home when we had to line up single file to come downstairs. We were not allowed to peek from the landing, and

The Day the Piano Arrived

we had to eat a complete breakfast at the kitchen table before we could see our dazzling Christmas tree and presents.

Calm and deliberate as usual, Dad took his time to assemble brass ornamental pieces which he produced from a soft leather bag. The intricate parts turned out to be a pair of candelabra which he mounted on either side of the "Pekinese faces." By the time they were in place, Mother and I were virtually struggling with each other for full possession of the piano stool. Dad, with just one look at me, indicated that Mother would have the first chance to play.

We circled around her and watched expectantly as she made a move to open the lid. It was locked! We were surprised and disappointed. Dad most of all. He kept his composure, but hurriedly searched the leather bag and his pockets. No key! He went outside to probe under the seat of the truck. Everyone joined in the search, even the houseboys, though they didn't really know what they were looking for.

Mother and I considered using a butcher knife to force the lid open, but Dad calmly asked Mother for one of her long metal hairpins. Scarcely breathing, we waited as he picked the lock. It worked! At the click of the lock, we let out a loud cheer which seemed to echo in the very depths of the piano.

Mother caressed the lid of the handsome spinet with tremulous fingers, opened it slowly, took a deep breath, and played a soft harmonic chord, and then the opening bars of the "Moonlight Sonata." The sound was too poignant to bear or the emotion to reveal. My brothers, sister and I ran from the room, eyes bright with unshed tears. In our rooms, each of us wept privately, overcome with joy and the realization that, even in this far-off land, we were home . . . the day the piano arrived.

The Master Painter

Ray Weirmack

'Tis morn' in California –
The Master Craftsman sets his easel
On ageless rolling sun-tanned hills.

He paints –
From His pallet flows a myriad of colors.

I gaze transfixed by his artistry –
The Heavens glow at His touch.

Crimson hues burn through
Light pastelled bluish hues.

He brushes in full puffy clouds, that sail the sky
Like phantom storm-lashed ships.

At last, His masterpiece complete –
The Master lays aside his brush.

Rembrandt-like, the panoramic scene
Glows in perfection for all the world to see.
A reflection of heaven—our Paradise to be.

Look up, you storm-tossed human souls!
See what art our Lord portrays
In His celestial gallery.

Here is the promise, yes, the hope;
The final salvation, for all who dwell
In earth-bound misery.

Away from It All

Helen Cannon

The Hoffmiesters had known Kitty and Greg Sharpe for nine years without letting themselves become envious. But this time Hilda Hoffmiester was having a hard time of it.

"Three months!" she said incredulously. "The Orient *and* Australia! *And* the South Seas! How can they afford it?"

Emil shrugged and rattled his newspaper. "Savings, I suppose," he mumbled.

Hilda set her jaw defiantly. "If they've got that kind of money you'd think they'd want a decent house. I don't know how they put up with just one bathroom."

Emil didn't answer. Hilda gazed absently across the street at the Sharpes' front window. Sharpes had a Plan E house. The street was part of an early "tract," with the same five house plans repeated in the same order for several blocks in each direction. Older homes now, mostly occupied by older people. Shifting her eyes momentarily to a tricycle in the driveway at the end of the block, she allowed herself a tiny frown at the thought of the four noisy children who lived there. But her mind returned quickly to the Sharpes.

"It hasn't been six months since they took that Caribbean cruise," she said. "And Alaska last summer, and the Lord knows how many times they've been to Hawaii and Acapulco. They must have spent at least fifty thousand dollars on travel in the last five years."

New Perspectives

Emil rattled the paper again, a little louder, getting impatient. "Well, they must have it or they couldn't be spending it."

Hilda considered that. Greg Sharpe was sixty-eight years old; she had figured that out from some date Kitty had inadvertently dropped once. Hilda knew they were still paying off their house; she had seen the payment envelope stuck in their mailbox for the postman to pick up. And at their ages, both of them retired, they couldn't possibly borrow money for frivolous junkets. They must have a safe-deposit box full of thousand-dollar bills . . .

All for travel. . . . It was ridiculous. Kitty almost never appeared in a new dress, and they drove an old Buick that seemed too asthmatic to pull the camping trailer they sometimes used. Hilda glanced across the street again, surveying the Buick with pitying distaste.

"They never buy anything," she muttered. "Then they go all over and eat in all those fancy places and stay in high-priced hotels. And come home and tell everybody about it."

The newspaper came down on Emil's knees with a slap. "What do you want me to say?" he exploded. "If that's what they like to do with their money, it's their business!"

"I know that." Hilda's voice became plaintive. "I'd like to travel, too, you know . . . We never go anywhere except to see the kids."

"Where do you want to go?"

She lowered her head, staring at her hands.

Stealing a quick look at him, she saw the expression of defeat that crossed his face. It wasn't fair to blame him; she'd had as much to do with their financial affairs as he had, and certainly he'd worked as hard before he retired as Greg Sharpe or anyone else. She smiled tentatively.

"Do you want a cup of tea and some of that date bread? I think it's cool by now. Remember, we're supposed to go over to Kitty and Greg's in a few minutes, and you know what you'll get there."

Kitty had picked up a wine-and-cookie custom from her continental travels—the wine usually pink and tasting of vinegar, the cookies little more than cornstarch with a hint of sugar. Emil fortified himself with two thick slices of the date bread before he felt ready to cross the street.

Kitty's face glowed as she opened the door. "Come in," she said in a distracted voice. "You'll have to excuse the mess; it's so hectic, getting ready."

Away from It All

Brochures and timetables littered the living room. Greg looked up, waving a booklet. "Got a little something on New Guinea," he apologized. "We were talking about changing our itinerary. Just give me a minute to check something out, if you don't mind."

"Now, honey," Kitty said gently, "Hilda and Emil don't want to hear about itineraries. Show them the brochures on Japan, why don't you?" She flashed a happy smile at Hilda. "This time we're going to take time to really see Japan—we're going up to Hokkaido and come back down the western coast of Honshu, places the tourists don't usually get to see."

Emil pulled a chair closer to Greg. "I'd rather look at pictures from those South Sea Islands," he said in a tone of comradely conspiracy. "You can just tuck one of those hula girls in your suitcase to bring back for me, if you want to."

Greg smiled tolerantly. "I'm afraid they've got away from that these days. We're thinking about a look at Bora Bora—they've got special tours set up to historical sites."

Kitty left the room and came back with a tray of tiny glasses half-filled with wine—white, this time—and a plate of pale, thin wafers. She passed it around and set it down without taking anything for herself. "Hilda, bring yours out to the dining room, will you?" she asked. "I've got the fall list from Saks, but I can't decide what I want to get to take with me. There's a beautiful raw silk suit . . ."

Hilda followed her obediently. There wouldn't be any new clothes, she felt sure. Kitty always talked about it, but in the end she always decided to wear what she had. She would talk about priorities, about economizing on certain things in favor of first-class travel and four-star restaurants. It seemed odd for two people who lived so plainly at home to insist on that sort of quality abroad; but apparently they found their pleasure in memories of that luxury.

The evening took its predictable course, lasting until all the illustrated literature had been exhausted. Emil stood up and yawned, finally, and Hilda was quick to take her cue.

"We really have to go. You'll be so busy, we won't try to see you again before you leave—so we'll wish you bon voyage now. And this time be sure to send post cards—you always get too involved, and we don't hear a word till you come home."

"We'll remember this time," Kitty promised. "And we'll expect you over for an evening as soon as we come back."

New Perspectives

Greg nodded quickly. "Yes, indeed. I know most folks don't like other people's slides, but you folks always appreciate them so much it's a pleasure to show them to you."

"You bet, we wouldn't want to miss 'em. Thing is, your pictures are really professional, not those blurry snapshots most folks come back with." Emil suppressed another yawn with difficulty. "Anyway, you have a good time."

"I think I'll just stow away in one of your suitcases," Hilda said. "I've always wanted to see the Orient . . . "

Hilda's wistful mood lingered after the visit, lasting into the next day and the next, leaving Emil with an uncomfortable feeling of guilt. He gave the problem five or ten minutes of thought, a few days later, and came up with what seemed to him a novel solution.

"Why don't we take a few days and run down to see Gert and the kids?" he asked heartily. "We haven't seen them since Easter."

Hilda sighed, glanced once more across the street at the Sharpes' empty house, and began packing.

By mid-morning the next day, having telephoned to be sure they wouldn't be imposing, they began the ten-hour journey. They no longer traveled the entire distance in one day; Emil's legs cramped easily, and Hilda's back wasn't as good as it had once been. But there were lots of tourist attractions where they could break the trip, all with handy motels. This time they chose Neptune's World, a marine park they had bypassed on previous trips.

As expected, the park was closed when they got there, but both of them were ready for the motel and a night's sleep. In the morning, fresh and alert, they spent two delightful hours watching dolphins and seals perform and wandering past glass tanks teeming with brilliantly colored fish. Emil congratulated himself as they drove back out to the highway—the idea of a trip had been a good one; Hilda was happy.

"Those porpoises," he chuckled. "They're clever little fish, aren't they? They act almost human."

"They're not fish, they're mammals," she said. "And I think these were dolphins, not porpoises."

Emil peered both ways and pulled carefully out into traffic. "Same thing," he said carelessly.

Away from It All

"No, I don't think so. I think it's the dolphins that are fish; I think I read that somewhere."

He spared a second from the traffic to frown at her. "It's just two different names for the same critter," he insisted.

"No, it's not. Or at least I'm almost positive." Hilda tried to recall exactly what she had read, but her memory was vague on the subject.

Emil was determined to prove his point. "What town's this?" he muttered. "Melville . . . I bet they've got a library. By golly, I'm going to stop, and we'll go and look it up."

"That's silly," she protested. Then the name of the town struck a response. "Melville—that's where Kitty and Greg used to live. He had a hardware store here, remember? And she taught school."

Emil grunted a non-answer. He circled a block in the downtown district, turned to circle another, and grunted again. "They must have a library. Looks like forty, fifty thousand people or so."

"We don't need a library," Hilda said crossly. "I give up. You're right, I'm wrong. Let's just go on to Gertie's."

"No, it's got to be here somewhere. Probably toward the edge of the business district. I'll find it." He swung around a corner too close, bumping a rear tire over the curb, and swore under his breath. But in the next instant he was grinning in triumph. "There—see? See there? Library, down that way."

Hilda looked at the sign and then at her watch. Emil paid no attention; his mind was on maneuvering the car into a parking space. Surveying the dingy brick building, Hilda tightened her lips. It was all a waste of time—and what if she were wrong?

"Well, I'll be goddamned!" Emil said suddenly.

"Now what?" Hilda followed his glance and blinked. Around the corner from them, not forty feet away, was an old Buick—if not the Sharpes' car, at least its twin. "Why, Emil! That looks like Greg and Kitty's car."

"That's what I was thinking." Emil's eyes narrowed. He switched off the engine but made no move to get out. "Can't be, of course, but it sure looks like theirs."

"Do you suppose something's happened—they had to come back or something—some emergency?" As she spoke, Hilda realized she didn't want to know the answer. She looked at Emil, a piteous look of hope and apprehension. "It can't be theirs. Let's not stop here. Let's just go on."

187

New Perspectives

He shook his head and opened the door. She opened her own door hesitantly and stepped out. Stealthily, like two people engaged in a crime, they approached the Buick.

Emil went to the driver's side. Hilda, on the curb, bent down to look into the other side. In the middle of the front seat was a large stack of booklets, the cover of the top one picturing a beautiful beach and the words, "Gauguin's Paradise." She had seen that picture only a few nights ago in Kitty's living room. The back seat was piled with books; she saw the photo of a black man on the cover of one with "Outback!" in large red letters across his legs.

Her eyes met Emil's through the two windows, and she looked away quickly. She retreated toward their own car on tiptoe. Emil slid in as she did, and they sat in silence for a long moment.

"I don't understand," she said finally. "I wonder what . . . "

"Shh!" He nodded toward the library and slumped down in the seat, turning his head slightly away. "Get down, can't you!"

Hilda was unable to move. She stared open-mouthed as Kitty and Greg Sharpe came down the steps, Greg's arms loaded with more books. They seemed calm, untroubled. At the sidewalk, Greg shifted the books to his other arm and reached for Kitty's hand. They walked to the Buick that way, still talking, and in a minute the car pulled away. Hilda shook off her stupefaction and took her first breath in several seconds.

"Well, I never! Emil, do you realize what we just saw? Do you realize what they're doing—what they've probably been doing all these . . . "

"Never mind, Hilda." Emil's voice was surprisingly kind. "Forget it. It was two people that looked like Greg and Kitty Sharpe, that's all. And you're right—there is a fish called a dolphin, only porpoises are dolphins, too, so that's all right."

She wasn't listening. "Well of all the—I can't believe it! All this time, just one big lie after another!"

"Be still," he said in that same amazingly gentle voice. "Now, you and I are going on to Gertie's. And in a few days we'll be home, and who knows? Maybe good old Kitty's remembered to send us a card from some place or other. Not that it matters, of course—we'll get to see their slides, anyway."

Hilda looked nonplussed for a moment, then nodded slowly. "Yes, they're bound to have us over for the slides." She paused, swallowed hard, and went on. "And I can't wait to hear about all the sights they've seen, all the wonderful places they've stayed in, can you?"

"Can't wait," he said gravely. He turned the key and pulled out of the parking slot, displaying more expertise than he had shown in years. Hilda watched him, smiling slightly, until her eyes blurred with tears and she had to search for her hankie.

It Takes One to Know One

Marjorie Nesbit

Betsy Remington was at odds with herself and life around her.

Beyond the balcony the world was awash with late afternoon sunlight, but within her small apartment gloom lay as heavy as San Francisco fog.

Numbly she let the last three rejection slips fall through her fingers and disappear into the half-filled wastepaper basket.

Why had her usually receptive romance editors suddenly turned so cold? Didn't they realize she must sell if she hoped to pay the rent and eat regularly? Was she, God forbid, getting stale?

She ripped the half-filled sheet of paper from her typewriter and tossed it after the rejection slips.

"What the hell!" she said, addressing the voluptuous blonde on the wall calendar. "We can't all look like you. If my eyes were big and blue instead of near-sighted and gray, and my mouth curved up in a 'come and get me' smile instead of drooping at the corners—well, perhaps, romance writing would come easier."

Betsy had always known that writing was a lonely profession, but when you start talking to the pinup girl on the wall calendar it's time to take a good, hard look at yourself.

"Thumbs up, old girl. No one's over the hill at thirty. All you need is a little inspiration then; keep it simple, grab 'em in the first paragraph, remember an element of mystery to stir the senses—a seemingly insurmountable obstacle to make the breast heave with desire, and, finally, a happy ending!"

It Takes One to Know One

She was about to insert a new sheet of paper in her typewriter when her attention was diverted by a movement on the adjoining balcony. What was going on? That apartment had been vacant for months, since the landlord was asking an astronomical rental due to the fact that if you stood at the corner of the balcony and leaned dangerously over the rail you could get a very narrow glimpse of the sparkling waters of San Francisco Bay.

Then she saw a young man move out toward the railing, obviously engrossed in something beyond her view. Was it her imagination, or were his movements furtive? The very possibility caused a delicious stirring of her senses.

Of course, why hadn't she thought of it before? She would write about a mysterious man next door—a romantic, mystical man, seemingly unattainable. Research would be close and easy, and there was no time like the present to begin.

She carefully replaced the cover on her typewriter, filled a small watering can, and stepped onto her balcony.

Out of the corner of her eye she could now see he was examining three small plants. He was tall, thin, stoop-shouldered, and wore glasses. He seemed entirely unaware of her presence, and when he finally spoke she almost dropped the watering can.

"Damn it!" he said, "I think I lost one."

"My God!" she gasped. "One what?"

"Camellia," he told her. "See how the leaves on this one droop down."

"I wouldn't worry about it." She tried to sound reassuring. "Just needs a little time to get acclimated."

He had a nice smile.

"I'm Vince Halliday," he told her, "and I know you're Betsy Remington. I saw your name on the mail box. I hear your typewriter going at all hours. Are you, perchance, a writer?"

"Sort of," she told him. "Are you?"

"Good lord, no! All I ever get to talk to are computers."

He looked and seemed nice. Should she tell him she would like to do a little research on him purely for literary purposes? He certainly looked harmless enough, but sometimes appearances were deceptive. Secretly she hoped so.

New Perspectives

Before she could come to a decision he leaned over the balcony and said, "I've just arrived in town. Transferred from the Middle West. I love San Francisco, but I don't know a solitary soul and I'm lonesome as hell. You wouldn't have time for a nice glass of chilled wine, would you?"

"Matter of fact," Betsy lied, "I was about to fix myself one, but I'd much rather drink your wine than mine."

He laughed. "I think I can even scrape together some crackers and cheese. Just knock on my door. My butler will let you in."

Betsy did not change her clothes. She would have liked to, but that was too obvious. She contented herself with a little eye shadow and fresh lipstick. Then she walked the short distance to his door.

So far, so good, she thought. Step one—her pulse had certainly quickened at first sight. Step two—she had already bridged what would seem to be an insurmountable barrier spanning the space between her balcony and his. Step three—in the lap of the gods!

The door was open and he was waiting for her.

"Welcome to my humble abode," he said, spreading his arms wide.

"It doesn't look very humble," she told him. "Untidy, yes; humble, no."

"You got me," he grinned. "Untidy it is, but give me a break; I just moved in."

He disappeared into the kitchen and reappeared with two glasses and a bottle of white wine.

"I've had it on ice waiting all day for you." He held up the bottle. "1987—fresh off the vine!"

"Ah!" she laughed. "A true wine buff!"

"So what's your latest project?" He settled himself on the sofa beside her.

"I'm about to do a little research."

"For a story?"

"Yes, for a story."

"What are you researching?"

"As a matter of fact—" Betsy hesitated and helped herself to another cracker. "Lately my rejection slips have been mounting. I decided I'd take a little time off to discover what turns on the young women of today."

It Takes One to Know One

"Oh." His tone was polite but disinterested. "Where do you propose to begin?"

"Here," she said.

"But surely you don't think for a moment I would be able to enlighten you. I only like children when they belong to somebody else, and the same applies to most women."

"Then you're just what the doctor ordered. You're the unapproachable man next door—exciting and unattainable."

He took a deep breath and poured himself another glass of wine.

"Exciting and unattainable? This is, indeed, heady stuff. But you must realize women like the macho, athletic types with plenty of forceps and biceps and all that sort of good stuff."

"Oh, yes," she said. "But as soon as they get them they long for the pale, esthetic types who read far-out poetry, play classical music by candlelight, and take lonely walks on the beach at sunset."

"What do you know!" he grinned. "That's a perfect description of me!"

"Ah," she said. "And what kind of woman interests you?"

The near-sighted eyes searched her face.

"Pale, delicate-looking women with wide, thoughtful gray eyes that can't quite hide a seductive and passionate soul."

"I think," she smiled, "you would be wasted on my story."

"So do I. Why don't we just pretend we are two perfectly normal people who are interested in becoming better acquainted. Would you consider having dinner with me?"

"You're on!" she laughed.

"What sort of restaurant would you prefer? You're the San Franciscan."

"How about a small, intimate Italian restaurant with red and white checkered tablecloths, candlelight, and a phoney Irish tenor singing sad Italian songs?"

"I was right," he grinned. "I had you pegged for a romantic the minute I laid eyes on you."

"All research aside," she told him, "it takes one to know one."

When they were comfortably seated in a booth at Luigi's, candlelight flickering on the checkered tablecloth and glasses of ruby wine, Vince raised his glass and their eyes met and held.

New Perspectives

"Just think—a couple of hours ago I had no idea I was exciting and unattainable. Without that knowledge I'd never have had the courage to invite a total stranger to dinner."

Betsy returned his smile, feeling a wonderful glow of warmth and well-being which she was quite sure was not entirely due to the second glass of wine.

"How would it be—" Vince toyed with his French bread, "if we went back to my apartment? There's a full moon tonight and we could watch it come up from my balcony. I'm even supposed to have a view of the bay. I haven't found it yet, but the real estate agent assured me it was there."

"I know just how to find it," she told him. "I'll show it to you."

"Good!" He touched the rim of his glass to hers.

"I'm awfully glad you selected your neighbor to research. I applaud your choice. Research, you know, when properly conducted, can be as rewarding for the researcher as for the researchee."

"It's going to take a bit of time to ascertain which is which," she said, gazing up at him through what she hoped the candlelight had transformed into tangled black lashes.

The Unwelcome Guest

Don Donovan

Señora Estaban Ramirez, a refined widow of Castilian background, was the proprietress of a *pensión* in the city of Veracruz, Mexico. Her guests were ladies and gentlemen of quality. The señora was proud of her Spanish blood, and though a loyal and patriotic citizen of the Republic, towards *mestizos*—mixed bloods—she was condescending and towards *indios*—Indians—she was disdainful.

Among her permanent guests were Mr. Charles Tripp, a native of London who ran a prosperous business as an exporter of chocolate and vanilla, and Mr. Ronald Baker, a New Yorker, also in the shipping business. There was also Don Pedro Alejandro Solorzano, of Santander, Spain, who had various business interests in the city. Even the Danish consul, Mr. Christian Lawsen, another bachelor, was one of the Señora's guests. The well-bred widow ran a quality establishment, and she catered to people of the better class.

On a humid summer evening in the year 1872, beads of perspiration showed on the face of Señora Ramirez as she supervised the place settings for dinner. Suddenly the bell beside the entrance door rang and minutes later, Josefina, the principal maid, entered to inform her mistress that a gentleman, inquiring about accommodations, awaited her in the parlor. Entering the parlor she frowned as she observed a dark, diminutive Indian, appearing to be in his early sixties, attired in a wrinkled frock coat whose sleeves showed the glossiness of long wear. In his hands the stranger held a rather battered stovepipe hat that, when perched on his head, must have given him the appearance of a somewhat taller stature than his five feet, two inches.

New Perspectives

The lady greeted the caller with a frigid, "Buenas tardes, señor. What can I do for you?"

The little Indian gentleman politely returned the señora's greeting. "Buenas tardes, señora." Bowing courteously, he continued, "Your *pensión* was recommended to me by Colonel Tomas Sanchez. He told me that it was a quiet and restful establishment, and that he thought I would find it comfortable for the few days I would be in Veracruz. The Colonel and Señora Sanchez were your guests for a few days last summer, and the Colonel speaks very highly of your *pensión*."

The frown disappeared from the face of Señora Ramirez, to be replaced with a courteous but nevertheless patronizing smile. Indeed she did remember the Colonel and his wife. *Mestizos*, true, but on the whole, people of quality. The Colonel, he was a gentleman without doubt, and his lady, such genteel manners!

"Si, señor! I remember the couple well! Charming, both of them," she enthused. "The Colonel flatters and gratifies me to speak so well of my establishment. Please sit down, señor."

With a smile the little man bowed graciously as he sat in a cushioned chair that stood behind him. His appearance seemed comical as he held his huge hat on his lap, his small, delicate hands nervously steadying it in position. The top of the stovepipe reached to his chin, so that his torso was completely hidden from view, giving an appearance of a hat with a head attached to it.

Seating herself across from the dwarf-like figure, the señora sounded slightly apologetic as she inquired, "May I ask your name, señor, and also your profession."

"I am called Don Benito," he replied, "and my work is that of *abogado*—you know, a *licenciado*, lawyer—although at this time business other than the law occupies much of my attention."

Señora Ramirez thought it ususual for an Indian to be a lawyer. She hesitated, polite reserve mixed with compassion, as she admitted, "Yes, I do have one small room available. Adjoining the kitchen. But, señor, ah, I am afraid that one of your quality would find it austere and confining."

"I am a simple man, señora," replied her diminutive caller. "I am sure the accommodations you offer me would be acceptable."

"Very well," Señora Ramirez decreed, "I quite understand. The room is yours."

The Unwelcome Guest

"*Mil gracias, señora,*" the swarthy little Indian said. "A thousand thanks. I expect to be your guest for only a few days, however, since next week it is imperative that I start my journey to the capital. I do have pressing obligations there that must be attended to."

And so a bargain was struck between the genteel widow and the disarmingly unimpressive Indian lawyer.

As the guests entered the dining room at the dinner hour, they took their accustomed places at the long table which extended the length of the room. But on this particular evening, a small table had been placed in one corner of the room, off to one side of the entrance. Unfortunately, there just was not enough room at the main table for the additional guest, and this solitary table was especially prepared for Don Benito.

The situation was awkward, thought Señora Ramirez. The little Indian gentleman had polished manners; he was an educated man, and obviously he could more than hold his own in the trite, conventional conversation that flowed freely at her well-set table. But, after all, he was an Indian, and propriety must be maintained. Out of respect for the other boarders, Proper Society must be given its due. So went her musings as the excellent meal progressed.

Suddenly there was an interruption; again the entrance bell rang and shortly Josefina entered to usher in a tall individual attired in the glittering uniform of a colonel in the Army of Mexico. Gold epaulets bristled on his shoulders, and an array of military medals covered both breasts of his coat.

In a voice laced with anxiety, diffidently Josefina whispered to Señora Ramirez, "El Colonel, señora, he wishes to speak with Don Benito."

Looking up, a bit perplexed, Señora Ramirez replied, "If the Colonel so wishes, Don Benito is there—at the table in the corner."

"Si, señora," the maid said. Then, at Josefina's direction the handsome colonel approached Don Benito and bowing respectfully said, "Señor Presidente, a message by telegraph has come from the capital. It is imperative, it seems, that you return there immediately. An emergency, señor. One that requires your personal attention."

"Gracias, Colonel San Juan," Don Benito answered quietly. "While I gather things from my room, be pleased to wait for me in the parlor. I will join you momentarily."

The Castilian widow's guest arose. To the hushed room, "*Con su permiso,*" he excused himself as he bowed, smiled gently to Señora Ramirez, and departed. As he passed, his embarrassed hostess curtsied as gracefully

New Perspectives

as she could, and, her face flushed with chagrin, murmured, "Señor Presidente, mi casa es su casa." Mr. President, my house is yours.

And so it was that the Veracruz house of proud widow Ramirez became the home of Benito Juarez, the revolutionary President of the Republic of Mexico.

The Wedding

From the novel, *Another Part of Town*

Betty Matulovich

Chapter 20

Mr. Olsen wasn't nowhere around. I tried to think if he knew Mr. Charlie and might be home getting ready for the wedding, like half of West Oakland was. Nobody else was out here on the pier, either. Maybe it being Sunday explained the lack of activity. I made for the edge of the dock, trying to decide which of Mr. Olsen's boats I would borrow. As it turned out, I didn't have a choice; only one old sorry-looking boat was down there. I climbed down the ladder and stepped carefully into the rowboat. I had hoped to find better than this, but I wasn't turning down no means of escape.

I began to row, falling into a steady rhythm, thinking about how lucky I'd been, being able to sneak out of the house while everybody was busy, right out the front door and down the front walk. Then streaking for the pier that I was now rapidly leaving behind, I started thinking about the wedding—most everybody in town, at least our part of town, would be there—everyone but me. I felt sad. But I kept on rowing; I was free and I planned to stay that way. Where I was headed, I wasn't sure. Then I thought of the tramp steamers and the big freighter I'd seen one day when I was with Papa, Seb, and Uncle Ivan over on the San Francisco docks. That was it. That's where I was going—on a steamer as a stowaway to the Hawaiian Islands.

New Perspectives

I started to row faster, then I noticed that water was slowly spreading across the bottom of the boat. Sudden fear picked up my rowing to a speed that made my muscles throb, but the water was coming in faster than I could row. I let go of the oars and started scooping water out of the boat with my cupped hands. I was so busy I didn't pay attention to a distant rumble—until it got louder. Sitting still, listening now with the water dribbling through my fingers onto my lap, I felt the hair on the back of my neck rise up as I recognized the sound. In panic I swung around to see what direction it came from, bumping one oar loose, sending it flying far out into the water. My breath wailed out a sob. I watched the oar float away in the fog. The *fog*!

I looked around me, a lump in my throat like I'd swallowed a golf ball. The morning mist had turned to thick, rolling gray without my noticing. Suddenly, all I could think about was putting my feet on dry land. This had to be the worst fix I'd ever got myself in; here I was, out in the bay in a leaky rowboat that was fast filling my Sunday shoes; the fog was rolling over me and I could hear the rumble coming across the water that told me I was, for sure, right in one of the ferry lanes. Cold bumps puckered up all over me; my throat closed up so tight I couldn't even get a holler out, and all this was happening because Mama and Aunt Clara was planning to marry me off to some dumb cousin I'd never even met.

Well, I wasn't going to do it. No sir. My head kept working through a fuzzy haze. Even if it meant I was going to miss Mr. Charlie and Melissa's wedding that was due to happen at St. Mary's Church in—I looked at my pocket watch—about two hours. Well, my first plan of escape from a life of marriage was a flop. Now if I could only get back to dry land I had a better idea: I'd go over to the train yard, catch a ride like I'd seen hobos do, and ride so far out of town nobody would *ever* find me. I looked down past the watch that Uncle Ivan had given to me in what seemed another lifetime now to see the water was still raising and so was the pant legs of my wool Sunday suit. They had shinnied by now four inches above my bony ankles, showing my favorite bright red socks that Mama had said I was *never* to wear with my Sunday clothes. "Look like clown," she had said. I looked like a clown all right. I felt like one, too. I had a sudden flash of Mama whacking me for ruining my good suit and missing the wedding, and not wanting to marry the girl she had picked out with Aunt Clara's help. My second flash was—I hardly *ever* had second flashes—that I probably was going to die out here in my red socks, alone in the fog, from freezing or being run over by a ferryboat, if I didn't go and drown first. And nobody would even miss me while they was all having a good time. Nobody, that is, except Mama, who would be waiting at the church door to kill me.

The Wedding

I sighed as I looked down at the bottom of the boat, my shins wavered red through the swirling water. It come to me that it hadn't been no good from the beginning; even if I'd got clean out to some hidden rice paddy in China, Mama would of come and found me. The throb of the engines grew louder; I felt numb. Anyways, as I looked at it—one way or the other I was pretty soon going to be a goner...

I was on my knees, blubbering, trying to make my boat go somewhere except in circles with one oar, when I heard the throttled-down sound of a small powerboat.

"Help! Help! Somebody help me!" I was standing up, rocking the boat, when I saw Mr. Olsen come sliding out of the fog in his motorboat.

"Yonny! What you be doin' out here? An' how come you be doin' it in my boat?"

The roar of turbine engines sent Mr. Olsen into action. His blue eyes was about to pop out of his face as he threw me a rope. "Make fast! Make fast!" he yelled. Tears streamed down my face and I was crying like a baby, but never in my life had my fingers moved so swift.

"It's tied, Mr. Olsen."

"Hang on, Yonny! *Hang on*!

My knuckles turned shiny white where I gripped the side rails as Mr. Olsen screamed his motor through that fog and I felt the airlift as that rickety boat came off the water. My teeth clattered together with the sudden yank, and as my head snapped back I saw just behind me the shape of the ferry-boat's hull...

It turned out that Mr. Olsen had took a walk down by the dock, as he usually did on Sunday mornings, and noticed the rowboat missing. Thinking it might have come loose and drifted out into the bay, he had come looking for it before it got into one of the shipping lanes. If it hadn't been for Mr. Olsen always being so picky about his boats, I'd probably already be asking Saint Peter for directions. I shivered, part from my wet clothes but mostly from what I was thinking.

Mr. Olsen was still talking—he'd yelled back at me all the way to the pier—his eyes when he looked at me were still bugged out. But by the time we climbed up onto the pier, I think he was more mad at me than scared. Even when I told him why I had to try to run away he didn't seem to understand.

"I bain tank you no hear right, Yonny. You bain only puny kid yet. Ja?"

New Perspectives

I guessed everybody thought I was a puny kid, everybody, that is, except Mama and Aunt Clara, who were both trying to ruin my life. Mr. Olsen was still talking. "What they *say*, Yonny, is they fixing up for you to marry this girl when you grow up. Like make a contract."

Well, I knew a little bit about contracts; they was what Papa signed when he bought new furniture. I sat still, thinking over what Mr. Olsen had just told me, feeling strange. I sure didn't think it was right for parents to go selling their kids. One thing made me feel a bit better, though, if Mr. Olsen was telling me straight: I had a couple of years to figure out some way to get out of that contract thing.

I sighed as I leaned back in the cab Mr. Olsen had called to get us to the church on time. He had wanted to take me to my house to change clothes, but I told him the house would be locked. Anyways, I didn't have another Sunday suit. Besides, it didn't much matter what I looked like, since it wasn't me getting married—yet. I still wasn't positive sure I believed Mr. Olsen.

The taxi squealed around the corner, stopping with a jolt in front of the church. I got out, dragging my wet rear end loose from the leather seat. Then, as Mr. Olsen paid the fare, I looked up to see a long black car with Melissa in the back seat turning the corner off of Seventh Street. Suddenly time turned backwards. I was that dumb kid with chocolate on his face again, trying to hide behind a cardboard box, seeing her eyes on me, hearing her laughter . . .

I shot across the sidewalk and up the church steps like a cat with turpentine on its tail. I pushed through the heavy side door and into the foyer. The inner doors were all wide open. I went through the far right one, planning to go along the side aisle until I found an empty seat over against the wall. A big hand slapped down on my shoulder, yanking me backwards.

"*There* you are, Johnny! Your ma's been looking all over for you. Come on, before the bride gets here!" I recognized Manuel Lopez; he was one of the guys that Mr. Charlie had asked to be an usher. I tried to pull away.

"No! No! I want to sit over here on the side!"

Manuel seemed to suddenly see me. "Geez, what happened to you? Ya fall in a sewer?" Manuel always had a way of putting a guy at ease. He didn't let go of my arm, though; he was half-dragging me now towards the center aisle. People were looking around, frowning at the disturbance.

"Ya hafta sit with your family, ya dumb kid!"

I gave up. It weren't no use trying to get away. Manuel pushed me ahead of him, his hand on my back, when I slowed down; my shoes squish-squished in the awful silence. I stopped and felt the hand again nudge me

The Wedding

forward. Slowly I moved, staring ahead of me at the narrow red carpet rolled right up to the altar railing in spotless, glowing beauty.

Mama turned as Papa, his eyes opening wide when he saw me, slid quickly over to let me in beside him. For one second Mama looked glad to see me. Then I guess she *really* saw me, because her mouth flew open like a beached fish trying to get air. I had a strong feeling that if she wasn't in church she probably would of screamed. Her hand covered her mouth and her eyes rolled scary wild in her pasty dough face. Then Papa was grabbing her arm and pulling her down tight beside him as she started to get up. Papa had a silly grin on his face, like he hoped everybody around us would think things was just fine.

"Shhh! Shhh, Maria! Is all right!"

I knew Papa's calm whisper, plus his hold on her arm, was the only things keeping Mama from getting at me. Trembling, I watched sidelong as my mama bowed her head. She looked like she was praying; if she was, I sure hoped the Lord would put a good word in her head for me. I snuck a look at Seb. As usual, he was looking like he was big stuff, his nose all wrinkled up like the tide was out. I didn't feel so good. I guessed my whole family, and everybody in church, and God all figured I was the biggest dummy they'd ever seen. All except Papa. I looked up at him. He smiled at me, his eyes soft. I guessed Papa must of got into some dumb jams, too, when he was a kid, because he most always seemed to understand the messes I got myself into—him and Uncle Ivan . . . Uncle Ivan. A sharp pain of loss twisted inside of me.

I jerked up in my seat as the bride music boomed out. Everybody around me stood up. I got up, too, shivering in the cool breeze that blew up the aisle. Didn't seem like a kid ought to feel so low down . . .

Everybody turned to look at Melissa standing in the entry door with the light behind her, all lacy white and strawberry gold. My friend Melissa; my heart swelled. For a minute I forgot how low I felt—feeling happy for her and for Mr. Charlie. The music crashed and she moved slowly straight forward, like it was a signal. She looked little—all alone, but I had heard Mama talking to Aunt Clara, saying, "Melissa say her father dead, she no want anyone else give her away—she walk alone."

Melissa was moving funny. First she walked straight ahead, then off to the left side, then two steps to the right, like she was dancing. I noticed her bridesmaids were zig-zagging the same way behind her. I never saw a wedding where they came in like that before . . . My eyes fell to Melissa's feet

New Perspectives

and the puddle she was now stepping to the left to miss. Behind her I saw other ugly splotches that I knew only my slopped-over shoes could have made. All my misery and problems plumb up and vanished right there on the spot. Suddenly my only concern was my sudden death; at my own mother's hand or from the heart failure I was having as my chest went slurp, like it was going down the kitchen drain. Maybe even God was going to get mad at me this time.

Through blurry eyes I saw Melissa smiling at me as she bobbed and weaved. I tried to smile back. Then I turned my head, not wanting to look any more at the terrible mess I'd made. I saw Mr. Charlie walking out to the altar rail. He didn't look like he saw any mess—for a split second I forgot my own problems. Mr. Charlie looked more like he'd just seen the sun come up forever.

Melissa was past me now, and in another minute I heard Father Muldoon beginning to talk. Across the aisle a movement caught my eye. Peeking sideways I saw Mama's cousin Hazel, and beside her—a vision—an angel, sitting right there in one of the pews of St. Mary's Church. If not an angel, then the most *beautiful* girl I had ever seen in my whole entire life. My head whirled—I was in the hills fishing, in a secret shaded place, gazing into purple shadowed pools . . .

I shook my head to clear it, feeling the hard pew behind my knees. I stared at the black fan of lashes brushing snow-white cheeks, feeling like somebody had hit me on the head, then snuck around back of me and hit me again. Cousin Hazel sat down and I saw the vision's golden hair falling like sunlight down to her dinky waist. She sat down slowly beside Cousin Hazel. I felt Papa pulling me down to my seat. My heart was a great white stallion, like in a Saturday Western matinee, racing wildly across high desert country. Then a thought stunned me, setting my whole body to shaking, and if I hadn't had heart failure yet I was sure having it now, as my poor heart flipped over like a Sunday morning hotcake on the griddle with the thought—was this the girl I was supposed to marry? Then a worse shockwave hit me as I suddenly remembered what I must look like to *her*.

Sudden gloom pressed me down in my seat. How come when a special girl come along I was either too young, like over at Idora Park, or my face was all over chocolate, or, like now, when I was a total wrecked-out mess. I looked down at my wool pants, aware of the sour smell coming from them. They were shrunk half up my leg, and those bright red socks, that I suddenly hated, were clinging to my legs on one side and sagging down on the other. I slunk down further, wishing I could crawl under my seat, feeling her eyes still looking at me. I stared at my sandy shoes, then I couldn't stand it any more. I had to see

The Wedding

her again. I tried squinting from the corner of my left eye. All that got me was a big cramp. Finally I plain turned my head, looking square at her. Then something in her eyes made me forget my shriveled-up suit, my soggy socks, and my knobby ankles, because suddenly nothing else in the world mattered except *us*; those sparkly eyes said so. My eyes wouldn't come unglued from hers, that were saying something else. I got the feeling it was something like a—a promise . . .

Music filled the church, my head, my heart. Melissa and Mr. Charlie, smiling fit to bust, were walking back down the aisle. Any fool could see they were in their own world. I was in my own world, too. I was sitting up tall again. All thoughts of breaking that contract had vanished; Rosita, the girl of my dreams up to now, and her Mama's tamales were fading fast. I even began wondering how old a guy had to be before he could get married—I was a goner and I didn't care . . . all I could think about was that shimmering, purple-eyed p r o m i s e   .   .   .

Vernal Equinox

Ann C. Krauss

Today, the master weaver returned
To prepare the tapestry of spring!
The thread tones are bright and vibrant
On a background of chartreuse velvet hills.
Joyfilled birds sing in welcome chorus,
Perched in once brown and gnarly trees;
Soft pink petals of cherry blossoms
Burst, spilling their color in the air
And burgundy leaves of rose bushes
Add their dark winey contrast everywhere.
With a song in my heart, I join the avian chorale
In thanks for the glories we are sharing . . .
As the warp and woof of nature's hues
Are woven into the tapestry of another Spring!

Mother's Day

Gail E. Van Amburg

She was an attractive woman, tall and thin, with dark hair and eyes. Some say she resembled Myrna Loy, others Katharine Hepburn. We likened her to a young Lucille Ball, and suspected she was the inspiration for "I Love Lucy."

She had a whacky sense of humor, by her own definition, and smiled a lot; even when there wasn't a lot to smile about.

The kids in the neighborhood brought her ailing pets to heal, the adults brought her yardage to sew and problems to solve.

She may not have resolved the neighbors' personal problems, but she did remedy a lot of wardrobe woes.

"If you can't say something nice about someone, don't say anything at all," she told us, and practiced what she preached.

We never heard her speak unkindly of anyone. She was too much in love with life and the people around her to be bothered with pettiness.

Perhaps it was her faith and courage we remember most.

When we were too weak to accept the severity of her illness, she gave us strength; when we questioned "Why you?" she said, "Don't cry, God must need me more than you do."

Her grandchildren knew her for only a short time. Her great-grandchildren will never experience the joy of knowing the woman whose courage, kindness and love touched so many.

Alice Marie Veronica Goldt Westington was her name. My sister and I called her Mom.

The Nest

Wanda Giuliano

"Coo... Coo... Coo..." The sound seemed to come from the patio. Frowning, I stood in the kitchen listening. "Coo... Coo..." I put the cup down in the sink and walked into the living room. Lightly I opened the drapes and peeped out.

The sight of the orchids, some gloriously blooming, some in the process of blooming, filled my heart with contentment, soon dispelled when I saw the gray pigeon squatting in the large pot at the left side of the patio.

"The birds!" I cried out. Hastily I slid the glass door and stepped out. The pigeon looked up, alarmed, obviously scared by my presence. Still, he didn't move.

"Shoo!" I shouted. The pigeon squirmed, then took off shrieking. "Darned birds!" I muttered in distress. "They'll ruin all my plants." I was trying to straighten the crushed petunia when my attention was caught by something whitish lying between the leaves. "Oh, no! Not again!" I groaned, when removing the leaves I discovered two tiny eggs. I was about to pick them up, when, flapping his wings, the same gray pigeon landed on the patio sill. Was he staring at me?... Trying to send a message?... Or was I imagining things? Birds don't think!... Or do they? A strange feeling invaded me. What can I say? I shooed the bird off again, but I left the eggs in the pot.

A few days later I was in my daughter's house. Jennifer, who is expecting her first child, lives in a small rural town, where the San Joaquin River runs quietly. The place is not very big, but there is enough space, with lots of trees and green pasture. A very peaceful place, too peaceful for me. I'm a city lover. Looking outside the large window I saw the horses grazing in the grass. A little further, two cows were standing immobile. I wondered how long a cow can stay in one place without moving.

Turning toward my daughter, I said, "You really like it here, don't you?"

"I love it all, mother. I always dreamed of living on a farm." Her eyes shone, a slight smile turned up the corner of her mouth. She always had that smiling mouth. Nothing about her had changed; she was still my little girl.

Smiling to myself, I glanced out in the open. One of the horses was galloping, circling the fence, round and round, neighs resounding in the air. The placid cows, startled, roused from their immobility and scampered elsewhere. It surprised me to see how fast a cow can run. Laughing, I turned toward Jennifer; she was in the process of feeding a very young puppy. Holding him like a mother would hold a newborn baby, she was dropping milk into the eager mouth.

"I found the puppy by the ditch; he was left there to die . . . people have no heart . . . they are cruel . . . "

There was such sadness in her voice. Her soft beautiful face, slightly lowered, intent on caring for the puppy, brought back to my mind a painting of a Madonna with a Child that I admired in a gallery exposition not long ago.

"I named him Bosco," she said, refilling the dropper.

"Bosco? What an unusual name!"

"Right," the smile returned on her lips. "I got it from a bottle of syrup. There was a dog's picture on the label, and this name, 'Bosco.' I liked it." She had said it decidedly.

I nodded and accepted Bosco just as I accepted "Fellini" for the cat. Of course, she got Fellini's name from the movie *Breaking Away*.

Later, while preparing lunch, I opened the window, letting the warm sun in. The chirping of many birds filled the air.

"The pigeons returned to my patio—built another nest."

"They did?" She looked up at me, a half smile on her face.

"Yes, for the third time now!" My annoyance was evident. "I already destroyed several eggs that were laid before. I . . . "

"Mother!" Jennifer interrupted me, her hazel eyes looking at me with disbelief. "How could you do such an ugly thing?"

"Ugly?" I looked at her in surprise.

"Yes, Mother, ugly." She confirmed.

New Perspectives

"But Jennifer," I protested, the patio is full of plants . . . the birds always make their nests in between the flowers."

"That doesn't justify you, Mother; that was a terrible thing you did."

"I did?"

"Yes, those eggs were going to be babies . . . little baby birds . . . " There was an odd tone in her voice.

I tried to reason. "We don't make much fuss about splattered or boiled eggs, do we, Jennifer? Those eggs could also have been little baby chickens."

With a gesture of her hands, as dismissing me, "We don't eat pigeons' eggs, Mother!"

Her logic confused me. Looking at her pretty, saddened face, I remembered the scores of cats, dogs, and birds that she seemed to always find, and I had to cope with over the years . . . At all times those big imploring eyes, that small voice . . .

"The poor cat is starving, Mother, he has no home . . . the car almost ran over him . . . "

"Oh! Mother, the puppy is hurt! I found him whining, right by our door."

"Those cruel kids! They broke the bird's wing. Please, let's fix the poor wing."

And what about the time she came in screaming, scaring the life out of me?

"Mother . . . Mother . . . a kitten is caught in the elevator! Kids threw him in the first floor's opening! Call the firemen!" And the firemen came and saved the kitten . . .

The same big eyes were staring at me, full of accusation. My daughter is a born crusader, and I'm guilty and on trial for . . . murdering innocent baby birds! . . .

"Okay, Jennifer, what am I supposed to do?" Did I sound tired?

She looked at me, perplexed, "Well, Mother, even if you get rid of more eggs, the pigeons will come back. " She paused, then repeated with conviction, "They will . . "

"Heavens," I exclaimed, "I hope not! You have no idea of the mess they'll make."

"Do you remember, Mother, what you told Lois when she left home at eighteen? 'The swallow always comes back to the nest.' She did come back, didn't she? And her room got all messy again, but then you didn't care anymore."

Did I remember? It was not too long ago. How many years? Six? The time rolled back to the past.

"Mother?"

"Yes, Lois, what is it?"

Lois was looking at me, a shadow in her eyes. "I'm going to live with Judy." She had said it in a hurry, so as not to give me time to get the full meaning of these simple words.

If the roof had fallen on my head, I would probably have felt the blow less. I sat on the unmade bed speechless, glancing around the messy room, straightening the pillow to give myself time to hide the pain. I finally succeeded in saying, with an almost normal voice, "Are you sure that yours is the right decision?"

"Yes, Mother," she knelt by me. "Please, Mom, try to understand. I know how you feel, but I'm not a little girl anymore."

Silently I caressed her long, dark hair, my mind in chaos.

"You are so young, barely out of high school."

"Yes, it's true, but I've got a job now, and I'll live on campus, sharing room and board with Judy."

"It won't be easy, darling."

"Maybe so, but I have to do what I feel is the right thing for me." Then getting up she made a large gesture of her arms, as if to embrace the entire room, and with a perfect pirouette said, "See all this? No Lois, no mess!"

"I would rather have you and the mess." I joked, feeling a knot in my throat.

Lois left a few days later. She hugged and kissed Jennifer, who could hardly hide her tears. Jennifer adored her older sister. She hugged and kissed me, whispering, "Who knows? I may come back."

I nodded with a forced smile. "You will. The swallow always comes back to the nest." She did; when disillusioned and longing for all the things left behind, she knocked on the door again.. I silently thanked God and let her in.

"What are you thinking, Mother?"

New Perspectives

Jennifer's voice brought me back to the room. I smiled, shaking my head, but I had a hunch that she knew what had been going on in my mind. She knew of the countless hours I had spent sitting by the phone, waiting for Lois to call. She knew that her words had awakened memories. Jennifer was a very sensitive girl.

After a week in the country, I was ready to go back home. I left early in the morning, promising Jennifer to visit her soon again.

Time goes by so fast! The orchids were all in bloom. The eggs were still in the nest. Every morning the pigeons alternated brooding. One day, opening the patio's glass door, I heard sharp chirps. The eggs had hatched! I stepped outside and bent over the two little creatures in wonder. They were so naked, trembling. I wanted to help, do something . . . cover them . . . I glanced around. It was then that I saw the two pigeons perching on the roof, looking at me as if in apprehension. I retreated inside. The chirps of the hungry birds become less strong. They were being fed.

The skinny birds were beginning to grow. One of the two was gray. A cute little fellow, he had a star-like white spot on his breast; the other one was more common, the color a yellowish gray.

I called Jennifer, long distance.

"Oh, Mother! You kept the babies!" she shouted in delight. "I always thought of you as the greatest mom in the world!"

Heavens! And I thought I was a fool! Jennifer was succeeding again in confusing me.

The birds were now learning how to open their frail wings, learning to fly. After a few tries they landed on the nearest plant, and at times flat on the floor. The patio was a mess; I did my best in cleaning here and there, but in vain. The little scoundrels were everywhere; up, down, in between the plants! I must confess that I felt a kind of affection for them, especially for the one with the white spot.

It was quite a few days later when I saw the mother pigeon going up and down the patio sill. I didn't move, just kept looking from inside. The little ones were also pacing up and down the patio, obviously excited, opening their wings, attempting to fly, to reach the mother. Then, at once, they flew to her side and stood there chirping. I felt their indecision.

"Go . . . " I murmured. "Fly . . . Fly . . . " And almost unconsciously I slid the glass door, stepping out. That did it! Frightened by my sudden presence, the pigeons shrieked and flew away. Anxiously I followed the birds with my eyes until they disappeared on the roof across the street. "Good-bye," I said, a little sad, a little happy.

Flowers and plants were looking great again. I was pulling a dried leaf off, and glancing around, my heart filled with contentment at the sight of the newly bloomed orchids drenched by the sun, when I heard a flutter of wings. A bird perched on the patio sill.

"Shoo . . . " I was about to cry out. The word died on my lips. The gray pigeon, who seemed to stare at me, had a star-like white spot on his breast.

Aren't I Pretty?

Andrea Crankshaw

"Mommie, we're bunnies."

"Mm."

"And you're the mommy bunny, and I'm the baby bunny."

"Uh huh."

"And we live in a house in a tree. And we eat honey. And sometimes we eat cookies." The child paused. "Mommy, what do bunnies eat?"

"Mm." Karen tore herself away from the newspaper reluctantly. "What do bunnies eat? Well, they like lettuce, and carrots, and all kinds of vegetables."

"And honey?"

"No, bears eat honey. Bunnies like green things."

The little girl dashed off and Karen searched for the story she had been reading. Two paragraphs later, the child was back, wrapped up in a fluffy yellow blanket.

"I'm a yellow bunny. See how sweet I am?" She made cooing noises and nuzzled her mother's arm.

"Umhmm."

"I have *six* wedding dresses. Do you want to see them?"

"Sure." The child scampered away. Karen rubbed her eyes and wished briefly for a husband—or at least five uninterrupted minutes with the evening newspaper. Giving up her attempt at political enlightenment she looked from

Aren't I Pretty?

her bay window over at the crisp blue and gray Victorian house across the street.

The little girl returned, a white baby blanket draped over her blonde curls. "This is my wedding dress. Aren't I pretty? Do I really need to get my hair cut before the wedding? How many days is it? Aren't I *so-o-o-o* pretty?" Melissa chattered, tilting her hips flirtatiously.

Karen smiled and stroked her daughter's cheek, delighting in the soft freshness of her baby's skin. "You're very pretty, Melissa."

The little girl's brown eyes beamed with pleasure and she asked, "Mom, what's a wedding?"

"It's when two people who love each other decide they want to live together, so then they get married."

"But Aunt Sylvia and Roger already live together. Why are they having a wedding?"

"Because, umm . . . "

The telephone bell rang shrilly. Karen thankfully gave up the attempt at explanation and went to answer it.

"Hello?"

"Hi, Karen, this is Jonathan."

Karen's heart leaped when she heard his voice. She worked to keep her own voice light and playful.

"Jonathan! How's my favorite artist?"

He laughed. "Well, I'm glad someone can still call me that. The way this show has been going together I wouldn't be surprised if the critics declared me nothing more than a talented house painter."

"Well, so long as the houses you paint are on canvas, what's your complaint?" Karen teased.

"Gee, thanks. Here I take time out of this hectic evening to give you a call, looking for a few kind words, and what do I get? Early critics!"

"I'm just trying to help you get used to it. I wouldn't want you to fall apart under the pressure." Karen twisted the telephone cord around her fingers.

"So how have you been?" Jonathan asked. "Did the models work out for the spread you were talking about?"

Karen laughed and regaled him with the logistics of trying to get sixteen-year-olds to frolic in summery beach clothes while a damp fog rolled in around the Golden Gate Bridge. She savored the opportunity to talk about something besides bunny rabbits, and drew it out as long as she dared.

Reluctantly she realized that she didn't know where Melissa was. "Jonathan," she said urgently, "can I call you back? Now I'd better check on my daughter."

Karen replaced the phone on the kitchen counter. A glance into Melissa's bedroom revealed only a heap of discarded blankets. A light brown bear in a jaunty red cap watched glassily as she went down the hall. The bathroom door was closed. She pictured her lipsticks streaking the walls, the medicine cabinet contents half-swallowed, the soap bottles spilling their slippery bubbles. She tried to open the door. It was locked.

We'll have to call the fire department, Karen thought. They'll come up here with axes and shovels and break down the door and the landlord will evict us for destroying the property. Don't scream. "Melissa," she said, as calmly as she could, "unlock the door."

Silence.

"Melissa," Karen said more loudly, her tone balancing precariously between anger and fear, "are you in there?"

There was a soft noise from inside the bathroom.

"Melissa, open the door."

There was more rustling, then the doorknob turned with an ineffectual squeak.

"I can't."

Relieved to hear the girl's voice, Karen said firmly, "Try again."

The child fiddled with the doorknob.

"I don't know how."

"Turn the little button thing just the way you did before."

A miracle! The bolt turned to give up its grip and the door opened.

Looking down toward child height, Karen's eyes were struck by the bright silver glint of the haircutting scissors. Slowly and fearfully she opened the door wider to see her daughter's face beaming up at her.

Where fifteen minutes ago there had been a bouquet of the most delightful blonde curls any mother could wish for, there was now a three-inch path of light fuzz. Her little cherub looked like a cross between a Marine and a French poodle.

Aren't I Pretty?

Karen squeezed her eyes shut and willed herself not to scream. "Melissa!" she cried out in spite of herself. "Oh, Melissa, what have you done?"

The child's smile faded. "Aren't I pretty?"

"Oh, Melissa, whatever made you cut your hair?"

"I wanted to be pretty." She whimpered as she began to understand that Mother was not pleased. "Don't you remember, you said the only thing I needed to look pretty for the wedding was to get my hair cut. Don't you think I'm pretty?"

"Oh, Melissa, I just meant we needed to trim the ends a little. I didn't mean for you to . . . " Karen's scolding ceased when she saw the hurt and confusion in the little girl's eyes. She stroked Melissa's head, her hand recoiling slightly at the bristly feel of it. She shook her head sadly, not wanting to think about her sister's wedding. Maybe she could make Melissa a little bonnet, she thought, and cover it with lace and pink ribbons. "Oh, my precious darling," she said, gathering the child in her arms. "You'll always be pretty to me."

About the Authors

Myrtle (M. L.) Archer's prize-winning novel, *The Young Boys Gone*, enjoyed success in the United States, Canada, and Germany. Her fiction, articles, and poetry have appeared in anthologies and in such periodicals as *New Frontiers, Mature Years, Westways, Ski Magazine, Contempora, Fiction,* and *Spectrum.*

Frank Bette, who by trade operates an antique repair shop, is at heart an enquiring poet. A transplant from Germany, his European background gives his work a unique flavor that is humorous and profound. While he teaches neat little lessons, his observations slyly poke fun at human nature.

Lucile Bogue, after a career in education on four continents, began a writing career fifteen years ago which included drama, poetry, novels, and a biography. Several of her plays have been published and produced. *Salt Lake*, a historical novel published by Pinnacle Books, was nominated by Western Writers of America for the Golden Spur award. Most recently, a dance/theatre biography, *Dancers on Horseback*, was released by Strawberry Hill Press.

Genevieve Bonato credits the Writing for Publication class offered through the Alameda Adult School for getting her writing off the ground. Her articles have appeared in the Alameda Times Star, Island Journal, Castro Valley Courier, and, most recently, Across the Generations--a Vista College publication.

Delbert B. Campbell was born in Indiana in 1929. He completed a twenty year career in military service, then completed a twenty year career with the IBM Corporation. Being retired, he writes as a hobby. He is currently enrolled in a poetry writing course in Berkeley.

Helen Cannon is the author of three published novels: *A Better Place I Know, Seasons Change,* and *Where the Truth Lies.* Other works include personnel training programs, stories and teaching aids for adult low-level readers, short stories, and verse.

Andrea Crankshaw is a technical writer for a computer company in Alameda. Although she has worked as a writer during most of her career, she has only recently directed her efforts toward writing fiction. In addition to raising her son, she enjoys sailing, swimming, and reading.

Lola Curtis, a retired executive secretary, wrote her first story at the age of seven and has continued writing as a hobby. She authored an informational booklet, *The Elderly and the Nursing Home*, which was published in 1978.

Roberta Tennant DeBono is a writer/artist. She and her husband, Ken, and son, Daniel, have recently formed an independent publishing company, Ankh Press. Their latest title, a Sci Fi/fantasy novel, is being distributed nationwide. She is currently working on a novel of supernatural horror.

Marilyn K. Dickerson is a native Alamedan whose novel *Lord Hap* was published by Avon Books and subsequently translated and released in

About the Authors

Germany. At the present time she is actively engaged in screenplay writing and prefers it to writing books.

Don Donovan was born in Oakland and now lives in Alameda. He taught social sciences in Oakland public schools for thirty years. A graduate of St. Mary's College, with a Master's degree in History and Sociology from San Francisco State, Don has traveled extensively in forty-five countries on five continents.

Cecil Fox, a retired probation officer, has been a freelance writer for several years. His essays, human interest articles, and humorous fillers have appeared in such publications as Capper's Weekly, California Correctional News, *Byline Magazine*, and *Mature Living*.

Wanda Giuliano, born in Naples, Italy, has been a Californian since 1954. Her love for writing began as a young girl when she wrote songs, poems, and short stories in Italian. Much of her work reflects that early influence. Married and residing in Alameda, she has two grown children.

Roque Gutierrez was bred in the orchards of Fresno, tempered on the streets of Oakland, and is now basking in the tranquility of small town Benicia. "Alas," he laments, "nothing ever comes out the way I planned it. But, I guess, that's the beauty of writing. Nothing is ever as it seems."

Shirley Johnsen spent her early teen years in the copper fields of Northern Rhodesia and her early married life in the "Grapes of Wrath" environment of the San Joaquin Valley. A V.L.B., (very late bloomer), after retiring she received her B.A. in Health Science and began a new career as a freelance writer.

Joe King, eager to be near his mother on such a traumatic occasion, was born in Mesa, Arizona, during the Coolidge Era. At age four they moved to Oakland, where he grew up, attending Lincoln school, Oakland Tech, and U.C. Berkeley. He enjoys socializing, writes occasionally, reads when he must, and presently writes a weekly column for the Alameda Journal.

Ann C. Krauss has been writing short stories and poetry since 1983. She is an active member of Writers West, Alameda Poets, and the Chaparral branch of El Camino Poets.

Grant Lowther is an eighteen-year-old poet and writer of short stories. He has been writing poetry since the age of sixteen and stories and essays since the age of seven. His lifetime literary goal is to make all of his words flow freely from pen to paper and flow just as freely into the minds of his readers.

Jean Lucken, an Oakland teacher, joined Writers West in 1978 after publishing *Play Away*, a book of humorous plays for teenagers. She published three more books for students before winning the Mindy Gates O'Mary Tribute Award from the National League of American Pen Women for her short story, "Tender Terror."

Linda Marlow's newspaper career began in 1964 when she covered the Republican Convention. Eagerly awaiting her next assignment, she discovered that it was to be the obituary desk! She moved to Alameda two years ago via Mill Valley, Honolulu, and San Francisco. She aspires to write screenplays, TV scripts, books, and short stories.

New Perspectives

that it was to be the obituary desk! She moved to Alameda two years ago via Mill Valley, Honolulu, and San Francisco. She aspires to write screenplays, TV scripts, books, and short stories.

Elizabeth Matulovich, the mother of eight, has completed one novel and is currently writing a romantic adventure novel set in Alaska. Her poetry, publicity, and general interest articles have appeared in the Daily Review, Oakland Tribune, Alameda Times Star, Island Journal, Trading Post, and *Byline*.

Sybil McCabe worked as an editor for publishers of school texts for twenty years. She authored twelve social studies books and helped educators in Monrovia, Liberia, write books geared to the needs of the African children. Her current interests are magazine articles and animal stories for young people.

D. Leah Miller was born in Cheverly, Maryland, and moved to Alameda in 1987. She is an artist, amateur photographer, film buff, and an avid reader who enjoys psychological thrillers and horror stories. Screenplay writing is her ambition for the future.

Marjorie Nesbit, a native of Canada, has spent all of her adult life in California. Her interest in writing goes back to her high school days, when she served on the staff of the school paper. Her material has appeared in *Farm Wife News*, *Mothers Today*, and *Woman's Day*.

F. "Perky" Peling moved to Alameda from San Francisco ten years ago. She has since retired three times, once from the School of Humanities at San Francisco State University, where she learned from and envied all the published writers, whom she hopes soon to emulate.

Allen J. Pettit, after spending his youth seeking decadence and moral degradation in rural Mississippi, "sipped the wine and prowled the brothels of the world." He started a promising career as a writer after many years of flying in the service and for the airlines. His death in 1988 was the loss of a great storyteller.

Jean Tucker's poems have appeared in *Prairie Schooner*, *Poet Lore*, newsletters, and other varied markets.

Gail E. Van Amburg, social editor-photographer for the Alameda Journal, has been a member of Writers West for eight and a half years. She is a native Alamedan.

Ray Weirmack was born in Alavieska, Finland. In 1985 he received a B.A. degree from Cal State University, Hayward, where he was on the staff of Pioneer, the biweekly newspaper. His articles have appeared in Iron River Reporter, Detroit Free Press, Milwaukee Journal, Captain Billy's Whiz Bang, and the Alameda Times Star.

Mary Jo Wold is co-owner with her husband of ComputAccount in Hayward. Her philosophical bent and pursuit of her "laughing place" is expressed in poetry. She is a twenty-five-year member of the Distaff Singers of Oakland and currently is president of the Chabot Club of International Training in Communication Organization.